The Jackals

Alice Dolbeau

Ordering Information:

Prime Seven Media
518 Landmann St.
Tomah City, WI 54660

Printed in the United States of America

- **Eugenia and Konstantina** – You are my treasures and the source of my strength and creativity.

- **Steve Harris** – From the very beginning, you've stood by my side on this wonderful journey around the world.

- **To you, the reader** – Thank you for placing your trust in me and holding my book in your hands.

Table of Contents

THE WITNESS

A Day Like Any Other

Sarah woke up to the soft, persistent hum of her alarm clock, the familiar sound mingling with the sounds of the sleepy town she called home. The gray light of dawn peeked through the curtains of her small bedroom, casting a muted glow that seemed to echo her own sense of monotony. Stretching her arms above her head, she let out a sigh, bracing herself for another day that felt all too ordinary.

It was a day like any other. She rolled out of bed, her feet meeting the cool wooden floor, and shuffled toward the bathroom. Her reflection greeted her in the mirror—dark circles under her hazel eyes, hair a tangle of waves, and a face that felt tired, worn by the mundane routine of her life. She splashed her face with cold water, hoping to wake herself up, but the sensation was fleeting. Dismissing her reflection, she methodically brushed her teeth, her mind wandering to the meeting scheduled for later that day at work.

After barely finishing her coffee, Sarah hurriedly dressed in her standard office attire: a simple white blouse and black slacks. Looking down at her reflection, she felt like she was putting on a costume. Someone else's life, not her own. Was this what twenty years of hard work led to? A job as an administrative assistant at a small marketing firm where her values were eclipsed by the need for survival? As she fastened the last button on her blouse, the weight of self-doubt settled heavily on her shoulders.

Despite her lukewarm feelings about her job, she found solace in the camaraderie of a few close colleagues. Jenna, her spirited friend with fiery red hair and an infectious laugh, was the bright spot in the often dreary office atmosphere. They shared coffee breaks and whispered about their dreams and aspirations, but sometimes, Sarah felt a deep-seated envy. Jenna had aspirations of moving to the city, of chasing dreams bigger than their small town could contain. Meanwhile, Sarah felt like she was fading into the background, lost in the blur of days that felt alarmingly similar.

As she locked the door of her modest apartment behind her, the crisp air of early spring enveloped her, sending a small shiver down her spine. She filled her lungs with the fresh scent of dew-kissed grass and blooming flowers, hoping to shake off the haze of anxiety that had wrapped around her like a heavy fog. Sarah took her usual route to work, passing the bakery where the scent of fresh bread lingered in the air, mingling with the sweet aroma of warm pastries. The bakery owner, Mrs. Anderson, greeted her with a bright smile, and for a moment, Sarah felt a flicker of warmth in her heart. They exchanged pleasantries, and for a split second, Sarah felt seen, like she existed beyond her daily routine.

But as she made her way through the quiet streets, the familiar scenery began to feel oppressive, the isolation of her town amplifying her sense of entrapment. Each grocer's sign, each worn-down shopfront, seemed to echo her own sense of stagnation. She felt an insatiable yearning deep within her—a desire for adventure, for excitement, for a life that didn't feel like a never-ending cycle of repetition. But with each step, that yearning morphed into a bitter pang of guilt. Shouldn't she be satisfied? She had a steady job, a roof over her head, and friendships that, while comfortable, felt predictable.

Arriving at the office, the sense of familiarity enveloped her like a worn blanket that was both comforting and suffocating.

The fluorescent lights buzzed overhead, and the hum of conversations filled the air, punctuated by the clicking of keyboards. Sarah settled into her cubicle, organizing the scattered papers on her desk. She tried to focus on the tasks at hand, sifting through emails and reports, but her mind drifted. The clock ticked steadily, each pass further fraying her patience.

Around lunchtime, she decided to step outside for a brief reprieve. The sun beamed down, warming her skin, and the energy of the town was electrifying. People bustled about, their faces filled with purpose as they moved through their errands. She found solace in the familiar café where she often grabbed her lunch, and as she stood in line, she couldn't shake the feeling that something was amiss. A subtle tension hung in the air, a feeling that prickled at the back of her neck.

After grabbing a sandwich and sitting at a corner table with her phone balanced between her hands, she engaged in mindless scrolling. The café buzzed with life, but Sarah felt detached, the conversations faded into white noise. Jenna's words popped into her mind—a reminder that life was fleeting, and she wanted to be bold, to take risks. Yet, here she was, sinking deeper into the confines of her familiar life.

When she finished her lunch, she glanced at her watch and realized she had time to spare before heading back. With a resolve to clear her mind, Sarah decided to take a stroll through a small park nearby, a place she often ventured to when she needed to escape the walls of her office.

As she walked along the familiar path, the trees rustled softly, and the sound of laughter floated over from the playground filled with children. The scene painted a stark contrast to her inner turmoil. Everything felt so vibrant—it reminded her of her own childhood days filled with play and excitement. But now, the vibrant energy amplified the dull ache of yearning she harbored deep within.

Deeper into the park, she felt the world quiet down—the laughter diminishing as she meandered away from the playground. That edge of solitude started to feel like a comfort until she happened upon an area obscured from the main path. It was a narrow alleyway, shadowed by towering trees and the buildings surrounding it. Curious, Sarah hesitated. She wondered why she had never noticed it before.

The moment she stepped toward the alley, she was greeted by the sudden, bitter gust of an evening breeze. It carried with it unsettling sounds that twisted her stomach—a series of muffled voices, rising and falling in agitation. She stopped in her tracks, feeling an instant flutter of apprehension. Her instincts shouted at her to turn back, but her curiosity, mingled with an unsettling bravery, propelled her forward.

As she peered into the dimming alley, the sight paralyzed her. The scene before her was horrifying, so utterly shocking that her mind struggled to comprehend it. A man, his face twisted in rage, was grappling with a smaller figure—a woman, her face contorted in terror. The sounds of struggle heightened: shouts and the sickening thud of bodies colliding against brick walls echoed ominously. Sarah's heart thundered in her chest, and a tremor of disbelief coursed through her.

She was frozen, torn between the instinct to retreat and the morbid fascination that gripped her. Finally, with an adrenaline-fueled burst, she ducked behind a nearby dumpster, her breath hitching in her throat. Peering cautiously over the edge, she realized she had stumbled into some grotesque scene of violence.

"Help! Somebody help!" the woman screamed, her voice tremulous with desperation, clawing at the air. Sarah's heart sank deeper, a horrifying realization dawning on her. The cries were a call for aid—how could she stand idly by? But the thought of stepping out into the light of day, of confronting that raw, unfiltered horror, was terrifying.

As the man struggled to overpower the woman, shadows danced around them, accentuating the chaos in the alley. English words, mingled with threats, devolved into a cacophony of fear and anger. Each plea for mercy tore at Sarah's conscience, igniting a fierce internal battle within her—a desire to run and hide versus a need to intervene, to make it stop.

Just then, the man raised his arm, and Sarah's breath caught in her throat. It was a blade glinting ominously in the twilight. Fear rushed through her veins as reality twisted into something grotesque. Time seemed to slow as she grappled with her next move, her mind racing with fragments of consequences—if she intervened, she could become a victim too. But if she ran away, she would be complicit in the violence.

Instinct took over as she clutched her phone, her fingers trembling as she dialed 911. It felt surreal, an out-of-body experience; she was a mere spectator to a horror show, and yet she was somehow responsible for breaking the cycle. The call connected, but all she could hear was her own heart pounding, drowning out the operator's voice.

"Hello? 911, what's your emergency?" the calm voice asked, but Sarah could barely hear over the din of chaos before her.

"Please, there's a fight... a woman is—" Her voice trembled, cutting off as she watched the struggle intensify. The man pressed the blade close to the woman's throat. The terror she felt surged, clenching her chest tighter than ever.

"Ma'am, calm down. Can you give me the location?" the operator urged, and Sarah's mind scrambled for the words, but all she could see was the violent scene overtaking her senses. The cool night air turned hot, suffocating her as she clenched her phone like a lifeline.

With a burst of clarity, she managed to whisper the alley's location before ending the call. She knew help was on the way, but a deafening sense of urgency pressed upon her. She couldn't just stand and watch. It was now or never.

Sarah steeled herself, heart racing, and stepped out from behind the dumpster. "Hey! Stop it!" she shouted, her voice trembling but resolute. The man momentarily turned, and in that fleeting instant, the woman seized the opportunity, pushing him away with whatever strength she could muster.

"Run! Get out of here!" The woman's voice rang out, a raw sound of desperation that echoed through the alley. Time froze. Sarah's pulse thundered in her ears as she darted forward, instinctively moving to help the woman.

In that split second, the man's expression shifted—a predatory glint flooding into his gaze as he turned back towards Sarah, the blade catching the last rays of dying sunlight. The glimmer froze her in place, paralyzing her with fear, and for a moment, she felt as if the world around her had crumbled to dust.

Sarah's heart raced, pounding relentlessly against her ribcage as the realization of the danger she was in washed over her like a wave. She turned, adrenaline overtaking her senses, and bolted away from the scene. The alley blurred in her periphery as she ran, tearing through the familiar pathways of her life—a mere moment ago, her biggest worry had been the monotony of her daily routine. Now, she had been irrevocably changed.

Days of comfort and complacency had evaporated. The fear she felt seemed to echo endlessly as she sprinted towards safety, heart pounding in sync with the dissonant reality that had invaded her life. Each breath felt heavy, laden with the weight of what she had witnessed. The normalcy of her world had ruptured, and she wasn't sure if she could ever get it back.

As she approached the main road, her body shook with fright, each step a reminder of the violent scene that had unfolded mere moments ago. Her mind raced with thoughts of the woman, the danger still lurking behind her. What would happen now? Would the police arrive in time?

A chill swept through her. She felt utterly powerless, a mere witness to a horror she could have never imagined. As the fluorescent lights of her workplace glowed in the distance, she halted, breath heaving.

Standing on the sidewalk, she was disoriented, the world spinning around her. She could hardly breathe as reality slammed into her—she had witnessed a violent crime—and there was no escaping it now. It coursed through her, seeping into her thoughts, threatening to drown her in a sea of fear and self-doubt.

But amidst the swirling chaos of her emotions, one thing became crystal clear: she had become a reluctant witness. And with that realization came the weight of responsibility, the agony of choice. Would she report the crime or would she run away, allowing fear to dictate her actions?

Her heart raced as she battled with indecision, torn between the urge to flee and the need to act. She took a deep breath, her pulse echoing in her ears. Whatever lay ahead, she knew, would change the course of her life forever.

The Implications of Silence

Sarah stood frozen at the precipice of a decision that felt far too weighty for her shoulders. The chill of the night air wrapped around her like a shroud, but it was the memory of the crime she had witnessed that truly sent shivers down her spine. She could still hear the muffled shouts, the sickening thud of a body hitting the ground, and the growl of the engine of a car speeding away. It echoed in her mind, relentless and haunting, a reminder of the danger that lurked just beyond the flickering streetlights.

She leaned against the cool brick wall of her apartment building, heart racing, her breath coming in shallow bursts. The decision loomed like a specter—should she report what she saw to the police? The thought sent her pulse racing faster. What if they didn't believe her? What if they dismissed her as just another hysterical woman making allegations for attention? She couldn't shake the feeling that speaking up would only invite more trouble into her life. She could become a target, a living witness for the kind of person who made sure such witnesses never lived to tell their stories.

Paranoia seeped into her thoughts like smoke—dark, curling tendrils that obscured her reason. What if the killer came after her? The images of his face—cold, calculating, and twisted with a kind of sadistic glee— flooded her mind, and she felt panic begin to rise. He might know she had seen him. What were the chances he had caught even a glimpse of her glaring in horror from behind the trash cans just a few feet away? Her heart thudded at the thought. He could be anywhere, appearing as an everyday person in her town, waiting, watching.

She squeezed her eyes shut, trying to force the whirlpool of thoughts to recede. Sarah pushed off the wall and attempted to steady herself. She had to breathe. She could not let fear control her. Yet, the shadows cast by the lamplights seemed to shift ominously, and every flicker of movement made her skin crawl. Perhaps staying silent would protect her. Perhaps if she simply kept her head down and put the whole experience behind her, it would fade away, a bad dream she could simply wake up from.

But was that right? Was it fair to the victim in the alley, the man whose life had been stolen in an instant? He deserved justice, but would voicing her knowledge really achieve that? Or would her presence in the story only weave her more tightly into the tangled web of violence that enveloped their small town? She could almost hear the whispers of the townsfolk—the judgment in their eyes, the doubt lurking just beneath the surface, the skepticism toward someone new in their midst.

In their quaint little community, outsiders were often viewed with distrust, particularly by those who held sway over local matters. Connections ran deep, and the currents of loyalty could be unforgiving. Sarah herself had felt it, the subtle exclusion that came with being a newcomer, no matter how friendly the people of Maplewood had seemed. It was a place where familiar faces carried more trust than the truth; ignorance was bliss, and she suspected that law enforcement might turn a blind eye to avoid rocking the boat.

Her thoughts turned to Jenna, her only real friend in this town. Jenna had stepped in during Sarah's early days in Maplewood, offering friendship and warmth when Sarah had felt like a castaway. They had shared late-night conversations over mugs of steaming tea, gossiped about their lives, and confided in each other. Jenna often spoke about her desire to help people and her frustration with the status quo, her fierce loyalty a trait that drew Sarah in. If anyone would understand the weight of the decision she faced, it would be her.

Sarah pulled out her phone and sent a quick message. "Can we meet? I need to talk." She stared at the screen like it held the solution to her dilemma, fingers hovering above the "send" button. What could she even say? Would Jenna understand her fear? Would she provide the urging that Sarah needed to step into the light and speak the truth? The three little dots appearing meant Jenna was typing back, and Sarah waited with bated breath.

"Of course! Meet at The Kettle around 7?" Jenna replied almost instantly.

The Kettle, a cozy little café with rustic decor and a warm atmosphere, was a haven for Sarah, a place where she felt she could breathe without the weight of her fears clawing at her throat. The sun would soon dip below the horizon, casting a golden hue over the town, and she found solace in the idea of sitting across from Jenna, where laughter and honesty bloomed even in darkness.

As Sarah walked through the door of The Kettle, the familiar smell of coffee and baked goods enveloped her. She spotted Jenna at their usual corner booth, her curly hair glowing under the café's soft lighting, fingers dancing on her phone. Jenna looked up and beamed when she saw Sarah—her smile bright and infectious, a contrast to the storm raging inside Sarah's mind.

"Hey! I missed you! Are you okay?" Jenna's voice was kind, her gaze probing yet supportive.

"Hey," Sarah replied, sliding into the booth opposite her. "I—I've been better." She lowered her voice, leaning in, her urgency spilling out as she tried to keep the atmosphere light despite the heaviness in her heart. "I witnessed something…something terrible the other night."

Jenna's expression shifted to concern, her eyes widening. "What happened?"

Sarah glanced around the café, the sense of needing to keep her voice low weighing heavily on her. She swallowed hard. "I saw a man get killed." The words felt foreign in her mouth, an ache settled in her stomach as they left her lips. "I was just passing by... and he—he just fell. I saw the whole thing."

Jenna's hand flew to her mouth, disbelief mixing with horror in her eyes. "Oh, my God, Sarah. Did you call the police?"

"I don't know yet." The vulnerability in her voice made her feel exposed, raw. "Part of me thinks I should, but…what if they don't believe me? I'm new here. I'm an outsider." "

You're not an outsider. You're my friend," Jenna insisted, leaning forward, a fierce light igniting in her eyes. "You have to tell them. It's the right thing to do."

"But what if I become a target?" Sarah whispered. "What if he comes after me?" The gravity of her fear hung in the air like a thick fog, stifling her resolve. A wave of vulnerability washed over her as thoughts of the killer crept back into her mind—dark eyes, cruel smirk, dangerously good at blending into the background.

Jenna's fingers intertwined with Sarah's, giving her a reassuring squeeze. "You're not alone in this, Sarah. I'm right here with you. We'll figure it out together. You cannot let fear control your life."

Tears stung Sarah's eyes, and she blinked them away, feeling the warmth of Jenna's support wrap around her like a comforting blanket. The weight pressing on her chest lightened ever so slightly. Jenna had always been there, her unwavering loyalty a beacon when shadows loomed large. "But what if something happens? I don't want to put you in danger too."

"Let's not think about that now," Jenna replied firmly. "Think about the victim. Think about the injustice. His life was taken from him. Don't let your silence lead to more violence."

Sarah felt the fight in Jenna's voice seep into her own resolve. The thought of that man's stillness, the finality of his fate, twisted her insides. He deserved more than to be a mere faceless casualty in a story brushed aside by indifference. She was his witness, and her voice mattered—if not for her safety, then for his memory.

"What if they don't believe me? What if they, like, find some way to twist my words?" Sarah grappled with her doubts even as she felt a flicker of determination igniting within her. Could she really step into the unknown? Would her words carry weight?

"Then you keep speaking," Jenna encouraged. "You keep telling everyone. You find a way to make them listen." The urgency in her voice was palpable, conviction shining in her eyes.

"Okay," Sarah breathed, her heart pounding fiercely as a swell of determination washed over her. "I'll do it. I'll go to the police."

Jenna's smile radiated the warmth of a sunrise breaking through a storm. "Yes! And I'll go with you."

"Really?" Sarah questioned, the very thought of solidarity making her chest swell.

"Of course! We're in this together," Jenna affirmed, her eyes sparkling with fierce loyalty. "You don't have to carry this burden alone."

The weight that had wrapped around Sarah's heart began to uncoil. Whether she was ready or not, she had taken a crucial step toward reclaiming her voice. The tumult of paranoia and fear may linger like shadows dancing at the edges of her consciousness, but she would not let them suffocate her.

"Thank you, Jenna. I—" again, the tears threatened to spill, tears of gratitude and mixed emotions as everything she had been wrestling with came flooding forward. "I don't know what I'd do without you."

"Here's to doing the right thing," Jenna raised her coffee cup in a mock toast. "Let's bring justice to that poor soul."

They shared a moment of companionship, their gazes locking in a silent agreement. In that instant, Sarah understood that courage wasn't a solitary journey—it was a shared path, traversed by those willing to stand by each other in the face of danger. The whirlpool of fear began to recede, and though the edges still felt sharp and dangerous, she was not facing this alone.

As they exited The Kettle, the world outside felt eerily calm, as if it were holding its breath. Sarah inhaled deeply, filling her lungs with crisp air. She felt the weight of her decision settling inside her like a palpable force—a determination fuelled by a desire for justice that overshadowed her fears.

Steeling herself, she glanced down the street and felt determination blooming within her, mingling with the fear. She knew the path ahead would be fraught with challenges, but for the first time since that night in the alley, Sarah felt a glimmer of hope begin to pierce through the darkness. Today marked a turning point, and she was ready to fight for the truth—for the man who could no longer fight for himself.

Together, they stepped forward into the unknown, ready to confront whatever might come their way. The implications of silence weighed heavily on their shoulders, yet Sarah felt a growing sense of purpose pushing her forward, defying the shadows that threatened to engulf her. She would no longer be defined by fear; she would be a voice not just for herself but for the countless others silenced by the violence of indifference.

The Decision

As Sarah stood outside the police station, the weight of her decision pressed heavily on her chest. The early evening sun cast long shadows on the sidewalk, and she could feel the tendrils of anxiety creeping into her mind. She glanced up at the imposing building, its façade cold and unwelcoming, a stark reminder of the world she was about to enter. Every fiber of her being screamed at her to turn around, to run back to the safety of her apartment, but she knew she couldn't. Not anymore.

She took a deep breath, the air thick with the smell of asphalt and the faint scent of honeysuckle from nearby bushes. For a moment, she allowed herself to picture the life she had lived only days ago: the mundane routines, the predictable conversations, the comfortable dullness that had enveloped her life. But that existence felt like a distant memory now, overshadowed by the horror she had witnessed. A woman had been brutally murdered, and she had seen it all.

With trembling hands, Sarah pushed open the heavy door of the station and stepped inside. The interior was stark, filled with stark fluorescent lights that buzzed overhead, illuminating the stark white walls decorated only by a few framed commendations for commendable service. The reception area was barren, save for a counter manned by a weary officer who barely glanced up as Sarah approached. Her heart raced as she found her footing, a deep sense of dread pooling in her stomach. This was the moment she had been both anticipating and dreading.

"Can I help you?" The officer's voice was bored, almost dismissive, as he finally tore his gaze away from the computer screen to meet her eyes.

"Um, I need to report a crime," she stammered, her voice shaking as she wrestled with the fear that threatened to choke her words.

The officer raised an eyebrow, leaning back in his chair. "What kind of crime?"

The question felt like a litmus test, a measure of her courage. As she opened her mouth to explain, the memories came rushing back like a tidal wave, overwhelming her senses. The flash of the knife, the terrified expression on the victim's face, the gut-wrenching sound of flesh meeting steel. She swallowed hard, trying to push the images away, trying to compose herself. "I witnessed a murder," she finally managed to say.

His skepticism was palpable. "Really?" he replied, his tone dripping with skepticism. "When?"

"Just a few nights ago," she said, her voice gaining confidence as she recounted the dark alley, the struggle she had witnessed, the screams for help that echoed hauntingly in her ears. "It was… it was awful. I saw everything. Please, you have to help me."

He tapped his pen nonchalantly against the desk, considering her for a moment. "Look, lady, it's not that I don't take your claim seriously, but we get calls like this all the time. People get confused, see things that aren't there. Without evidence, it's going to be hard to move on this."

"But there were witnesses!" she insisted, her desperation mounting. "I can't be the only one who saw it. Someone else must have seen it too!"

"Maybe," he replied, shrugging. "But let's take it one step at a time. What makes you think you even saw a murder? People get into fights all the time, especially down at the bars around this area."

Her heart sank. She felt small, any sense of power she had diminished by his indifference. It didn't help that the surrounding walls seemed to echo his doubts, the sterile environment stifling her courage. The entire room felt like it was closing in on her. "I know what I saw," she insisted, her voice barely above a whisper.

"Then let's hear it." He leaned forward slightly, a gesture that felt more condescending than inviting. "Start from the beginning. What exactly did you see?"

As the officer prepared to take her statement, Sarah's mind swirled with the details. Each recollection was visceral, replaying in her mind like a glitching film. She took a steadying breath, desperate to summon the strength to relay her story. "I was walking home from work when I heard yelling. I thought it was just some fight, you know? But then I heard a woman scream. It scared me, and I ducked into the alley to see what was going on..."

As she spoke, she struggled to maintain her composure. "There was a man... he was attacking her. I couldn't see his face clearly, just the knife glinting in the light. I didn't know what to do. I thought about running, but then I froze. I was terrified. I just—I just stood there. I watched as he..." Her voice wavered, and she felt the tears threatening to spill.

"Okay, slow down." He scribbled on his notepad, as if her grief was simply an item to be checked off. "What did the victim look like?"

"Blonde hair, wearing a red jacket," she mumbled, her voice barely audible. "There was so much blood... I thought I was going to be sick."

The officer glanced up at her, clearly weighing her words, and she felt her resolve wavering. Had she made the right choice? Was this all a futile effort that would lead nowhere? "How do we know you didn't just hear a fight?" he asked, his tone more blunt than she had expected. "There wasn't any crime scene discovered or any reports of missing persons. It's a quiet area. People don't just disappear."

"Because I would report it!" she exclaimed, her frustration breaking through. "You can't just ignore this. I know someone is dead. I know what I saw!"

His eyes narrowed slightly, assessing her with skepticism before finally relenting with a sigh. "Fine. Let's go through the details again." With a movement that felt disinterested, he gestured for her to continue.

As she recounted the moments that had seared into her mind, flashes of the crime replayed like a broken record, each moment underscoring her trauma. "I heard her pleading for her life, and then I saw the knife. He was so merciless," she murmured, the weight of her revelation heavy on her shoulders. "I thought he would turn around and see me. I thought I would die too."

"Did you call anyone afterward?" he questioned, pen hovering over the notepad.

"No!" she cried, anger and fear mingling in her voice. "I was too scared! I just ran home and locked the door, and I couldn't sleep. It made me feel sick, just pretending nothing happened."

"Did you tell anyone?" His tone was still devoid of concern, switching gears to the technicalities. "Family? Friends?"

"I told my friend, Jenna. She told me I should report it. I thought that by coming here, I was doing the right thing..." Her voice trailed off, uncertainty creeping back in. "But now... you're making me feel like it doesn't matter."

His expression softened slightly, but it was mixed with a weary resolve. "Look, it's not that it doesn't matter. But you should know that coming forward is a big deal. It's not just a report—it becomes part of an investigation. You might have to testify, and that can take a toll. Some people don't realize that until it's too late."

Sarah felt her heart sink. She thought of the emotional weight of reliving the experience, the stares of strangers in the courtroom, the defense attorney's probing questions making her feel like a fool for witnessing such a horrific act. Would she be believed? Would they see her as a victim or just another story? "I still think it's important," she said at last, her conviction reigniting. "I have to do something. Silence isn't an option."

"Alright," he replied, visibly begrudgingly as he resumed his note-taking, even as he maintained a demeanor that suggested he didn't fully believe her account. "But understand this: it's going to get messy, and the system isn't perfect. There may be a lot of red tape and a lot of waiting. Are you ready for that?"

Saying she was ready felt like an understatement, yet Sarah nodded determinedly. "I have to be. That woman deserves justice."

With a sigh, the officer finally set down his pen. "Alright then. Let's get started. I need you to recount everything you remember."

As she continued her account, she sensed a shift in herself—a transition from being a passive observer of her own life to an active participant. She may have felt invisible before, but in this moment, she had a purpose. She wanted to honor the victim, to bring her truth to light, to ensure that no one else would have to endure the terror she had witnessed.

As she bravely recounted the details—how it all unfolded, the words exchanged between the attacker and the victim—her hands began to shake, a reminder of the raw fear that still thundered in her veins. The officer wrote furiously at times, pausing occasionally to ask for clarification, each question sending her deeper into the heart of her memories. Her breathing quickened, matching the escalating tension in her chest as the darkness of that night washed over her like a tidal wave.

Once they finished, Sarah stepped back from the desk, her heart still racing. It felt surreal; she had finally reported the crime, something she'd been dreading yet yearning to do simultaneously. Part of her felt a rush of relief, while another part was still steeped in anxiety, realizing the enormity of her actions and the potential repercussions they could carry.

"Thank you," she whispered, unsure of what else to say, the air heavy with the silence of unspoken words.

"No problem," the officer replied, his tone neutral. "You'll need to check in with detective tomorrow. He'll want to ask more questions." He leaned back in his chair and waved her off, returning to his screen, his professionalism somewhat restoring Sarah's faith in the process.

Stepping out of the station, Sarah paused, allowing the fresh, cool air to envelop her. It took a moment for her mind to process what had just happened. The relief she had anticipated didn't come rushing in as she had hoped. Instead, there was dread, an unshakeable feeling that things were about to change irreversibly.

As she walked to her car, unease thrummed beneath her skin. Had she made the right choice? Would she become a target? The streets felt different now, the fear that had been swirling within her turning into a palpable force. It was too quiet. The city hummed with life, yet she felt utterly exposed. The thought of Ethan, the killer, lurking somewhere in the shadows sent shivers down her spine.

A low growl echoed across the stillness, and her heart raced. Jackals roamed the outskirts of town, and she could almost hear their distant howls as if they were warning her of impending danger. Those haunting cries felt like a sign, a reminder that something sinister was lurking just out of sight.

As she entered her car, her hands gripped the steering wheel tightly. She spent the drive home replaying every emotion she had felt during her interactions at the station, the officer's skepticism, her own fear, but also the deeper need for justice that had driven her to report the crime. Beyond the façade of normalcy, she could feel the weight of her decision settling heavily on her chest.

Bracing herself for what lay ahead, she needed to remain vigilant. This wasn't just about her anymore; it was about the truth, about justice for the woman whose life had been cruelly snatched away. As she turned onto her street, she felt a renewed sense of purpose blooming within her, both invigorating and terrifying. Each step she took toward acknowledging her experience brought with it layers of anxiety and resilience.

Arriving home, she felt the familiar safety of her room wash over her, yet the echoes of that night still haunted her. She knew reporting the crime was only the beginning, a step into an unknown world of complexities and fear. She slowly unpacked her bag, the familiar items a comfort, while the images of the crime still flashed in her mind. But beneath that swirl of despair lay a growing flame of determination; she had taken a stand, and she wouldn't back down.

As the evening deepened, she sat on her couch, staring at the news blaring in the background, stories of unfortunate events swirling through the air. Each flickering image and breaking news report felt like another reminder of the shadows edging closer to her reality. Deep down, she understood that her actions had set off a chain of events—a ripple through the very fabric of her life.

Tomorrow would come with its own set of trials. She could feel it in her bones. The uncertainty of what lay ahead both thrilled and frightened her. The desire for safety clashed with the pull of justice as fear battled against a newfound sense of agency. She had stepped into the light, but with that light came a darkness she could not yet comprehend.

With thoughts in turmoil, Sarah finally allowed herself to sink into the couch, wrapping a blanket around her. Closing her eyes, she took a deep breath, whispering a silent prayer for the woman she had seen. Tomorrow was going to be a fight—one she was determined to win, whatever the cost.

THE HUNTER

The Calm Before the Storm

In the muted light of the early dusk, Ethan sat in the small cluttered room of an unremarkable apartment that clung to the edges of the city, a space filled with shadows and secrets. The walls were lined with jagged scars of paint peeling away, remnants of a past that clashed with his meticulously curated present. Despite the chaos that enveloped him, he thrived in the controlled chaos of his mind, where shadows loomed larger than life. Everything about him projected unyielding calm, a fortitude seasoned with a hint of madness, youthful fervor tempered by years of haunting experiences.

He leaned back against the tattered sofa, a hand deftly running through his unkempt hair as his sharp blue eyes traced the cracks in the ceiling. With every breath, he orchestrated a symphony of creation tinged with destruction, his mind tirelessly churning through the intricate plans he had laid for Sarah. The power he felt coursing through him was intoxicating, a heady rush that cascaded over every ounce of his being. To rid her from the narrative was not merely an objective; it was his right, his destiny.

The memories came rushing forth unbidden, peeling away layers of his calculated demeanor. His childhood had been marred by violence, a chaotic home where vulnerability was met with viciousness, and compassion morphed into a weapon wielded against the weak. There was a time when the walls of his family home had reverberated with the echoes of screams, the trauma intertwining with his very essence. Each argument, each physical altercation had chipped away at him, shaping him into the predator he had become.

He remembered the moment it had clicked—the precise alignment of circumstances that had drawn him into the dreadful dance he now thrived in. It was the day he realized that control was an illusion for the unworthy but a reality for the strong; he had promised himself never to be weak again. The sanguine satisfaction of domination over others filled the hollow void that had once threatened to consume him—a void so deep that even light could not reach its depths.

Images shifted and blurred into the foreboding present as he recalled the chaotic encounter on that fateful night. In his mind, every detail unfolded in vivid high resolution: the frigid air swirling with tension, the flickering streetlight casting grotesque shadows against the brick walls, the silenced screams that echoed in his ears. Sarah had stepped decisively into his life, her ordinary existence an inviting challenge to him. She had stolen a pivotal moment of his life, unwittingly turning his carefully calculated world into a transient dream threatened by the specter of chaos and exposure. The memory of her wide eyes flashing with horror ignited a twisted sense of exhilaration within him.

He envisioned her now, that fragile balance of terror and determination igniting a fire in her green eyes. The woman would prove a worthy adversary, he mused. But adversaries were simply another part of the game he played, the pieces moved on a chessboard. While she was desperate and afraid, Ethan was invigorated by it. Her fear, swirling around him like sweet perfume, filled the gaps where he felt understood against the chaos inside.

As twilight encroached upon the city, he meticulously prepared for the next step in his plan. The dim light cast airy shadows that danced against his skin, amplifying the contours of a figure that exuded dark charisma. He opened the drawer of the small table beside him, revealing an array of items—tools of his trade, each so carefully chosen. Knives glinted menacingly, their sharp edges reflecting the dim light like diamonds, and a breathable mask lay tucked at the bottom—a vestige of precaution that he would soon don.

He closed his eyes for a moment, allowing the sensations of the room to seep into him. This place was where the synergy of a stalker and prey unfolded, a theater of the twisted game he relished. Soon, he would become the shadow that chased her, the embodiment of her darkest fears.

With a deliberate rhythm, he donned a fitted black jacket over a dark sweatshirt, his movements precise and assured. There was an art to the preparation, an aspect that transcended the act itself. Every motion was instinctive, a well-rehearsed dance he executed flawlessly. Each item was a part of him, each step toward the unknown both thrilling and exhilarating.

His thoughts shifted to the web of information he had meticulously woven about her. Sarah was no longer a mere name; she was a series of data points, a carefully constructed persona that he had dissected. The café where she worked served as a stage, its mundane atmosphere laced with an undercurrent of secrets he alone knew. He reveled in the confluence of the ordinary and the horrific; it fascinated him when such mundane lives unwittingly drifted into darkness.

As the evening deepened and the last light of the sun brushed against the skyline, he felt a pulse of excitement resonate in his bones. Soon, he would step into her world, a harbinger of chaos disguised as a shadow. Her life would twist at his command, leaving nothing but ripples of terror in her wake, and he would be the architect of her undoing.

Images of their last encounter flashed through his mind, her trembling frame pressed against the brick wall as she tried to comprehend the nightmare before her. The gurgling of adrenaline fueled his thoughts as he savored the memory—the sheer terror in her eyes, the jagged breaths that escaped her lips. Control fluctuated in such moments; he became both predator and prey. It was exhilarating.

He clenched and unclenched his fist, the thrill electrifying his veins as he momentarily lost himself in his thoughts. The clock on the wall ticked methodically, a metronome to the symphony of his dark intentions.

But even as he exulted, a thread of unease whispered below the surface. Memories of his childhood surfaced—harsh reprimands for being weak or cowardly. In the cold shadows cast by the stark lighting of his apartment, he caught glimpses of his father's rage and his mother's fading spirit. Each encounter had left permanent scars, silent reminders of a life spent battling against his own fears, now projected onto his victims.

Ethan's lips curled into a twisted smile as he turned away from the frailty of memory with practiced ease, shoving the feelings of doubt back where they belonged—in the depths of his subconscious. Resolution washed over him in waves, a tide pulling him off the shoreline of hesitation and toward the cliff of action. A kill was a kill—nothing more, nothing less. A necessary assertion of power that disproved the myths taught by his childhood about justice and mercy.

It was time to take back control. He meticulously planned her movements, watching her transition from the café to the bus stop, carefully cataloging the paths she took. All her weaknesses mapped like the intricate patterns on an ancient tapestry, waiting for the right hand to unravel it.

As darkness blanketed the city, he exited his apartment, locking the door behind him with a deliberate click that reverberated through the quiet halls. Outside, the streets were bathed in a pale amber glow that illuminated his path—a lure inviting shadows to dance just out of sight. The streets were alive, yet strangely vacant, an irony that spoke to him in hushed tones. He thrived in the spaces that pulsed with the heartbeat of fear yet harbored the illusion of safety.

Driving through the familiar streets, he became acutely aware of the dread swirling just beneath the surface of the city's bright lights. The atmosphere felt electric, charged with an impending storm. Each traffic light served as a reminder—time was running out for Sarah. With every approaching glow of red, anticipation mounted.

The shadows became his allies, softly draping over him as he navigated the streets where they shared an unbreakable bond, shaping him into who he had become. He reveled in the silence—the disquiet before the storm. There was a particular thrill in being the unseen puppet master guiding precariously dancing marionettes through the dark. As he parked his car down an ordinary street a few blocks away from her home, he let the silence wrap around him.

He observed Sarah's movements through the window, studying the way she flipped her hair over her shoulder, oblivious to the nightmare that was about to unfold. Moments like these heightened the tension, transforming the mundane into something sinister. The calm before the storm hung palpably in the air, a delicate curtain that promised to rise into chaos.

Checking the time, he felt satisfaction wash over him, knowing that the stage was set. Every second that ticked by intensified his thrill, elevating his resolve as he transformed from mere observer into a predator with blood on his hands. He readied himself, strapping the mask securely over his face; it was time to end the game and take control of the narrative that had briefly slipped through his fingers.

As he stepped onto the sidewalk, he could feel the world dimming around him, the breeze carrying promises of upheaval and madness. Streetlights flickered and buzzed, casting eerie shadows that flickered against the concrete. With each step, he blended seamlessly into the night, a demon rising within a city of dreams, unshackled and free.

The air grew thicker with the weight of the impending encounter— he could sense it, the crackling anticipation tinged with the bittersweet taste of inevitability. The storm was coming. And as he prowled toward the inevitable chaos, Ethan embraced the darkness with open arms, knowing that even as the hunter, he had become prey to the fear he instigated in others.

Tonight, it would all culminate—the spiral of madness woven into the fabric of life would finally unravel, leaving a tapestry of terror in its wake. Everything was falling into place, and he reveled in the familiar refrain of anticipation, punctuating the calm before the storm that would sweep through the heart of Sarah's world.

The Pursuit Begins

Ethan leaned back in his chair, a disheveled pile of papers strewn across the desk before him. He felt an unsettling thrill as he stared at the police report detailing the crime Sarah had witnessed. The ink still glistened, fresh and full of opportunity. Shivering with excitement, he ran a finger over the words, his pulse quickening. She had reported it, she had taken the bait—now, the game was on.

The flickering light bulb overhead cast shifting shadows against the walls, and overhead, the darkened ceiling fan whirred lazily, matching the rhythm of Ethan's thoughts. Each stroke of adrenaline worked through his veins, invigorating him for the task ahead. He picked up a crumpled map of the town only to drop it back down in favor of his phone, pulling up the police report online for another look.

From that report, he gleaned a wealth of information about Sarah— her last-known location, the route she frequented, the places she might call sanctuary. Obsession coursed through him like a drug; he could feel each heartbeat echoing the fundamental truth: She had seen him, and now she could not be allowed to speak of it again.

Ethan could almost hear her voice, a whisper unfurling in his mind. "Please, I didn't want to see anything. I don't want any trouble." Her pleas, a mere moment lost in time, were now twisted remnants of a chase yet to unfold. He chuckled softly, the darkness of that moment resonating within him, thrilling him. There was a power to it that he reveled in, a control he was determined to maintain.

The clock on the wall steadily ticked, accompanying the mental countdown to his hunt. He wouldn't let her escape. She had seen too much, and now she was his. Gathered documents and notes fuzzy with anticipation, he stood abruptly, setting off into the growing dusk.

Ethan navigated through shadowy alleys and quiet streets, his mind alight with the thrill of the chase that awaited him. He pushed open the door of his van, a nondescript vehicle that blended seamlessly with the darkening surroundings. He closed the door with a thud, a sound swallowed by the stillness of the night. He knew the town like the back of his hand, each twist and turn etched into his memory. His pulse quickened as he envisioned the map in his head; despite being small-town America, it held secrets like any other vast city—vulnerable spots, alleys that led nowhere, and shadows that cloaked intentions.

As he roared out of the parking lot, he envisioned Sarah's movements, her familiar routines enriched by the knowledge he had gained from her report. Where would she have sought refuge? What places felt safe enough for her fleeing heart? Would she trust her friends, or would paranoia guide her to isolation?

Stalking through the night, Ethan reveled in the dance of predator and prey. He imagined her navigating the same streets and sidewalks she had walked countless times. He pictured her with a warmth he noticed in her voice and in the softness of her face when she thought of safety. But that warmth would soon chill when she realized there was nowhere to hide.

He pulled up to a corner café that would be a regular stop for her. Faded lights hung above the entrance as patrons came and went, oblivious to the dark game unfolding just beyond the shadows. Ethan parked, running his fingers along the smooth steering wheel, the scent of leather mingling with his warm breath. He scanned the area, deliberate and calculated, his instincts sharp. If Sarah had chosen anywhere familiar to her, this would have been it.

Minutes passed, and just as Ethan began to fret, she emerged, a ghost of herself amid ordinary activity. She moved cautiously, eyes darting, her shoulders hunched as if trying to blend with the shadows. A thrill ignited within him—there she was. He leaned forward, revelry blossoming as he wrestled with a yearning to snatch her from that moment and into his own darkness.

There was no beauty in the chase without a little fear, he thought. He grinned, his teeth bared, as he watched her tension while mingling in the crowd, swallowed by the enticing veil of anonymity. It was a bittersweet irony; she had stepped into the sanctuary, yet it was merely a deceptive facade. He felt the chatter of families and friends around her was a lullaby—a false sense of security promising safety. But Sarah would learn soon enough that the darkness pursues even in the light.

With the thrill of the hunt in his veins, he followed her, a specter haunting the edges of her reality. He mirrored her movements, slipping through the throngs of conversations and laughter—the ringing sound of dishes clinking as coffee came pouring. She paused, glancing over her shoulder, a fleeting moment of instinct where previous worries now danced behind her eyes. He pressed lower, merging into the shadows as adrenaline surged through him, unwavering.

Ethan pulled into a side alley, waiting to see which way she would take. The smells of closed restaurants drifted in his direction, tainting the air with oil and grease but rendering him unbothered. His excitement pulsed as he envisioned the lengths she might venture to save herself, anticipating her next steps while he planned his own.

It was this volley of strategizing and stalking that fascinated him the most, the heady intoxication of every calculated move. He relished in the thrill of being a step ahead; he had always been the predator. Would it ever get old? In a world where nothing felt truly alive, this was his art.

Ethan had stalked through the shadows of countless towns before, each one a canvas he painted with moments of chaos designed to rip truth from the fabric of unwary souls. But no one had given him quite the exhilaration Sarah did. She churned through his thoughts like the twisting bark of trees swaying in the night. Every image of her left him fixated, hyperaware of how she had begun to evolve in his mind's gaze—a reflection of the danger she posed and the fragility of what her survival meant to him.

He followed her as she turned down streets he knew by heart. He could map her patterns by instinct alone, watching as she moved from place to place. The whispers of her past scrubbed around him like the storm clouds gathering on the horizon. Where was she going? Who would she trust? Each new movement signaled a strategy on his part, for he could not merely play along; he had to emerge victorious, unmasked.

As night deepened, the atmosphere thickened with impending dread. The shrill sound of the wind rushed past, engulfing him, absorbing his thoughts and heightening his adrenaline. All around him, shadows flickered beneath dim streetlights, calling to him with sweet temptation—would he linger here, tangled in the beauty of a hunt gone awry?

Yes, he'd been here too long. Sarah wouldn't remain blind forever; she would sense the weight of darkness pressing in close, and he could already envision how she might start outsmarting herself, how the paranoia could weave a web of her own making.

Eventually, she retreated into another café—this one darker, with the permanence of looming shadows that denied light entrance. He tightened his jaw, eyeing the place with equal measures of restraint and excitement. Would she stay there too long? Would she let her guard down? He was a mere hunter, lurking in the periphery; waiting was his true art.

Ethan moved on instinct, scoping out the entrances while contemplating the paths he could take—the windows, the alleyway, a fire escape perhaps? But he'd have to play it safe, keeping close to her without triggering the alert she didn't yet see. Instead, he opted for methodical torment, feasting on the fear that would set her heart racing.

Watching from his wheezing van, he began sharpening his view into the café beyond. They had replaced the usual seating with red cushioned chairs that had seen better days. Flashes of laughter broke through the edges of his concentration, but the world felt layered, as though encapsulated in honeyed glass. He focused on Sarah, isolating her amid the blurs and hums.

There she was, sitting at a window table across from another woman—Jenna, he deduced from the fleeting glimpses he'd glimpsed previously. To have the gentleness of friendship beside her would only serve to confuse her instincts. He longed to disrupt that bond, sever the connection of familiarity that might provide her solace.

Sarah's laughter trickled through the glass, crystal clear amidst the daunting ambiance. His fingers gripped the steering wheel, slowly crushing the plastic, as his heart thundered in his chest. Resentment bubbled over within him, a violent storm raging against the beauty of her laughter, a reminder that while she was safe, she was still vulnerable. He couldn't let that connection linger; if anything, he craved to unravel it all.

The café's lights flickered momentarily, a dulled backdrop to the colors of his thoughts. Sarah's face glowed with an infectious smile—he hated it. He needed to sow fear, to ingrain the frights pulling her deeper into paranoia. But how long would she remain undisturbed? How far would she venture before she recognized the sudden absence of safety in the air?

He parked, washed in a coating of tension, the haunt of the hunt lingering, twisting around him. His instincts told him to wait, to bide his time until the opportune moment seized itself. He could still see her from the reflection against the window, oblivious to the danger prowling beneath the surface.

Time slithered by as he read the movements around her, the ebbing tide of joy erupting within that café. He imagined himself slipping inside—what would it be like to see that smile extinguished? Would her laughter shift to fear? Would panic stretch her features taut until each muscle quaked with recognition of her peril? And what of her friend, blind to the approaching darkness?

The air in the café felt too light, too inviting; he needed to change that. Shroud her world with shadows while wrapping himself in her memories; he would almost enjoy it.

As if following the blueprint of his imagination, the moments stretched endlessly, fragmented glances between conversations pushed him deeper into a manic rush. The pit of excitement welled within him as he envisioned that stepping stone—that point of no return. His chest tightened, inching upward as he prepared himself; there was a thrill in the idea of strategically engulfing every ounce of warmth Sarah had shared through laughter, extinguishing it like snuffing out a candle.

With determination hardened into resolve, he turned the corner and stepped from his van into the darkness. He had to slip closer; this intrigue had to breathe life in suspense. He would clip the strings holding her together, pulling each thread until she spun into chaos.

And despite the fleeting unease that tickled the back of his mind, he couldn't ignore the sheer excitement that this hunt was about to unleash—where madness merged with passion, and dark whimsy came alive in each stalking step. He was drawing closer to her, the sound of her laughter fading into echoes as he navigated the alleyway leading to the café's back entrance.

Silently, he crept around the corner, allowing the shadows to envelop him, a loyal embrace just waiting to engulf a light into the 40 The jackals abyss. Quinn, the barman, leaned over the bar wiping a glass; the soft tunes of distant music filled the night air as laughter and chatter thrived in the café. Ethan edged closer, muscles tense as he gauged Sarah's every movement, watching for the right moment to plunge into her world.

The race was on. The hunt was about to reach a fever pitch. Before the night closed around her, he would have her. She was his now—the jewel of his obsession waiting just beyond his grasp, waiting for that moment when he could tip her world upside down, drown her in darkness, and silence the witness once and for all.

The Killer's Mind

Ethan sat in the dimly lit room, the glow of the dying embers casting flickering shadows across the walls, creating shapes that danced mockingly to the rhythm of his racing thoughts. The peeling wallpaper, once a cheerful shade of yellow, now faded to a sickly hue, mirrored the decay he felt inside. The air was thick with the stench of metal—blood, regret, and desperation mixing into a toxic cocktail that lingered in his nostrils. He breathed it in, letting it fill the hollow spaces of his soul, a twisted comfort in a world that felt more alien by the day.

He rubbed his temples, fighting against the itch of his memory, the constant replay of that night—the chaos, the screams, the thrill of the hunt. His mind raced back to Sarah, the witness who had dared to linger too long in his world. She had seen him; she would talk. A scoff escaped his lips at the absurdity of it all. Did she not understand? She was nothing but a fleeting moment in his carefully crafted life. The truth was, she was merely an obstacle, one he had never intended to face.

Yet, as the weight of his existence pressed down upon him, Ethan couldn't shake the sense of determination that rose within him like a tide. He had spent countless hours buried in thought, dissecting the very fabric of what made him tick. He needed to remind himself of the world in which he lived, the corrupt landscape that shaped his perspective—a world that had done nothing but fail him.

He thought back to his childhood, the jagged pieces of his past slicing through the fog of his intellect like shards of glass. His father, a ife-long employee of a factory, returned home each night with resentment painted across his face, gnashing his teeth in the dark, always blaming the world for the burdens he carried. Nothing Ethan did could ever remedy the hollowness within that man; no matter how hard he tried, he became just another reflection of disappointment, an extension of his father's failures.

His mother, too, was lost in her bubble of oblivion, taking refuge in the haze of alcohol that swept her away from the bleakness of their reality.

She had long stopped being a mother, her laughter replaced by the empty echoes of broken promises and half-hearted apologies. She would often sit in her chair, eyes glazed, mumbling incoherently as if speaking to ghosts. In those moments, Ethan learned that trust was a commodity reserved for the naïve, the weak, and that attachment to others only led to pain—a lesson he would carry like a shield into adulthood.

The streets he grew up on were unforgiving, filled with broken dreams and shattered lives. He learned early on that weakness was a sin and survival depended on strength—a lesson drummed into him by the very society that had cast him aside. He observed the world with a detached curiosity, noting the way people scowled at the less fortunate, how the fabric of their lives enforced a hierarchy based on power and influence. He had decided, then, to navigate the darkness rather than be crushed beneath it.

As a teenager, Ethan felt the flickering embers of rebellion ignite within him, fueled by a burgeoning desire for control. He saw others yield to the whims of fate, and it disgusted him. The cycle continued—a perpetual dance of violence and despair. Some succumbed to the chaos, while he learned to harness it, to embrace the unpredictability of existence and mold it into something he could wield against those who dared to threaten him.

Every event in his life, every heartbreak, every whisper of doubt, further molded Ethan into the man he was now—a predator ready to pounce on the weak when opportunity presented itself. He justified his actions as a form of justice, an unspoken balance he sought to achieve in an unjust world. Those who drew breath without purpose, he believed, were simply occupying space that could be better utilized. In his warped worldview, wiping them out was a service, a cleansing, a necessary evil.

But lurking beneath the bravado was the truth of his existence: he was scared, desperately so. The fear of rejection, the gnawing uncertainty that threatened to unravel him at any moment, fueled the fire of his resolve. He had surrounded himself with shadows, physical manifestations of the nausea that spewed from the depths. Yet, in the back of his mind, there lingered an insidious voice—the ever-present whisper of inadequacy that gnawed relentlessly at his soul. What if he was not strong enough? What if he failed?

It was this very fear that propelled him forward, compelling him to seek validation in the chaos he unleashed. Each victim was like a rung on a ladder, propelling him upward through his own perception of success. With every act, he reclaimed a piece of his identity—his power, his control over circumstance. But like all things built on a foundation of sand, it was precarious, teetering on the edge of collapse. The anticipation of falling was exhilarating and terrifying all at once, and Ethan found himself addicted to the rush.

His mind drifted back to Sarah again. She'd dared to defy him, to disrupt the fragile ecosystem he'd created. The adrenaline surged through his veins at the thought of her pendulum swinging between life and death, wrought with doubt and fear. But it wasn't just her—she represented a challenge he had to face head-on, a test of his resolve. If she escaped, it would take everything he had built and turn it to ash. He felt a strange mixture of anger and admiration; her courage felt audacious against the backdrop of his fears, illuminating his own weaknesses.

But even in his dark thoughts, Ethan was conflicted. Would he ever be able to silence that voice in his head that screamed for acknowledgment and respect? Did he want to continue down this spiral of violence and chaos? Or was there a part of him clinging to the remnants of a conscience he had buried long ago? The existential dread squeezed at his chest, stifling him, and compelled him to confront the shadow— the embodiment of what he truly feared: being forgotten, ignored, and discarded just like the countless others he had seen crumble beneath the weight of despair.

Could he reconcile who he was with who he pretended to be? The ambition to maintain his identity was palpable, reflecting a desire for power, yet drowned in a quiet desperation. He was stuck in a cycle of violence, and at any moment, he could slip's guts and leave behind someone aching to forget the pain he inflicted. But the truth echoed within the dark recesses of his mind: If he didn't act, he wouldn't last long in this game. It was survival of the fittest, and life had never shown him mercy.

The flicker of the embers began to wane, and a chill crept into the air. He needed to act; the inertia threatened to paralyze him. Actions demanded resolution, and resolution beckoned him; there was no turning back now. He had to confront Sarah—not just to suppress a loose end, but to protect the only version of himself that mattered—a predatory version, a version not hogtied by the emotional turmoil that threatened to drown him.

In that instant, clarity consumed Ethan. The world around him faded to a dull roar, and all that mattered now was the chase, the thrill of the hunt igniting something primal within him. The darkness would be peeled back, revealing the truth of his existence for the final confrontation that lay ahead.

He envisioned Sarah's terrified face—the pleading eyes that would reflect her mortality. The vulnerability that had once disgusted him now stirred a sense of power unlike anything he had experienced before. Fear would cocoon her, an intimate embrace he intended to relish, savoring the agony and despair like a fine wine. He would be the orchestrator of her fate, the puppet master pulling the strings in a dance of life and death.

In his mind, Ethan finalized the absurd narrative that justified his actions. He was simply reclaiming order—a cruel but necessary role in a world that had offered him nothing but chaos. He watched society crumble through his experiences, the fractured relationships corrupting the sanctity of social fabric. He could not allow this woman, this unwitting witness, to dismantle the vestiges of control he had painstakingly carved out. As the clock ticked on, he resolved to seize what he needed—to eliminate the threat and etch his legacy into the dark corners of existence.

With each breath, he prepared for the hunt. Ethan would descend upon her like a predator, savor every moment suspended in electrifying tension. This was not just a matter of surviving; it was about conquering, achieving a final victory against a world that had perpetually assessed his worth with a scornful glance. He would step into that light, allowing the darkness to engulf Sarah, and, in doing so, reinforce his warped reality—a reality where justice reigns within his grasp, free from judgment and bathed in authoritative control.

The shadows whispering around him felt like a warm embrace, wrapping him in determination, assurance, and strength. He was ready. It was time to lunge forward into the chaos, release the hounds of his own making, and let the cards fall where they may. Sarah had become a crucial part of his existence; in her defeat, he would find his redemption.

Ethan straightened, his resolve solidifying with each heartbeat. The storm was coming, and he intended to be the one to wield it, permitting no more interruptions, no more distractions. Sarah would not escape him. She would serve as the final cog in his machinations—the keystone that bound his fractured world together. The sun would set

tonight, casting long shadows over the landscape, and he would emerge as the master of its twilight.

Fleeing Shadows

The Escape

Sarah's heart pounded in her chest like a drum, each beat echoing the urgency of her situation. The weight of Ethan's relentless pursuit pressed down on her shoulders, a tangible force compelling her to move. She pushed through the door of the café and felt the cool night air hit her, a stark contrast to the stifling atmosphere inside. Every instinct screamed at her to run, to escape the gruesome reality that had shattered her once-ordinary life.

The streets were eerily quiet, the kind of unsettling silence that wrapped around her like a shroud. She glanced over her shoulder, half convinced that she might see Ethan lurking in the shadows, his eyes gleaming with predatory excitement. Each step she took felt heavy, as if the concrete beneath her was trying to pull her back into her old life—a life where she wasn't running for her life.

She turned left into a side alley, the dim streetlights flickering overhead. The ground was slick with rain, each puddle reflecting the scant light like a shattered mirror. She could hear the distant sound of a siren, a reminder that help was out there but so far away. Her mind raced, flitting from one thought to another: What would happen if she got caught? If he found her? She had to keep moving. There was no other option.

The alley narrowed, the walls closing in around her. A sudden noise startled her—a scuffle of feet behind her. Fear sliced through her, sharp and unexpected. She ducked into an alcove, pressing her back to the cool, wet brick, her breath hitching in her throat. Silence enveloped her. She strained to listen, ears tuned to the faintest sound.

Then she heard it—footsteps, slow and deliberate, mingling with the sound of her own heartbeat. She stifled a gasp, shutting her eyes as if that would somehow make her invisible. Images of Ethan's face flashed in her mind, grotesque and looming. How could one man inspire so much terror? She felt the tremors of panic rising within her, stifled by sheer will.

The footsteps faded, and she opened her eyes, her heart still racing. She couldn't stay in one place for too long. She should move, should run. Forcing herself to breathe deeply, she slipped out from her hiding spot and continued to navigate the alleyway. Shadows danced in the periphery, twisting and turning in a macabre ballet of flickering lights.

As she emerged into another street, she was struck by the stark contrast to the alley's oppressive darkness. The streetlights illuminated the pavement, casting a yellow glow that felt both warm and inviting but also exposed her vulnerability. She had to find shelter—a safe haven from the monster hunting her.

Turning right, she sprinted down the street, keenly aware of every sound around her. The distant murmur of a late-night gathering at a bar provided a strange comfort, but also a reminder of how close she was to normalcy—how easy it would be to slip back into the life she once knew. But that life was gone; all that remained was the overwhelming sense of danger lurking just behind her.

Her breathing turned ragged, each inhalation tasting of fear. She could feel the chill of panic creeping up her spine, chilling her to the bone. A part of her wanted to scream, to cry out for help, but the other part—the part trained by terror—knew better. No one could help her now.

She spotted a small convenience store a few blocks down, its neon sign flickering. It seemed like a beacon of safety. Clenching her fists at her sides, she pushed herself towards the entrance, each step a defiance against the growing darkness gnawing at her heels.

Inside, the fluorescent lights buzzed, casting a harsh glare on the shelves piled high with snacks and drinks. The store was nearly empty, the late hour keeping most customers at bay. She moved quickly down the aisle, her gaze darting to the exit. She could feel the adrenaline coursing through her veins, propelling her forward while simultaneously weighing her down.

The cashier stood behind the counter, engrossed in a mobile game, blissfully unaware of the storm about to crash through his doors. "Excuse me," she started, but her voice was barely above a whisper, barely breaking through the rush of desperation that filled her.

He looked up, his expression shifting from casual indifference to surprise. "You okay?"

There was a lurching sensation in her stomach. "Have you seen anyone suspicious? A man… he's been following me." Her words fell out in a rush, a floodgate that opened in a moment of sheer impulse.

His brow furrowed as he took in her disheveled hair, the wild look in her eyes. "No, I haven't seen anyone," he replied cautiously, glancing toward the glass door as if expecting a monster to walk through.

Panic clawed at her insides. "I have to hide. Please," she implored, desperation scraping at her throat. "Just for a few minutes. I think he's close behind."

The cashier hesitated, weighing the potential risk of involving himself in something he didn't fully understand. But then the alarm in her eyes, the raw fear etched in her features seemed to move him. "Okay, go to the back. Quietly," he instructed, pointing toward a door. "There's a stockroom."

Without waiting for more encouragement, she darted toward the door he'd indicated, pushing it open and slipping inside. The cool air in the stockroom contrasted sharply with the anxious heat of her skin, and she leaned against the wall, allowing herself a moment to breathe.

The space was cluttered with boxes and bags, the smell of cardboard overwhelming. She crouched behind a stack of crates, pressing her back against the wall. Her pulse thudded in her ears as she listened, straining to catch any sounds from outside.

Minutes stretched on like hours, the silence amplifying her every breath. She felt her mind spiraling, thoughts racing. What if he came in? What if the cashier changed his mind? Panic wrapped its fingers around her throat, tightening like a noose. The darkness of her surroundings mirrored the uncertainty swirling in her head.

Just then, she heard it—the faint jingle of the bell on the door, followed by footsteps that made her heart race anew. She held her breath. Was it him? Had he found her?

The footsteps moved around the store, slow and deliberate, as if he were playing a game—his hunt painstakingly precise. Sarah squeezed her eyes shut, willing herself to remain silent, to not draw attention to her presence. Each creak of the floor made her jump, each rustle of plastic wrapping felt like a warning.

Time passed, each second dragging on, stretching the anticipation until it felt unbearably thick. She could hear him speaking to the cashier, his voice low and unfriendly. A shiver coursed through her; the moment rushed to her like a tidal wave.

"What was that noise?" Ethan's voice slithered through the air, a sickening sensation gripping her heart. The cashier stuttered, fumbling over his words in a vain attempt to act cool. "I… I don't know. Just, you know, stock stuff…"

"Just stock stuff?" Ethan's tone turned venomous. "I think someone's playing games."

Sarah held her breath, fully aware of the danger that pressed towards her. What would she do? She needed to get out of there. She had to.

In one swift motion, she surged to her feet, sprinting towards the back of the stockroom. There was a small window just high enough for her to reach if she jumped. She could escape—she wouldn't let this monster get her. Not now, not ever.

With a burst of adrenaline, she launched herself into the air, her fingers barely grazing the ledge of the window. She scrambled, pain shooting through her shoulder as she pulled herself up. The sounds of

Ethan's presence grew more pronounced in the store, and the urgency pushed her to move faster.

She kicked her legs, feeling the chill of the night air against her skin as she finally cleared the windowsill. The streetlight outside greeted her with its sickly fluorescent hue. She dropped to the ground, her legs stumbling beneath her. Without a second thought, she took off into the night.

The adrenaline surged in her veins as she tore down the street, the wind whipping through her hair. She was alive. She was free. But that fleeting sense of relief was quickly overshadowed by the certainty that he was still hunting her.

She turned a corner, navigating through the break in the maze of asphalt and concrete. The shadow of a building loomed ahead, a dark mass offering a momentary shield from prying eyes. The alley offered sanctuary, but also more vulnerability.

It felt as if she were caught in a nightmare—every instinct screamed for her to keep moving, to find safety, yet she had to grapple with the reality of her surroundings. Each shadow became a potential threat, every flickering light a reminder of the danger lurking in the depths of the night.

The alleys twisted like the corridors of her mind—cluttered and filled with echoes of despair. She pressed on, knees aching, breaths coming in ragged gasps. She had no destination in mind; she simply needed to put as much distance between herself and him as possible.

As she rounded a corner, the emptiness of her surroundings shifted beneath her feet. Suddenly, she felt exposed, and the quiet gnawed at her. Where was everyone? The streets should have been alive with life, but instead, they were devoid of presence, amplifying the sense of dread settling deep in her stomach.

She pressed on, her feet pounding against the pavement. A quick glance over her shoulder sent a wave of nausea through her—no sign of him. But the looming uncertainty over whether he was right behind her was what kept the panic fresh.

Rounding onto a block where a series of closed shops lined up like tombstones, she found herself in a precarious position. She hesitated, glancing down the darkened street to the left and then to the right. She heard the sound again—the echo of footsteps that sent her heart racing anew.

Desperation clawed at her thoughts. She couldn't stay here. Not now, not ever. She ducked into an alley bordering the shops, her mind racing with the need to survive. The darkness engulfed her, a friend and foe all at once.

Suddenly, a cacophony of despair echoed through the stillness as she heard a voice call out, sharp and penetrating. "Where are you, Sarah?" The call was taunting, reverberating off the walls, wrapping around her like vines.

Ethan. He was already closing in, and her heart sank in response to the urgency.

She pressed herself against the wall, resolute in her determination to remain hidden. The desperation coiled tighter with each passing second. Panic flooded her veins, and she squeezed her eyes shut, willing the moment to pass, wishing for just a brief reprieve.

She could hear him move closer, the sound of his footsteps disrupted by a gentle rain beginning to fall. She inhaled deeply, wincing at the thought of his victory. Each drop that hit the sidewalk felt like a countdown, marking the seconds left to act.

The chant of her name brushed against her consciousness, a haunting lull where comfort and terror intertwined. "Sarah. Sarah." It echoed, playing upon her deepest fears until she felt she might unravel.

In a show of defiance, she forced herself to move once more, darting across the narrow road to another alley just a few feet away. She distanced herself from the echo of his voice, plunging deeper into the dark embrace of uncertainty.

The desire to be seen fought with the primal fear of being caught; she had to keep climbing, to find another route—another avenue to escape.

She veered left, wrapping around buildings, letting the darkness guide her. Eventually, she found herself stepping onto a street that felt both familiar and foreign.

Lights flickered against the drizzled pavement, shimmering in muted hues. To her right, she saw clustering shadows—four figures huddled near the entrance of a vacant parking garage. Relief flooded through her, but it flickered when she remembered Ethan's threat.

She needed to reach safety. This could be her only chance.

With resolve, she approached, the thunder of her heart barely muted by the sound of the rain that now fell heavier. "Please," she called weakly, her voice breaking against the drumming of the storm.

The figures turned, expressions shifting from surprise to concern as they noticed the panic etched across her face. "Are you okay?" one of them began, stepping forward, hands raised in a gesture meant to soothe.

But before she could respond, before she could even plead for help, a shadow moved through the downpour, a figure gliding seamlessly through the mist of the night—Ethan, emerging from the depths like a phantom unleashed.

Time seemed to pause, seconds stretching like elastic as the blood drained from her face. "Sarah!" he bellowed, and the strangers around her flinched, echoing her own freeze as dread washed over the crowd.

Run!" she screamed, instinctively diving toward the shadows of the garage as a flood of adrenaline coursed through her body. Every fiber of her being screamed to escape, to put space between her and the hunter.

The strangers hesitated, fear etched on their faces, but she knew they had to choose—fight or flight. As she barreled past them, she couldn't tell if they followed, didn't have the strength to look back.

She sprinted deeper into the garage, the echoes of her footsteps reverberating against the concrete walls, a loud reminder of her desperation. Each breath was a battle, both a lifeline and a reminder of vulnerability, and she pushed on.

Ethan's voice bled through the garage as he pursued her—the predator unfazed. She scrambled past cars, fingers grazing their cold metal surfaces as she searched for a place to slip away, a corner to hide in.

In the dim light, she spotted a service door ajar at the far end. Perfect. Heart racing, she bolted toward it, leaning into the door as it swung open, welcoming her into the darkness beyond.

The corridor was narrow and damp, the air stale with the smell of rust. She pressed further, the labored sound of her heartbeat mixing with the rush of her panicked breath. She was outside again, she managed to think, as she emerged into an even darker space—a world behind the scenes.

The rain still fell, but this time it felt like an ally, loud enough to drown out her senses. As she focused on each step, her legs wobbled beneath her, but she couldn't stop. She wouldn't stop.

Glimpses of a nearby alley caught her eye, and her heart screamed the desperate urge to flee. Before her is where her path could twist again, and she dove into the darkened passage, the shadows weaving around her like a second skin.

With every ounce of her being, she pressed forward, the cruel nature of the night indistinct, wrapping her in ambiguity, but she didn't care. She was a wild creature, ready to fight or run. Every heartbeat urged her to survive.

With a final, desperate leap, she bounded into the open street, air rushing against her skin like liquid freedom. The ambush of adrenaline thrust her forward, panting against the reality that surrounded her—a relentless hunt, a fierce desire to live.

As she allowed herself a moment, just a hair's breadth of respite, she realized she wouldn't give up. She wouldn't let fear claim her, and in that moment, she found the strength she didn't know she had.

Ethan would have to work harder than ever before because she planned to survive. She vowed silently against the night, racing forward, not looking back—her battle against the shadows had only just begun.

New Alliances

The air was thick with tension as Sarah dashed through the darkened streets, the echo of her panting breath mingling with the sound of her racing heart. She had only narrowly escaped Ethan's pursuit, and with each corner she turned, she felt the weight of the shadows pressing in. The distant wails of jackals, haunting and lonely, were a grim reminder of the danger she faced.

Stumbling into an overgrown park, Sarah cast a furtive glance over her shoulder, slowing her pace to gather her thoughts. She clutched the fabric of her jacket tighter around her, its warmth a meager comfort against the chill of fear. She needed shelter, but in her current state, trust felt like a luxury she couldn't afford.

As she navigated through the tangled underbrush, she spotted the glow of flickering lights ahead. Cautiously, Sarah crept closer, the sounds of soft laughter floating on the night air. Intrigued and curious, she pushed aside a cluster of thorny branches and emerged into a clearing.

Before her stood an old, ramshackle house, its porch sagging under the weight of time—and perhaps too many secrets. A group of five people sat around a fire pit, their faces illuminated by the dancing flames. They were a motley crew, laughter and camaraderie radiating from them, casting a stark contrast to the dark world Sarah had just escaped.

"Pan those marshmallows, Jess!" a tall man with messy brown hair yelled playfully, poking fun at a girl who was trying to balance more than one skewer over the fire. She wore oversized glasses that slipped down her nose, her cheeks flushed with the heat of the flame.

"Hey! I can do it!" Jess shot back, her laughter infectious and inviting. Sarah watched from the shadows, battling with her instincts. Every fiber of her being shouted caution, yet the warmth of human connection was almost magnetic.

"Come on! Just help me! I need to make sure we have enough for everyone!" Another voice exclaimed, this one belonged to a woman with curly black hair, her laughter melding beautifully with the others.

Sarah hesitated. They seemed friendly enough, but the weight of her reality pressed down upon her—Ethan was still out there, searching for her. She wished she could just let go for a moment, to feel the safety in numbers, but the voice of reason reminded her of what she had witnessed. Trust was a fragile thing.

"Maybe I should just keep moving," she whispered to herself. But her feet remained planted, drawn to the warmth of their laughter. The firelight danced tantalizingly, invigorating a flicker of hope inside her.

"Hey!" shouted the tall man suddenly, swinging his gaze in Sarah's direction, as if sensing her presence. "You okay over there?"

Caught, Sarah stepped forward hesitantly, her heart racing as they turned to regard her. She squared her shoulders, refusing to show her fear. "I—uh, I heard you all from the woods," she managed, her voice shaky but firm. "I'm sorry for intruding."

"Not intruding at all! Come join us!" the curly-haired woman called enthusiastically. "There's plenty of food if you're hungry."

"Or if you need to roast some marshmallows," the tall man added with a grin, gesturing towards the fire.

As she stepped closer, Sarah felt the warmth radiating from both the flames and the small group gathering around them. She took a seat on the edge of the circle, her instincts battling it out with her hunger and growing need for companionship.

"I'm Ryan," the tall man introduced, extending a hand in greeting. "This is Jess, Tara, Mike, and Sam." Each person waved or nodded in acknowledgment, their smiles inviting.

"Sarah," she replied, shaking Ryan's hand. He had a strong grip, which somehow reassured her.

"What brings you out here, Sarah? This isn't exactly a safe place to be on your own," Mike asked, his brow furrowing slightly in concern. He had a rugged appearance, and his deep voice seemed to resonate with an underlying kindness.

"I...I'm just passing through," she replied, her words tinged with hesitation. The inclination to confide in them battled with her instincts screaming for caution. But the weight of her ordeal—the fear, the need to share—hung heavily on her heart. "I had a rough night."

Ryan's expression shifted to sympathy. "Hey, we've all had rough nights before. Join us around the fire—it's a lot more welcoming than what's outside." The invitation was earnest, and Sarah felt a momentary crack in the armor she had built around herself.

An unsteady breath escaped her as she pondered her options. Could she trust them? But their faces radiated genuine compassion. She could see it, an unspoken understanding surging between them. Slowly, she decided to lower her guard.

"Okay," she said, her voice steadier than she expected. She took a deep breath, settling into the warmth. "Thank you."

Jess handed her a roasted marshmallow, still hot and gooey. For a moment, the sweet taste absorbed her anxiety, giving way to a fleeting sense of normalcy. They shared stories, each laugh echoing into the night like a drum beating back the darkness.

"I'm a student at the local college—you won't believe the crazy stuff we do for fun," Jess said, her eyes gleaming. "Last month, we almost got arrested for trespassing on an old estate."

"What? Why would you do that?" Sarah asked, genuinely intrigued, captivated by their lighthearted conversation.

"It started as a dare," Tara chimed in, wiping marshmallow off her face. "But you should've seen the look on the officer's face when he caught us! Classic awkward moment."

Laughter enveloped them and began to ease the knots of fear within Sarah. She felt alive, a sensation she thought was lost to her. Yet, even in this moment of tranquility, dark clouds hovered at the edges of her mind, whispering warnings.

As the conversations ebbed and flowed, Sarah's gaze met Sam's. He had been quiet until now, observing the exchange. Something about his withdrawn demeanor caught her attention.

"Have you ever found yourself in a place where you had to choose between trusting people or running away?" she asked, her voice uncharacteristically vulnerable.

Sam regarded her intently. "Every day," he said slowly. "It's hard to decide who to let in when trust has been broken before. It's like a game of survival."

His words struck Sarah like a thunderclap. She caught a glimpse of something deeper in his eyes—a kindred spirit battling with demons of his own. "You too?"

"That's the reality, isn't it?" Sam continued. "You hope for the best, but you can't shake the feeling that danger is always lurking around the corner, waiting to pounce."

This truth weighed heavily on Sarah. Did they understand the gravity of her situation? She studied their faces, searching for any signs of betrayal, yet found nothing but acceptance and recognition. These strangers had extended a lifeline, albeit a fragile one.

As the evening progressed, Sarah let herself engage a little deeper. She learned Tara worked as a nurse, sharing stories about patients whose lives had changed in an instant. Ryan had once been a musician with dreams of touring before life's responsibilities chained him to the town.

In the soft glow of the firelight, Sarah felt her heartbeat syncing with theirs, a rhythm of camaraderie. "What about you, Sarah?" Ryan asked. "What's your story?"

For a moment, Sarah hesitated, her heart betraying her tongue. Should she share the truth? What if they turned against her? But then she remembered why she was here—because she needed people. "I... I witnessed something terrible," she murmured, as if the weight of her admission would shatter the trust they had formed.

"Terrible? What do you mean?" Jess questioned, genuine concern etching her brow.

"Something that could put me in danger," Sarah replied, meeting their eyes, gauging the understanding behind their expressions. "I'm not safe right now."

Silence cloaked the group, a collective breath frozen in time. Shadows flickered as the fire crackled, and she could almost hear the wheels turning in their minds.

"Why don't you stay with us for the night?" Mike suggested after a moment, his voice calm but firm. "We can help keep watch. There's safety in numbers, right?"

For a heartbeat, Sarah felt the walls she had built around her begin to crack. Could she really lean on them? "Are you sure?"

"Absolutely," Ryan affirmed, like a promise more than mere words.

And just like that, she took the leap. "Okay. I'll stay."

The shifting premise of their dynamic transformed her fear into an unexpected comfort, as she slipped into the safety of this makeshift alliance. They were, after all, strangers bound by the common thread of survival.

As the fire waned and exhaustion began to tug at her limbs, Sarah felt her heart soften with gratitude toward her newfound allies. They made plans to keep watch, divided into shifts, each offering reassurances that everything would be okay.

Yet, there always lingered a shadow of anxiety rooted deep inside her. The evening had been filled with warmth, but the specter of Ethan loomed ever larger. Slight rustles in the distance outside the clearing sent shivers through her spine. Could he already be onto her?

Her thoughts spiraled, but she forced herself to focus on the camaraderie surrounding her. Encouraged by laughter and gentle banter, she found respite for just a moment longer, a sanctuary amidst the chaos.

But the foreboding presence didn't let her rest completely. She hadn't yet dealt with the reality of what was still lurking outside the circle of light, and as fatigue washed over her, she understood that rest was fleeting, fraught with the awareness that danger was never far away.

This fleeting comfort was just a temporary refuge, a transient alliance built on shared humanity and mutual desperation. As they prepared to hunker down for the night, she kept a watchful eye on the dark edges surrounding them, refusing to let her guard down entirely.

Sarah nestled behind the warmth of the fire, and as her eyelids grew heavier, she vowed that come dawn, she would have to make decisions weighted with the knowledge of uncertainty—that trust could be both a balm and a weapon. In the shadows, the threat continued to simmer, its fangs bared and ready to strike.

In this night of uneasy camaraderie, she understood: the tightrope of survival was a dangerous dance, and one misstep could send her tumbling into the abyss once again.

The Weight of Fear

Sarah's heart pounded tirelessly in her chest, a frantic rhythm that drowned out the symphony of the night. Each footfall on the gravel path felt like an echoing alarm, alerting the world to her presence. She didn't dare look back, afraid that if she did, she might see his shadow lurking just beyond her, a chilling specter weaving through the trees. Her mind raced with dark thoughts, each more unnerving than the last, as the branches above her swayed ominously, creaking like old bones in the wind.

Despite her prudent decision to leave the familiar and seek refuge in the unknown, a sense of isolation closed in around her like a tightening noose. The deeper she ventured into this wilderness, the more susceptible she became to the gnawing fear that slowly edged its way into her consciousness. With every snap of a twig or rustle of underbrush, her chest tightened, an unwelcome reminder that danger could be lurking just out of sight. This was not the thrill of adventure she had longed for; it was a plunge into a darkness that threatened to swallow her whole.

Paranoia seeped into her thoughts, manifesting vividly like a volatile nightmare. She blinked rapidly, trying to shake loose the visions that swirled in her mind. What if Ethan was always one step ahead, always waiting for the perfect moment to pounce? Each moment spent alone stretched out infinitely, transforming the once comforting solitude into a cavernous void where her fears took shape, looming larger and more grotesque with every passing heartbeat.

In fleeting moments of stillness, the world around her faded, replaced by sharp, haunting memories. Those moments flashed before her eyes—the aftermath of violence, the raw fear etched onto the faces of the victims, and finally, the piercing gaze of Ethan, alive and vibrant in her mind. In those eyes, she saw a reflection of danger that sent icy tendrils of dread curling through her veins. She was haunted by his presence, a ghost that whispered her name as she tried to flee the man who had turned her life into a nightmare.

"Sarah," he seemed to call her name on the wind. The sound chilled her blood, echoing ominously as she stumbled through the underbrush. She was sure she had heard a voice, a sinister and familiar drawl calling out from the darkness. Glancing over her shoulder in sheer terror, she saw nothing, just the moonlight peeking through the trees, creating eerie shadows that seemed to stretch and claw towards her. She let out a shuddering breath, struggling to regain her bearings as the overwhelming weight of her predicament crashed down on her.

It wasn't supposed to be like this. Just days ago, she had been an ordinary woman living her mundane life, quietly going to work and sharing meals with friends. Now, she was a fugitive from sanity, running from the chilling possibility that a killer was stalking her. Ethan's reputation as a predator seeped into her psyche, and with every step, her self-doubt blossomed into a pressing weight that left her feeling helpless. Maybe she should have stayed silent, tucked safely away behind her veil of ignorance, instead of becoming an accidental witness to a horrific crime.

Yet, naive hope flickered in the recesses of her mind. Maybe she could escape him. Maybe there was a way to break free from the shackles of fear that bound her. Each decision she had made since witnessing the crime was a step towards reclaiming her life, albeit imperfectly. But with every step forward, she was reminded of how vulnerable she truly was.

Ethan wasn't just a memory; he was a specter that clung to her, whispering doubts and fears into her ear. His presence loomed large, not solely as a physical threat but as an insidious force that bent reality to its will. As Sarah stumbled deeper into the woods, she wondered if she was losing her grip. The shadows cast by the towering trees became menacing figures, and the soft winds morphed into taunting laughter. Each sound amplified by her anxiety, forcing her to question her own sanity.

She had to keep moving. Keeping herself awake, alert, and aware of her surroundings was her only recourse. But exhaustion gnawed at the edges of her consciousness. Guilt flickered within her, biting sharply as she recalled each moment wasted worrying about her safety instead of finding a way to regain control of her life. How could she fight back when fear barricaded her from clarity? How could she confront the monster in her mind when he manifested into the shadows around her?

Sarah's thoughts swirled together, her internal monologue growing increasingly chaotic. The lines between past and present blurred. Brief memories of the alley haunted her. She saw flashes of blood, the weight of her decisions bearing down on her as if it were physically squeezing the life from her. She could almost hear the gasp of her breath mixing with the muffled cries for help. And there was Ethan—all-consuming as he unleashed terror on that quiet night.

Suddenly, she caught herself questioning if she truly reported the crime or merely imagined it. Did she want to escape her reality? Was she so desperate to turn back time, so terrified of confronting the weight of her truth, that she was willing to sacrifice her very self to get away from it all? Who was she becoming, spiraling endlessly into doubt and despair?

A dark swirl of discontent emerged inside her as panic clawed and tugged at her sanity. As her breath quickened, she fought against the hallucinations clouding her mind, desperately trying to parse fiction from reality. When would she learn that she was not lost in a nightmare? That she possessed the strength to refuse his dark hold?

With no destination in mind, she pressed forward into the depths of the forest, pretending the trees were shields, that they could protect her from the nightmares. For the first moment in days, a small spark of resolve ignited within her. What if she challenged her fears? A sense of purpose surged through her, pushing aside the whispers of vulnerability. Was it possible that confronting her trauma, rather than hiding from it like a child from darkness, could pave the path to healing?

As if nature itself responded to her determination, a nocturnal chorus began—a symphony of rustling leaves, melodic calls echoing through the air, and the distant howls of jackals resonating in the space between tree trunks. The sounds reminded Sarah of the life beyond her confinement, the freedoms once taken for granted. She could hardly remember a time when fear didn't grip her—when her world wasn't shadowed by impending dread. In that moment, she wanted to embody liberation, to rise above the fears that had stifled her for far too long.

If she were to face Ethan, she needed clarity, strength—something more than the ever-persistent urge to flee. She understood the only way to exorcise the haunting guilt of her past actions was to confront her fears head-on. It felt like a cliff's edge, fraught with uncertainty.

But Sarah was tired of running; tired of being shackled by her mind's own monsters. She was ready to channel that turmoil into a fire, igniting the bravery that lay deep within—igniting a resolve that, despite everything, she would stand tall.

The haunting memories wove through her mind like a dark tapestry as she embraced the fear. Tears brimmed at her eyes, but she wouldn't let them fall. They were a mark of weakness, a reminder of the fragility she had come to resent. With a determined heart, she wiped them away and steadied her breath, taking one last glance at the path behind her, what had once seemed so daunting. She would not look back again.

With this clarity, Sarah pushed herself forward, opening her heart to the wildness of the night, the shadows now less menacing and more inviting. She didn't abandon her fears but molded them to craft a resolve that would guide her onward. Momentum thrummed through her veins as she whispered a promise to herself. She could find her way through the labyrinth of despair; the light of resilience would guide her.

And for the first time since she fled, she felt her spirit align with her body, igniting a flicker of hope that surged within her. It sizzled in her chest, a promise that she would not be a victim but a survivor, ready to face whatever came her way. Driven by determination, she moved forward with renewed vigor, ready to reclaim her life beyond the nightmares, ready to confront Ethan with the courage born from her greatest fears.

THE JACKAL'S LAIR

Finding Shelter

The air was thick with foreboding as Sarah stumbled through the dense underbrush of the woods, her heart pounding fiercely against her ribcage. It had been nearly a full day since she last felt safe—since she had witnessed the brutal crime that had shattered her sense of security. She had fled from the city, desperate to escape the looming shadow of the killer who now hunted her with a singular, terrifying purpose. The trees loomed tall and twisted around her, their branches clawing at the twilight sky, and every rustle in the foliage sent shivers racing down her spine.

Just when she thought the darkness would swallow her whole, a glimmer of hope appeared—a shabby wooden hut nestled among the trees. The structure was small and weather-beaten, with peeling paint and a sagging roof that seemed to lean closer towards the ground as if it were trying to avoid the ominous gaze of the encroaching night. The crescent moon cast ghostly shadows around it, a stark contrast against the enveloping gloom. Despite its worn appearance, it presented itself as a potential sanctuary, a place where she could rest and gather her thoughts.

Caution battled against desperation as Sarah approached the hut. Her breath caught in her throat when she noticed the door, cracked and slightly ajar, as if inviting her inside. Instinct urged her to turn back, but the gnawing anxiety in her chest overpowered her reluctance. She stepped closer, her senses heightening with every careful footfall. The wood creaked beneath her weight, and the scent of damp earth mingled with the musty odor emanating from the hut, forming a bizarre comfort in the perilous night.

As she crossed the threshold, the air inside the hut was stale and cool, tempered by the dampness that surrounded her. Dim light streamed through a grimy window, casting eerie patterns on the dirt floor. Beams of moonlight danced across the sparsely furnished interior, revealing a small table and two rickety chairs. A crumbling fireplace sat in the corner, choked with ash and cobwebs—remnants of a warmth that had long since faded into memory.

"Is this a dream?" Sarah whispered to herself, a tremor in her voice. Though she longed for the semblance of safety, doubt crept into her mind as she surveyed her surroundings. She felt as though she were an intruder in a place long abandoned, with memories of its former life ghosting through the cracks in the walls.

The unsettling howl of a jackal pierced the stillness outside, sending a jolt through her. The distant cries echoed ominously, reminding her that the wild, untamed world surrounding the hut could be just as dangerous as the man she feared. Clenching her fists, she pushed the dark thoughts aside; she couldn't afford to be paralyzed by fear. She needed to focus. For the first time since she had fled, her mind was clear, primed for action.

Taking a deep breath, she began to explore the hut, her heart quickening as she moved around the small space. The floor was littered with leaves, dirt, and remnants of age—yet there was a sort of rustic charm to the place. She brushed her fingers along the walls, feeling the rough texture beneath her fingertips. The heaviness of the air pressed against her lungs, each inhalation a reminder of her panic, but she concentrated on the feeling of the wood instead. It steadied her.

A sudden thought broke through her haze of fear; she needed to fortify the hut. She would not allow herself to be an easy target. Scanning the area, Sarah spotted a rusted shovel propped against the wall. It seemed like the perfect weapon for her defense. Moving with newfound determination, she grabbed it, dusting off the dirt with her sleeve before gripping the handle tightly, its cool metal feeling steady in her hand.

"Okay, Sarah," she murmured to herself, the echo of her own voice serving as a small comfort. "Let's make this place secure." She crouched to gather fallen branches and debris, which could be used to barricade the door. With the shovel as her tool, she crafted a makeshift barrier, pushing the wooden slats and twigs against the doorframe until she felt satisfied—if anything or anyone came for her, they would have to work for it.

As she worked, anxious thoughts collided and swirled in her mind, prompting her to reflect on her harrowing journey. She cast her mind back to that ordinary day that had spiraled into chaos, igniting the series of events that drove her to this very moment. **What's happening to me?** she thought bitterly, reflecting on how her life had been ripped apart in an instant, how she'd gone from a woman going about her mundane routine to someone thrust into a living nightmare—a reluctant pawn in a deadly game.

Each scrape of the shovel against the dirt sent an electric jolt through her, making her acutely aware of how truly far she had come. **From passive bystander to active participant,** she mused, a hint of pride swelling in her chest. She had begun as a mere witness, but now survival was the only thing that mattered. She had to get through this; she had to make it out alive.

The sun dipped further below the horizon, leaving the woods cloaked in shadow as Sarah completed her barricade. Breathing heavily, she paused for a moment, resting against the wall of the hut. In the stillness, her heart slowed, but her resolve grew stronger. She would not let fear overcome her. She had faced Ethan once; she would face him again. **This time, she would be ready.**

Suddenly, another howl of a jackal echoed from deep within the woods, this time louder and closer than before. Sarah's heart leaped into her throat—her sense of sanctuary quivered under the weight of her paranoia. The distant calls were ominous, a reminder of the wild and unpredictable danger lurking beyond the thin walls of her sanctuary. She gripped the shovel tighter, its weight grounding her amidst rising anxiety, yet adrenaline coursed through her veins like fire.

Choosing a spot near the window, she lowered herself cautiously onto the dirt floor, listening intently to the sounds of the forest. The rustling of leaves, the scuttling of small creatures, and the eerie serenade of the jackals surrounded her, all blending into a sinister soundtrack. As she peered through the grimy glass, a shiver ran down her spine. The moonlight shed its unforgiving glare over the landscape, but it was not enough to wipe away the shadows dancing just beyond her view.

Wrapping her arms around her knees for comfort, Sarah closed her eyes briefly, attempting to align her breathing. **Think, Sarah, think.** She couldn't let herself spiral into panic; she needed a plan. First and foremost—she had to be proactive while waiting for her instincts to alert her to danger. It was crucial to stay sharp, especially if Ethan was still stalking her. She couldn't trust anything or anyone—not even shadows.

Time slipped painfully by as she sat in solitude, the weight of both the past and uncertainty pressing down on her. Moments turned into hours, and still, the haunting howls continued, accompanied by the rustling of foliage of something lurking just out of sight. She had no idea what time it was, only that darkness enveloped her entirely.

Suddenly, a sharp sound broke through the cacophony—an unmistakable crack! Sarah's heart leaped, thrumming wildly in her chest as terror mingled with the adrenaline surging through her veins. Someone—or something—was outside. Her body went rigid as she strained to hear, her grip on the shovel tightening impossibly. The door creaked as if pushed by a gentle hand, and fear turned to sheer panic.

Was it him? Had Ethan tracked her down?

She drew in a shaky breath; the world around her shimmered as she fought to steady her mind. There was no time for self-doubt; now was the moment for action. Summoning all the courage she could muster, she edged toward the door, crouched low, and prepared to strike. Every sound amplified as she braced herself, the tension electrifying the air.

Again, that sinister howl echoed through the woods, and beneath the sound was the unmistakable crunching of footsteps on the forest floor, getting closer, creeping ever nearer. A pulse of adrenaline shot through her, urging her to act.

The shadows began to shift outside the hut, and Sarah's breath caught deep in her throat. Every instinct in her screamed for her to flee, to break through the wall of the trees and run until her legs gave out. But instead, she stood her ground, ready to confront what awaited her.

In that moment, she realized she had transformed far beyond merely a witness of violence—she was the unyielding spirit refusing to be a victim. The impulse to fight surged within her like wildfire, propelling her forward with purpose. **Whatever comes next, I will face it head-on.**

Just then, an unearthly scream ripped through the night; her heart nearly stopped. It erupted just outside the hut—a cry that sent waves of dread cascading down her spine. Struggling to remain anchored in the moment, she gripped the shovel and steadied herself for what would come next.

The howl of the jackals crescendoed, their cries filling the air like the sound of a thousand echoes intertwining with shadows. There, lurking beyond the veil of darkness, was the unseen predator, circling like a vulture ready to feast on its prey. She could feel it. The beast was near.

In the dimness of the hut, with adrenaline coursing through her veins, Sarah prepared herself to battle against the suffocating grip of fear. This wasn't just a fight for her life; this was her last chance to reclaim her story from the clutches of terror and rewrite it in her own blood-soaked ink.

As tension hung in the air like a shroud, Sarah squared her shoulders and breathed deep, readying herself. She would not back down. No matter what came through that door, she would face it. She would fight.

And in that resolve, she found a glimmer of hope—a flicker of strength in the labyrinth of despair—and the battle for her survival had only just begun.

The Call of the Wild

The darkness enveloped Sarah like a shroud, thick and suffocating. The stifling air inside the hut mingled with the musty scent of decaying wood and damp earth, a reminder of the isolation that surrounded her. Flashes of moonlight filtered through the cracks in the walls, casting ghostly shadows that danced mockingly across the floor. As the last of her adrenaline began to ebb, her heart raced with the heavy weight of anxiety and fear. She had thought the hut would be a refuge, a haven where she could catch her breath. Instead, it felt like a cage.

Sarah leaned against the rough wooden wall, the splinters digging into her back, a further reminder of her precarious situation. The earlier panic that had driven her to this secluded spot started to dissipate, replaced by a gnawing sense of dread. Every creak of the timber, every whisper of wind outside, filled her mind with dark possibilities. The jackals were out there, their eerie howls a reminder of the wildness that surrounded her, a wildness that mirrored the chaos in her soul.

She wondered if they were aware of her presence, hidden beneath the fragile roof, trembling in fear. They instinctively knew how to survive, to hunt, to exist in their untamed world. But what of her? She felt more animal than human, caught between the overwhelming instinct to flee and the paralyzing fear that kept her rooted to this spot.

The memory of that night replayed over and over in her head—the screams, the struggle, the blood. She had been a mere bystander at first, an unwilling witness to a horror she never wished to see. And now, she was marked by her knowledge, hunted by the very creature that had unleashed that violence. The thought sent icy chills down her spine. She was no longer just a woman from a small town, living an ordinary life filled with daily challenges. No, she had become the prey in a predator's game, and the lines between victor and victim were blurred.

Attuned to the sounds outside, Sarah strained to listen, her breath hitching in her throat. The forest was alive at night, filled with rustling leaves and the occasional call of a night bird, yet it was the jackals that struck the most fear in her heart. They were the harbingers of her deepest insecurities, the embodiment of her helplessness. They echoed her thoughts, reminding her that she was trapped in a reality she couldn't escape. The fear was palpable, coiling around her like a noose, squeezing tighter with every heartbeat.

Could she outrun the shadows that lingered over her? The memories whispered lies, taunting her with the idea that no matter how far she ran, the darkness would always chase her down. She could already feel its fingers curling around her throat, a reminder that she was not in control. The blood on her hands was a mark of failure, and the overwhelming guilt crashed down like a tidal wave, nearly drowning her in its depths.

Her thoughts drifted to the moments before the crime, reflecting on her ordinary life filled with mundane routines and trivial concerns. If only she had taken a different route that night, or if she had decided to stay home entirely. But those thoughts were futile, spiraling into a dark vortex that further trapped her. She had to focus on the present, on the immediate danger surrounding her.

The hut felt stifling as the night wore on; she was aware of the oppressive silence that stretched across the clearing, punctuated only by the distant calls of the jackals. Each howl was a taunt, a cruel reminder of her vulnerability. She could almost visualize them moving under the silver sheen of the moon, their eyes glistening like shards of glass. The realization sent another wave of cold terror through her veins. What if they sensed her fear? Would they come to pray on her, as Ethan had?

Armed with only a flimsy stick she had found inside the hut, she felt ludicrous and absurd. She closed her eyes for a moment, trying to steady her breathing. Her heartbeat thudded loudly in her ears, a constant reminder of her fear. Could she even defend herself against a man who had taken life so easily, so effortlessly? The stick felt more like a promise of failure than a weapon.

Outside, the nocturnal world stirred, and Sarah strained to listen to the rhythm of the wilderness. It was in those moments of quiet that the isolation gnawed at her. She was utterly alone, cut off from the reassuring warmth of human contact. No one knew where she was; Ethan was hunting her, but each shadow could also be a body lying in wait, ready to pounce.

She leaned forward, her eyes glued to the rotting door, willing it to remain shut, willing herself to believe she was safe. Her senses heightened, turning her into an unwilling participant in a waking nightmare. The forest was a dark creature, lurking and breathing, waiting in anticipation.

And then she heard it—a rustle. A slight shift in the underbrush just outside her sanctuary. Heart racing, every instinct screamed for her to flee, to burst through the door and run until her legs collapsed beneath her. But deep down, the hunter's instinct kicked in; she couldn't afford to panic now, not when danger was so close.

She steadied herself and squinted into the darkness, searching for any sign of movement. Nothing. Just shadows and whispers of wind. The anxiety coiled tighter, gripping her chest like a vice. She fought against the rising panic, focusing instead on her breathing, reminding herself that she had faced tougher battles before. She had trained herself to find strength even in the worst of circumstances, but now, in this forsaken hut where she felt both predator and prey, the battle was internal.

With each breath, she felt a flicker of resolve. Fear had a way of manifesting into something larger, overwhelming thoughts and seizing control over her mind. But she was Sarah, not merely a reflection of her fear. She clawed at her memories for strength. What she had witnessed could tear her apart, but it could also be transformed into courage—a fierce, wild energy that could defy the darkness closing in around her.

She slowly rose, gripping the stick tightly as she moved toward the door. It was as if she existed in two worlds at once—the reality of her fear and the world of her determination. She could turn this vulnerability into ferocity; she could reclaim her agency. Anger surged through her veins, igniting a fire that had lain dormant for far too long.

And then she heard it again—a definitive rustling, louder, closer. Her heart dropped, and she froze. The shadows blurred at the edges of her vision as she listened intently, feeling the adrenaline rush through her. There was no mistaking it now; something was out there, circling her hideout. It wasn't the jackals this time but the manifestation of her own trepidation, the embodiment of every moment she had ever felt powerless.

The world outside was a canvas splattered with her fears—the jackals were a reminder that she couldn't just sit and wait, that action was her only hope for survival. She glanced around the hut, her mind racing, heart thumping in a manic rhythm against her ribs. Howling trails of her mind's despair painted her external world, and she dared not to let it take hold.

With quiet determination, she took a step towards the door. The moment felt like an eternity, her breath shallow and quick. Every second stretched endlessly; fear surged against her ribcage, an insistent drumbeat of doubt and disbelief.

Crouching low, she pressed her ear against the rough wood, straining to uncover the source of the disturbance. There it was again, faint yet persistent. The tension within her coiled tightly as she prepared for the unknown, every instinct pulling her taut like a bowstring ready to snap.

With every second that passed, it became a matter of survival. All those moments when she felt like a ghost in her life exploded in a wave of clarity; she wouldn't be a victim any longer. She would fight, with every ounce of strength she had.

But as she braced herself, a louder crack pierced the quiet—wood splintering followed by a low growl resonating from outside. Her breath caught in her throat, and fear hit her like a wave, threatening to drown her again.

In that haunting moment, she remembered the jackals—how they hunted with a predatory grace, following the scent of fear. She was their prey, but now, she could play the part of the hunter. If she could anticipate the moves of her enemy, she could regain her power. It was a terrifying thought, but it lit a fire inside her.

As she silently positioned herself near the door, the rustling grew louder, approaching with an airy grace. Each sound sent jolts through her body, a stark reminder of her fragile reality. Then she saw it—a dark form slinking through the underbrush, not a jackal, but something more human, more sinister.

Just outside the wooden structure, eyes glinted in the darkness. The unmistakable predator was closing in, a tangible embodiment of her most unbearable fears. Sarah could feel her heart thundering in response, its echo vibrating through the still night.

The sound of heavy footsteps sent a cascade of horror ripping through her. Had Ethan found her?

Suddenly, the figure stopped just outside the door, and for a moment, time stood still. The world around her faded away, narrowing to the pulsing rhythm of her heart and the hungry breaths that echoed beneath the strained silence. Swallowing hard, she gripped the stick tightly, the smooth wood digging into her palm.

What would she do now? Would she confront the ghost of her tormentor, or cower back in fear? There was no turning back now; her moment had arrived, and she would not be defined by those dark moments any longer.

The sound of rustling leaves shifted again, followed by whispers that floated into the night like tendrils of smoke. It could not be merely a figment of her imagination—it was real, and whatever lay outside knew she was there, mere inches from being hunted down.

The jackals were howling again, their cries blending with the terror that swelled in her chest. Sarah steeled her resolve, her pulse quickening as she prepared for confrontation. The pull between fear and determination tightened painfully, but there was no alternative in sight.

She would either face him or be consumed by the weight of her own fear. A predatory instinct arose, awakening a dormant strength that begged to be unleashed.

Then, a sudden loud crack echoed through the stillness, as something heavy struck the door from the outside. Panic washed over her—the moment of confrontation was inevitable.

And with it, the embodiment of her fears would come crashing through the door.

The Calm Before the Storm

As night falls, the once soothing ambiance of the forest transforms into a suffocating blanket of dread. The fading light casts elongated shadows that dance among the trees, creating grotesque shapes that seem to leer at Sarah from the darkness. Each rustle in the underbrush sends a jolt through her, disrupting the fragile calm she clings to. The air, thick with the scent of moss and damp earth, feels heavy, saturated with the weight of her fears.

Inside the mounted hut, Sarah presses her back against the cool wooden wall, trying to center herself amidst the storm of uncertainty swirling in her mind. She takes a deep breath, but it catches in her throat, constricted by the terror that wraps around her like a vice. The memories of the past days play on a relentless loop in her thoughts—the crime she witnessed, the man who committed it, and the realization that she has become a target. Ethan is out there, a predator stalking his prey, and she can almost feel his presence creeping closer, like a shadow at the corner of her eye.

She glances at her surroundings, the light from the dying embers of the small fire casting flickering shadows that seem to leap and sway in sync with her growing apprehension. The hut, with its creaking wooden floorboards and makeshift furniture, provides minimal comfort. It should feel like a refuge, a place to catch her breath and gather her thoughts, yet it serves only as a reminder of her entrapment. The walls seem to close in on her, every creak echoing her fears.

Regret settles heavily on her chest. She had thought this would be temporary, a stop along her flight from the horrors she experienced. Instead, it feels like a cage, one that will be breached by someone unrelenting. Could she have done something differently? Should she have ignored that gut instinct urging her to leave the city after witnessing the atrocity? Every decision she made in the wake of that fateful night now feels tinged with a thick layer of shame, and she is left to grapple with the consequences.

With a trembling hand, she reaches for the coarse fabric of her shirt, clutching it tightly against her chest as if it can shield her from the onslaught of memories—each one sharper than the last. The echoes of the violent confrontation she stumbled upon still reverberate through her mind. The desperate cries, the sickening thud, the chilling realization that she was not just a bystander, but a witness. A witness with knowledge that could condemn a man to justice but also place her in a crosshairs.

Was it worth it? She wonders, feeling the weight of her decision curl around her like a serpent. What good is truth if it comes at the cost of her life? The internal struggle fuels her anxiety, building a wall of despair that threatens to engulf her. Sarah knows she can't go back now, but accepting the path forward fills her with dread.

The howls of jackals ripple through the night, an unsettling chorus that stirs something primal within her. The sound is both chilling and oddly familiar, a reminder that she is not alone in this harrowing wilderness. The creatures—their wildness, their cunning—feed into her fears, a symbol of the predatory nature lurking not only in the forest but within the very heart of humanity. At that moment, they feel like harbingers of doom, waiting for the signal to descend upon her fragile existence.

With every unintelligible call, her pulse quickens. She forces herself to breathe, steady and slow, but the rhythm is not her own. It races on, pulsing with the instinct to flee, to escape. But where would she go? Who could she trust in a world that has turned dark overnight? The comforting faces of her past flicker in and out of focus, replaced by visions of Ethan's cold, calculating gaze—his face a mask of malevolence that sends a rush of ice through her veins.

The fire crackles, a tiny rebellion against the encroaching darkness, but even its flicker feels muted, haunted by the imminent threat pressing in around her. She leans forward, the flames casting fierce light across her face, illuminating the fear that has settled into her features.

Sarah begins to mentally catalog her options, her eyes darting to the door, half-fearful, half-eager for any sign of an escape. Should she leave now, while there is still a sliver of hope? Would it be better to risk the woods than remain a sitting target? But every time she thinks of taking that step, her mind conjures the image of Ethan—a wolf in sheep's clothing, ever watching from the shadows, waiting for her naïveté to reveal itself.

Once more, her thoughts drift back to the crime. The moment everything changed, the irrevocable fracture that cascaded through her life. She had walked into that alley a mere observer, and by stumbling into reality's brutal grasp, she emerged from the other side battered, exposed, and hunted. The loss of her previous life feels palpable, as if she has been stripped of her identity, leaving only an echo of who she used to be.

Was this the cost of knowledge? The primal urge for self-preservation roars inside of her, sharpening her sense of reality. Decision-makers have lives that depend upon their wisdom. She'd learned that the hard way. The knowledge she carried felt burdensome, a weight pulling her deeper into despair while the forest around her thickened with night's embrace.

Another sharp cry from the jackals crescendos, vibrating through her very bones. They thrive in chaos, celebrating the edge of anarchy, and tonight they ready themselves for something gruesome. Bile rises in her throat—a visceral, instinctive response that nearly overwhelms her. What were wolves of the wild if not symbols of savagery? She shudders, and it feels as though the darkness is not only a cloak around her but an entity willing her demise.

She grips the makeshift weapon she fashioned earlier—a sturdy branch, rough and imperfect but the only thing that stands between her and the predator awaiting his chance. It strains against her palm, a reminder that this fight is hers. But the very row of stark reality begs her to question—what would she do with it? Would she fight, or would fear paralyze her at the decisive moment?

Thoughts whirl as the shadows lengthen, and she recalls snippets of conversations with Jenna, her closest confidante, where they talked about bravery and strength, about how true heroes find their courage in the most dire circumstances. But what if she wasn't a hero? What if she was simply a woman with a branch and no will to wield it? The uncertainty gnaws at her resolve, sowing seeds of doubt that threaten to bloom into paralyzing fear.

Night stretches on, oppressive in its silence—a startling contrast to the earlier chaos of the forest. She listens intently, each 85 The jackals creak of the hut raising her hackles, feeding the electricity buzzing beneath her skin. Thoughts of Ethan seep back into her consciousness, his menacing figure dominating her visions. He is close; she feels it in her bones. Instinct tells her to prepare, to brace herself for what is inevitable.

Yet, deep inside, a flicker of defiance emerges. She is more than a victim; this realization hardens her grip on the branch, grounding her in the present. Anxiety wars with determination, both battling for control over her psyche. She steels herself against a surge of panic. She has the power to fight, to unleash the storm brewing within her. The insides of her gritty battle evoke the first stirrings of a fighting spirit—one that cannot be extinguished by fear alone.

As seconds stretch into eternity, Sarah recalls the strength of tribulation. She recalls the stories of women who faced the impossible; the women who had walked through fire and emerged unscathed, leaving traces of their tenacity woven into the very fabric of their beings. The belief in survival fortifies her willingness to challenge her reality. She feels a heartbeat—hers—at odds with her fears, yet screaming for the chance to thrive.

Outside, the howls of the jackals reach a fever pitch, and adrenaline floods through her veins, sharpening her senses. Her breath quickens, and she can almost feel the approach of danger like a gathering storm. With each cry, she sees visions of Ethan, closing in around her—a dark silhouette that lingers just at the periphery, too close for comfort.

But she will not relent. Bracing against the wall, she twists her body to face the door, a deliberate act of confrontation against the unknown. The shadows that once felt suffocating now seem like challenges waiting to be met.

With a renewed sense of purpose, she mutters to herself, words born of desperation and determination. "You will not take me. I refuse to be a victim." The incantation of her own resolve echoes against the wood, and, in that instant, she becomes something more than fear—a force ready to fight back.

Just then, a scuffle disrupts the stillness outside, a sound unmistakable to her ears. It's a noise that could only belong to one thing—a presence that has come too close for comfort. Her heart leaps into her throat, pounding against her ribcage as dread coils around her heart. It's here—the storm she so desperately longed to prepare for is now crashing down upon her.

As a heavy silence settles into the night, Sarah grips the branch tightly, weathering the storm of emotions crashing over her. She readies herself for whatever is to come, steeling her mind against the fear that threatens to consume her.

With every passing second, she knows the confrontation is imminent, but this time, she's determined to face it head-on. The jackals may roam in the darkness, but she too is a creature of instinct, capable of survival against all odds. With the heartbeat of the forest echoing her own, she readies herself for the fight ahead, bracing against the storm that has finally arrived.

Night Terror

The Predator Approaches

Ethan moved like a shadow among the overgrown trees, his breath slow and controlled, blending in with the night. The moon hung high above, a silver coin spilling soft light across the landscape, illuminating the twisted branches and the gnarled roots that clawed at the ground. He had followed Sarah's path for hours now, feeling the exhilaration build within him each time he caught a glimpse of her faded footprints pressed into the damp earth. She was close, so close, and the thrill of the chase filled his veins with electric anticipation.

Each step he took was deliberate, calculated. The hunt was not merely about eliminating a witness; it was the intoxicating dance of predator and prey. She was fragile, a small flickering flame in the darkness, and he was a patient wolf, waiting for the right moment to strike. As he neared her last known location, his heart quickened with glee, anticipating the spark of terror that would light up her features when she realized she wasn't alone.

Sarah had reported him. Her voice replayed in his mind, the way she had stammered the words to the authorities, trying to convey the horror of what she had witnessed. He imagined her trembling fingers clutching the edge of the police station's counter, her eyes wide and panicked. That thought alone fed his drive. Instilling fear was an art form to him, one that he had perfected over the years. He breathed deep, inhaling the earthy scent of damp leaves and the faint musk of decay that came with the night, letting it ground him.

Moving silently, he ducked behind a large oak, grabbing onto the rough bark with his fingertips and crouching low. The moonlight cast eerie patterns across the ground, the shadows morphing into figures that danced around him. He chuckled at the thought that Sarah was likely somewhere nearby, haunted by those shadows, her imagination running wild in the dark. In that moment, he desired nothing more than to make himself known—just a rustle in the brush, a whisper carried by the wind—the very embodiment of her nightmares. The thought thrilled him.

He could hear the crackling of leaves underfoot, the rustling of small creatures that had settled in for the night. It was a symphony of life, yet he was the maestro of something darker. He relished the anticipation, the way it twisted his insides. A part of him existed within the thrill of the hunt, while another part remained in a haunting simmer of motivation—the need not only to eliminate her but to make her understand why.

As he navigated the uneven terrain, covered in a blanket of fallen leaves and enveloped by the scents of moss and wet earth, he zeroed in on the faint sound of Sarah's breathing. Her heart was racing, the cadence quickening as if sensing the danger that lurked nearby. What was it about fear that made the heart race like that? He relished that enigmatic heartbeat, the panic it inspired within her. It was an intoxicating rhythm, a living metronome that echoed through the night.

Ethan paused just beyond the edge of a clearing, where the moonlight pooled like molten silver. He had expected to reach this area sooner, envisioning Sarah's curled form cradled beneath the shelter of the trees. But she was not here yet.

He scanned the surroundings, noting the sharp shadows that twisted and stretched in the moonlight. In the distance, the sobering howl of a jackal echoed through the trees—a reminder of the dangers that lay hidden within the dark woods. He grinned, imagining her frightened response to the sound. It was almost funny how oblivious she was to her surroundings, how vulnerable she remained in this moment.

Ethan's eyes narrowed as he caught sight of a flicker of movement at the edge of the clearing. A flash of her dark hair caught the light, a reminder of her beauty even in despair. She was here—close enough for him to reach her in mere moments. He crouched lower, blending back into the shadows, his heart racing with the thrill of imminent confrontation.

Deliberately, he calculated his next move. She might have friends who would come looking for her; she might even make noise, hoping to scare him away. But after what he had witnessed in the alley, he understood that her newfound bravery would only make her more reckless. He had studied her, learned every hesitation and every sudden burst of energy that flared when things breached her façade of normalcy. He knew how to manipulate that fear, and in some sick, twisted way, he had crafted a plan that would guarantee his dominance, no matter how afraid she tried to act.

The darkness provided cover, yet he could see her mingle with the faint light, moving aimlessly, looking back over her shoulder as if sensing something—a primal instinct rooted in self-preservation. She had no idea how closely she was being watched. He grinned at her naivety, enjoying the game of cat-and-mouse that he played with her.

Within minutes, he noticed the way she stepped into the clearing, glancing nervously around. He could almost taste her fear on the air, and it sent a shiver of satisfaction racing through him. Will she scream? Run? Freeze? Each possibility lit up his imagination, tantalizing him with the thrill of what was to come. He had to give her a moment—a moment to feel truly alone, vulnerable without any sanctuary in sight.

Then, from somewhere deep within the forest, there came another odd noise, punctuated by the rustling of bushes. It carried through the air, causing Sarah's body to tense—the way she stood, poised for flight held a profound elegance. Ethan savored it.

But he remained on edge, fighting against the shift from predator to waiting beast. With every second that passed, he felt the familiar pulse of adrenaline far beyond mere excitement; it brought with it a certain clarity and focus that redirected his thoughts.

In that instant, a stone clinked against the roots behind him, a sudden collision with the ground that disturbed the seemingly serene night. Sarah spun around, her breath hitching as she turned, a fragile deer caught in the hunt's glaring act. For an instant, their eyes met. It flickered with the candlelight of fear—a moment that stretched for eternity before crashing down around them like a tempest.

Ethan felt electrified, holding on to that fragile moment as time slowed. Her expression shifted from confusion to stark realization. He could almost hear the thudding of her heart echo through the chasm of the night as it raced toward danger. The forest seemed to hold its breath, waiting for what was to come.

The moment stretched on, each second an eternity, as Sarah took a step back. He shifted, the hunter preparing to pounce, relishing the power coursing through him.

Then, without warning, she turned to run. The sound of her footfalls against the forest floor sliced through the silence, sharp and frantic, echoing like a death knell. He unleashed a low growl, excitement thrumming in his chest as he shot after her, his figure becoming nothing more than a blur in the night.

Branches snagged at his clothes, scratching skin as he pursued her fleet form, his breath steady as he made sure not to lose ground. He could almost sense her panic rising as she darted through the trees, her frame stumbling, branches snapping underfoot, breathless gasps escaping her lips like desperate prayers.

Ethan reveled in it—the chase was the essence of the thrill. The thrill of being closer, the pulse quickening with every stride. She was nothing but prey, a puzzle to be solved, and he had all the time in the world to play.

Suddenly, the sound of a rustle ahead froze him in place. It echoed ominously, a jarring note that interrupted the rhythm of the chase. It was the jackals, their haunting calls slipping through the night. The howls seeped into the space, washing over them like a tide charged with foreboding. Ethan felt a shiver crawl down his spine; that meant she was close to their territory. But so much fear only emboldened him.

He pressed forward, closing the distance. Through the thinning trees, he saw her stumble again, the low ground buckling beneath her feet as she tried to sprint. The thrill of victory was almost palpable, surging within him like molten steel, growing in intensity, beckoning him to push onward. She darted from shadow to shadow, desperate, searching for a refuge that wouldn't exist until it was too late.

The chase—this was his realm.

A nightmarish atmosphere enveloped them as she spiraled deeper into the forest, light fleeing in hues of darkness, and once again, he felt the pulse of that ancient instinct: hunter and hunted.

But before he could reach her, the sudden noise crept back through the trees—a snapping of twigs, incoherent chatter somewhere nearby. For a moment, uncertainty flared. Was she not alone after all?

Ethan's heart raced as he recalibrated his approach, dark anxiety knotting in his chest. He could hear her breath, agonized and desperate, and it fueled the monster that dwelled within him. But in the back of his mind, a cold voice warned him not to act recklessly. Losing a moment was all it took, and he couldn't afford any distractions.

He remained cautious, trudging carefully forward, the thrill of the hunt intertwined with a cautious wariness. Shadows danced in a disorienting ballet around him, the dark twists of the forest casting long, eerie arms. How easy it was to lose oneself in the heart of fear.

And then something shifted—a sudden motion caught his eye. He turned toward the sound, instincts sharply tuned into every nuance of the night. Sarah's figure wove through the trees, her expression wild, and she stumbled again but caught herself just in time. He inhaled sharply; her delicate frame trembled under the weight of her mounting terror.

The howl rose again, fierce and raw, settling heavily on the silent tension that had engulfed them both. She froze for a moment, battling against instinct, against fear, and for a heartbeat, she looked as though she might turn back.

That was the moment he had been waiting for—the moment that could change everything.

Without hesitation, he surged forward, muscles coiling into action. The thrill coursed through him, rolling like a wave as he closed the distance between them with a predatory grace, fully intent on making her recognize her fate. Before long, she felt him creeping closer, the predator that lurked beneath the surface primed for confrontation.

But as he reached the clearing where he last glimpsed her, the world shifted once again with a sudden noise in the underbrush—an animal, a branch snapping, or perhaps something far more menacing. The sharp crack reverberated through the dark, puncturing the oppressive silence as it roared to life.

Both hunter and hunted stood still, their breaths hanging in the weight of the tense air. Ethan's heart thrummed in his chest as he watched Sarah turn sharply, her wide eyes searching the night. The game of cat and mouse held in a shimmering balance, hovering just on the cusp of chaos.

Then she looked directly at him, her expression torn between fear and defiance; that was when everything changed.

Ethan felt the tension thicken, a tautness pulled between them as silence descended like an executioner's blade. He could see the terror blossoming in her eyes—the predator approaching in a moment loaded with anticipation marked by a sudden fracture in the night. Would she fight? Would she flee? Or would she remain rooted in place, caught between the shadow of the hunter and the gnarl of the forest itself?

And, outside of their standstill, the distant howl of the jackals echoed again, a harbinger of the chaos yet to unfold, transforming the night into a stage where boundaries would break, where the blood of the innocent might spill, ushered forth by the one who relished in darkness.

The air hung thick with dread as uncertainty rippled between their senses, creating an electrical charge that foreshadowed what was yet to come. In that eye of the storm, woven tightly in a fabric of fear, Ethan prepared to close the distance, ready to return the hunt to life.

The Confrontation

As the night deepened, the cold air inside the hut was thick with tension, each rustle of the wind outside making Sarah jump. The sounds of the night felt alive—an orchestra of chirping crickets, the distant howl of the wind, and the unsettling calls of jackals echoing in the distance. Clutching the makeshift weapon she had fashioned from a broken chair leg, she strained her ears, listening for any sign of Ethan. The hairs on the back of her neck stood up, a visceral reminder that she was not alone in this lonely refuge.

Since finding shelter here, she had battled waves of fear that threatened to overwhelm her logical mind. The hut felt like a trap and a sanctuary all at once. Memories of the brutal crime she had witnessed swirled in her mind, mixing with the sharp adrenaline of survival. Each imagined footstep outside sent her heart racing, each creaking wooden plank a reminder of her fragile safety. Sarah had come to a realization: she was no longer just surviving—she was preparing to fight.

Suddenly, the faint crunch of leaves outside pierced the silence, and her breath caught in her throat. She couldn't be mistaken this time; someone was out there. Absently, she glanced around the dimly lit room, searching for something more substantial than the chair leg. Her heart thudded in her chest as the noise grew closer. The shadows in the corners of the room seemed to grow longer, each a reminder of her vulnerability. She had seen death before, and she would not let it find her again.

The door burst open, splintering wooden shards flying into the room as Ethan stepped inside, his silhouette framed against the moonlight. He looked like a specter, wild and menacing. The confidence in his stride was unnerving—a predator reveling in the anticipation of the hunt. Sarah's pulse quickened, but her grip on her weapon tightened. This was the moment she had feared yet somehow instinctively awaited: the confrontation.

"Sarah," he called, his voice a low growl that sent chills down her spine. "Did you really think you could hide from me? You are in over your head."

She felt anger bubble up inside her, a defiance that almost surprised her. "Get away from me, Ethan!" she shouted, raising the weapon in a trembling yet determined stance. "I won't let you hurt me!"

His lips curled into a twisted smile, and he stepped further inside, his eyes gleaming with a mixture of amusement and malice. "You think that will stop me? You're just a scared little mouse playing pretend."

Every instinct screamed at her to flee, but Sarah held her ground. A deep breath steadied her resolve. This was not just about her anymore; it was about standing up to the darkness that had invaded her life. "I'm not afraid of you," she asserted, her voice stronger now, cutting through the tension like a blade.

With a sudden, calculated move, Ethan lunged forward, and Sarah instinctively swung the chair leg. The impact sent a sharp pain shooting up her arm, but she felt a rush of adrenaline as it connected with his side. He staggered back, momentarily caught off guard. It was the opening she needed.

"You're faster than I thought, Sarah," he hissed, his tone shifting from taunting to frantic. His eyes flickered with rage, and for a moment, she saw the monster beneath his facade. "But you won't get away that easily. You shouldn't have reported me."

"I did what I had to do to protect myself!" she spat back, her anger fueling her courage. "You're a monster, Ethan. And I will not let you scare me anymore."

He laughed, the sound echoing painfully in the small space, repugnant and dark. "That's your problem, Sarah. You think you can change the narrative. But in the end, you're still just a witness. A fragile witness who should have known better."

Pain and fear washed over her, but underneath it all was something primal and fierce—a readiness to fight for her life. Sarah lunged at him again, desperation guiding her actions. She swung the weapon wildly, earning her first moment of victory when she connected with the side of his face. He stumbled, falling to the floor, and she quickly tried to move towards the door, but his hand shot out, grabbing her ankle.

In a panic, she kicked back, striking him hard in the chest, freeing herself from his grip. The adrenaline coursed through her as she sprinted towards the doorway, her eyes blazing with determination. This time, she was fighting for her survival, and she would not back down.

But Ethan wasn't finished yet. He sprang upright, his eyes blazing with fury, as he charged after her. Just as she darted through the door, he grabbed her by the wrist, yanking her back violently. The world spun around her as she fell to the ground, breathless.

"Why can't you see the bigger picture?" he seethed, looming over her like a dark cloud. "You've put everyone at risk. Nobody understands the game we're playing, but you and I? We share a bond, even if it's stained with blood!"

"You're twisted!" Sarah cried, scrambling to get on her feet. "You're no superhero. You're just a coward hiding behind your terrible actions!"

As she spoke, she could sense the breakdown of the man in front of her. The bravado he wore was a mask slipping, and if she could just drive him further into madness, maybe, just maybe, she could gain the upper hand. The light from the moon reflected off the sweat on his brow, and in that moment, she saw both the man and the monster he had become— lost and desperate.

"You think you understand me?" he spat back, stepping closer, his eyes narrowing. "You think you're brave for standing up to me? You've no idea what real strength looks like!"

"Then show me," she challenged, her voice steady despite her pounding heart. "But know this: I'll fight back. I won't play your game any longer."

With a primal roar, he lunged, but Sarah was ready this time. She dodged to the side, narrowly escaping his grasp, and with all her might, she swung the chair leg toward him again. It connected, this time catching him squarely in the stomach. He lost his balance, and she could see the shock ripple through him.

"You're nothing," she shouted, surprise coursing through her system as she felt the rush of empowerment flow within her. "Just a killer hiding in the shadows."

Ethan glared, rage boiling over as he regained his stance, the mask of confidence cracking. "You think this is about me? This is about you being a victim! A story to tell, and I will not let your version prevail!"

The desperate truth behind his words sank in—that he believed himself some sort of arbiter of fate, the twisted hero of his own dark tale. In that moment, understanding flooded her: a realization that his monstrous behavior stemmed from a place of pain twisted into lunacy.

"You don't get to decide who lives and who dies," she shouted back, full of righteous fury. "Your twisted sense of justice ends here, tonight!".

His countenance shifted, shifting from anger to something darker—desperation and perhaps fear. Sarah seized the moment, channeling her strength as she swung the chair leg again. This time, as the weapon connected, she felt renewed determination surging through her veins.

Ethan staggered and fell against the wall, and for a moment, they both paused. The air hung thick, silence enveloping them before it shattered as he let out a guttural scream of frustration. Even in the face of defeat, he wasn't ready to accept the reality of losing to her.

"Motherfucker!" he spat, eyes wild with rage and pain. "You'll never escape me!"

Feeling a surge of thrill mixed with fear, Sarah managed to keep moving, maneuvering around the room, her heartbeat thundering in her ears. Each breath was heavy with the anticipation of what was to come. She remembered Jenna's words—her friend's unwavering support—and it gave light to her otherwise darkened heart.

"Think about it, Ethan!" she yelled, dodging his next desperate advance. "You have nothing to prove! Let the police handle this—let justice take its course! Your twisted notions of power only serve to soil your soul further!"

His expression turned, eyes flickering with something akin to anguish. "What's justice, huh? A way for them to control your fate? To tell you how to believe? I grant freedom in my own twisted way!"

With every word, the fabric of his sanity frayed further, and it fed into her own resolve. Sarah lunged, dodging low towards the 100 The jackals ground and rising up to strike again, this time swinging as hard as she could.

The impact of the weapon against his temple sent him spiraling to the ground, and as he fell, the shadows that had once seemed so suffocating began to lift. He lay there, gasping as the power—his power—began to slip away.

As she stood over him, a wave of conflicting emotions washed over her—fear, anger, but also triumph. He had lost; she had won against the darkness that had haunted her.

"You're nothing without your violence," she said, her voice firm, each word a dagger piercing through his delusions. "And tonight, you will face the consequences of your actions."

Ethan struggled to get to his knees, blood trickling down his face. "You were always meant to be part of my story," he rasped, his words now slurring, desperation creeping back into his voice. "You don't realize how important you are to me…"

But Sarah would no longer be part of his narrative. She was the author of her own fate now, and she had fought like hell to reclaim her life. "No," she declared defiantly, "it ends now."

The tension hung thick in the air, the fight leaving Ethan as his eyes widened with a mixture of realization and defiance, but he lacked the energy to retaliate.

As sirens wailed in the distance, a sense of finality washed over her—her shaking legs still unsteady, but her heart now beating with hope rather than dread. For a moment, a flicker of humanity crossed Ethan's face, but it vanished as quickly as it had appeared, lost to shadows forever.

"Sarah! Are you okay?" A voice broke through the chaos, and she turned to find Jenna racing towards her, concern etched on her face.

"I'm—" she breathed out, voice trembling but steady, adrenaline subsiding, "I think I am. I think it's over."

The realization settled around her, and as they locked eyes, a precious flicker of understanding passed between them: in the darkest moments, courage can ignite within, transforming fear into strength.

As her friend's arms enveloped her in a fierce hug, Sarah felt the hollowness of loss begin to fill with resilience—a promise to herself that she would reclaim her life, scarred yet unbroken.

And as the police arrived, sirens blaring, Sarah looked back at Ethan—lost in the shadows—ready to face what was to come, to finally disentangle her story from his. For in this moment of confrontation, she had discovered an unshakeable truth: she was no longer just a victim trapped in a nightmare. She was a warrior on the path to becoming a survivor, and no darkness would define her existence again.

The Struggle

The darkness enveloped the hut as Sarah's heart raced, each beat echoing like a drum in her ears. The air was thick with tension, suffocating, and she could feel every fiber of her being on high alert. Moments ago, Ethan had been just a shadow in her life—a terrifying presence haunting her thoughts. Now, in this small wooden structure, he was here, real and dangerous, threatening to obliterate the small hope she clung to.

Adrenaline coursed through her veins, igniting a fire she didn't know she possessed. She took stock of her surroundings, scanning the dim light filtering through the cracks in the wooden walls. The remnants of a life once lived surrounded her—dusty shelves lined with broken clock parts and cobwebs. A rusted knife lay abandoned on a counter, and instinctively, she edged closer, hands trembling as she reached for it, willing her heart to slow down long enough to think clearly.

The sounds outside were muted, the night air filled with the distant howls of jackals—a haunting serenade that underscored her isolation. They seemed to taunt her, a reminder of the peril she faced. At that moment, the roar of fear was almost too much to bear, and she thought she might drown in it. But there was no time for despair. Ethan would be on her soon, and in that realization, she found clarity.

She gripped the knife firmly, its cold metal reassuring against her palm. There was no more running, no more hiding. This was her stand, her moment to turn from prey into predator. The memory of their previous confrontation surged back. Fear paralyzed her then, but agony and the instinct to survive ignited something primal within her. In the face of death, she would neither yield nor surrender.

Suddenly, the air shifted. She heard a noise—a twig snapping somewhere outside, the soft tread of footsteps drawing closer. Her breath hitched in her throat as she crouched low, hoping that the shadows would conceal her. Every instinct screamed at her to move, to flee or fight, but she was frozen in place. The realization that Ethan was outside, that he had come to finish what they had begun, sparked a fierce determination within her heart.

"Sarah…" His voice called out, smooth and taunting, cutting through the hushed night like a knife. "You can't hide from me. This is all just a game, and you know how it ends."

Inside, she recoiled at the sound of his voice. It was laced with a sickly sweetness that made her skin crawl, but she steadied herself. This wasn't just a game for her; this was life and death. She breathed slowly, focusing on her heartbeat, whispering a silent mantra to prepare herself for what was to come.

"Come out, come out, wherever you are," he continued, his words dripping with amusement. "You know I'll find you. I always find you."

The knife felt heavy in her hand, and the weight of it was a reminder of her resolve. She wouldn't go quietly, not this time. Even if he had hunted her down, even if the odds were stacked against her, she would fight with everything she had. The same fire that blazed in her chest refused to be extinguished, a defiance that flared bright against the darkness.

As Ethan stepped closer, she could see him through a crack in the wooden wall. He was calm, too calm, his eyes glinting with that predatory gaze that sent a chill slithering down her spine. He appeared almost relaxed, as if this were a casual stroll rather than a life-and-death confrontation. "You think you can escape?" he mocked, glancing around the perimeter as if he were surveying a battlefield.

The sight of him, standing there, instilled a sense of rage within her. A soft sound escaped her lips, not quite a growl, but a low, primal sound that resonated deep within her. She was no longer just a victim in this twisted play—it was her turn to act.

Staying as silent as the night surrounding them, Sarah seized her chance. She darted from the shadows, her heart pounding loudly in her ears, and lunged at Ethan with the knife raised high. The element of surprise was on her side, for a moment, his expression slipped—shock and disbelief flitted across his features.

But he recovered quickly, grabbing her wrist with surprising strength. "You really think you can do this?" he hissed, anger twisting his words into a venomous snarl. "You're just prolonging the inevitable."

With a guttural scream, Sarah twisted and fought against his grip, forcing her other hand forward, shoving the knife aimlessly, desperately. Their bodies collided and they stumbled back, crashing into the walls of the hut. The wooden structure creaked in protest as they struggled for control, their breath mingling in the fraught space between them.

"Let go of me!" she shouted, her voice raw, fueled by adrenaline and desperation. She could feel the warmth of blood trickling down her wrist where he held her, but the pain was secondary to the rush of survival that coursed through her veins.

In a fierce burst of energy, she managed to jab the knife downwards, feeling it nick his side. Ethan growled in rage, more animal than man in that moment. The desperate reminder that this was a fight for her life lent her strength, and she pushed harder, fighting against the terror that gripped her heart.

He shoved her back, sending her sprawling against the wooden floor. The wind was knocked out of her lungs, but she scrambled to her feet, fueled by a fierce resolve born from a desperate need to survive. "You'll regret this, Sarah," he spat, but he was struggling to maintain the upper hand.

The chaotic dance continued as they circled each other, anticipation hanging thick in the air. Each time she lunged, he riposted, an unsettling balance, a grim ballet of survival. Sarah's muscles burned with exertion, but she refused to relent. The memories of running, the fear, the hopelessness vanished with each step into the unknown.

It was a strange clarity that enveloped her now—she simply would not back down. A surge of fierce energy fueled her attack, and she pushed against the palpable dread looming in the air. Sarah felt the weight of the knife shift in her grip, becoming an extension of her will, a lifeline in the impending darkness.

Ethan's movements were a serpentine fluidity, each calculated and often defensive. He tried to throw her off balance, to undermine her determination, but deep within her soul, a fierce fire lit up. "Take your best shot, Ethan," she hissed, channeling her frustrations into her next attack. As she lunged again, she felt a surge of confidence wash over her.

He didn't expect this fierceness from her. The knife sliced through the air, narrowly missing his shoulder. It grazed his skin instead, and he stumbled back, momentarily thrown off course, leaving Sarah open for the next blow.

This was not merely a fight for survival—it was a reclamation of her spirit. In that moment, victory was not defined by the outcome of their struggle, but by the fight itself. She found strength in the possibility of defiance, in the act of facing this monster. With each clash of adrenaline and resolve, she felt more whole, more powerful—the battle was as much internal as external.

But exhaustion began creeping in, a heavy weight settling in the pit of her stomach. Her breath came in sharp gasps as her muscles screamed for respite, and doubt crept to the edges of her consciousness like an unwelcome shadow. Could she really keep this up? But then she felt the knife clutched tight in her palm, grounding her, reminding her of why she fought.

"No!" she screamed, shaking her head to dispel the weariness, pushing every thought of hesitation aside. Ethan, sensing a crack in her resolve, lunged for her again, hoping to leverage her fatigue.

Their bodies clashed as she fought to maintain her footing, the desperation of the moment revitalizing her spirit. The struggle became a blur of movement, sweat, and raw emotion. Pain sizzled in her limbs, but survival was paramount; it overrode her bodily suffering.

"How many times must I teach you this lesson?" he growled, frustration mixing in with his rage. He shoved her back with enough force to send her staggering, and in that split second, he sought to gain control, wrapping his hands around her throat.

Sarah's pulse thundered in her ears as he pressed down, the world around her fading to a distant blur. Panic set in, and she clawed at his hands, fighting for air. The terror was suffocating and profound. At any moment, this could end her fight. This could be her death.

But in the darkest depths of despair, she clawed deeper inside herself. A flicker of memory ignited—the faces of her friends, the laughter of Jenna, the warmth of her childhood home—each a testament to the life she fought for.

In a last surge of strength, Sarah kicked out, her foot connecting with Ethan's heavily planted leg. He yelled, loosening his grip for just a fraction of a moment. That's all she needed. Summoning the last reserves of energy, she twisted hard, breaking free from his grasp as she scrabbled for the knife once more.

The struggle intensified, their bodies slamming into one another, desperation blurring the line between hunter and hunted. She swept the knife forward, fueled by fury, but this time, it felt different. She had a clarity of purpose, a fierce determination to be more than just a victim.

"Get away from me!" she shouted, her voice breaking with emotion, raw and unrestrained. Sarah drove the knife forward, aiming for his chest. The blade connected with a sickening thud, and for a split second, silence fell.

Ethan's eyes widened, shock transforming into rage. He stumbled back, clutching at the wound. Blood flowed freely around his fingers, painting the cold, wooden floor. "You... you think this is over?" he gasped, his words laced with pain.

But Sarah knew otherwise. In that moment, she saw a flicker of fear in his eyes—fear of defeat, fear that he had underestimated her. She seized the opportunity, the adrenaline giving her strength. With a fierce shout, she lunged forward again, not intending to give him a second chance.

Then it all came crashing down as he lunged back, knocking her down, their bodies intertwining in a chaotic explosion of limbs. The knife slipped from her hands as they grappled for dominance. The floor was cold against her skin, contrasting with the heat radiating from their struggle.

Pain ricocheted through her body as he bashed her against the wooden surface unpredictably. In that visceral moment, Sarah felt the darkness creeping around the edges of her vision, the reality of what could happen sending her heart into a frenzy. But amidst the chaos, she reached deep into herself, realizing her will to fight had now taken on a life of its own.

Drawing breath as he wrestled with her, she fumbled to regain her weapon, desperate for its calming weight. She spotted the knife just within reach, its silver glint a beacon of hope in the dark.

But just as her fingers brushed against the handle, Ethan locked eyes with her, that wicked grin playing on his lips, like a demon promising her doom.

"Too slow, Sarah."

The strength in his body pinned her down, almost suffocating as she felt his presence loom over her. For a brief, terrifying moment, time slowed, her heart aching, fear pooling at the base of her spine. She realized he wasn't done yet; he wouldn't go so quietly into the night.

As she fought against him, the heaviness of despair threatened to crush her spirit, but she wouldn't succumb. With every ounce of willpower, she twisted and turned, maneuvering her body until she could grasp the knife again.

In a breathless moment of clarity, the urgency rushed back into her blood. Fighting against desperation, every fiber in her body screamed to survive. With one swift movement, she turned the knife around, pressing it into his side. The emotion erupted, a raw scream of defiance escaping her lips, drowning out the cries of the night.

"Get away from me!"

And through that scream, she felt herself emerging, not just as a survivor, but as a woman shaped by this struggle—a force pushed into existence by pain and fear, rising to reclaim her life.

But just as quickly, darkness descended once more, as Ethan's grip twisted, and the world spun out of control. The knife slipped from her fingers, sliding away from both of them in a moment of chaos. Sarah felt her heartbeat quicken, the realization dawning that their fates entwined, each desperate breath tightening the threads between hunter and prey.

As he lifted himself to strike again, the realization that nothing was certain loomed overhead—a moment hung in the balance, and the outcome of their struggle lay just out of reach. Would she finally succumb to the horror, or could she wrestle free from this nightmare?

The answer remained elusive—each heartbeat weighted with potential and dread, the knife's silence echoing like a warning in the shadows around them. The struggle was far from over.

The Final Confrontation

The Showdown

The wind howled through the cracks of the old mounted hut, sending shivers down Sarah's spine as she crouched in the dim light, knowing the darkness of the night was only shadowing an even darker threat. Her heart raced, pounding in her ears like a war drum, each beat a reminder of the danger she faced. The scents of damp wood and the crisp smell of leaves mixing with the earthy musk of the forest surrounded her, a dissonant echo to her spiraling thoughts. This was not how she envisioned her escape would end.

Footsteps. She could hear them now, muffled, but unmistakably close. Ethan was coming for her.

Bracing herself against a jagged edge of wood, Sarah steadied her breathing, grounding herself in the moment. Panic threatened to take over, but she forced herself to focus. She recalled her life before this nightmare—her mundane job, her supportive friends, the little things that made life worth living. This thought ignited a flame inside her. She was a fighter, and she had something to fight for. Drawing strength from those memories, she gripped the makeshift weapon she had fashioned from a broken plank of wood, its sharp edge a feeble reassurance against the terror that was closing in.

The door creaked open, a slow, deliberate movement that made her heart lurch. Shadows spilled into the hut, drawn like moths to the fleeting light of her flickering lantern. Ethan was silhouetted against the night, his presence soaking into the space, darkening it with every breath he took. He stepped inside, his eyes glinting with a predatory hunger that sent chills coursing down her spine.

"Hello, Sarah," he said, his voice a low, menacing drawl. "Did you really think you could hide from me?"

She stifled a gasp, fighting the urge to run. Instead, she held firmly to the weapon, raising it defensively, her knuckles white against the wood, her body coiled like a spring ready to launch. "Get away from me," she managed, her voice shaky yet defiant.

Ethan laughed, a sound devoid of warmth. It curled around her, a sinister fog of impending doom. "You think that can stop me? You don't understand your place in this, do you?" He stepped closer, and she fought the instinct to back away, forcing herself to remain steady. "I'm the hunter, Sarah, and you… you're the prey."

In that moment, fear clawed at her insides, yet she responded with a fierce determination she didn't know she possessed. "I'm not going to let you hurt me, Ethan. Not anymore."

The tension in the room swelled, electric and thick. Ethan's predatory smile widened, revealing teeth that looked more like a wolf's than a man's. "You really think you can fight me? Look at you, shaking in your boots, clinging to that pathetic weapon. How quaint."

As he moved closer, a sudden surge of adrenaline coursed through her veins. She thought of the moments leading to this confrontation—the helplessness, the fear, the torment of being chased. And she remembered something else: the fire of tenacity that had burned within her since she decided to take a stand, the very moment she reported him to the police. It was time to turn that fire into something more.

Ethan lunged forward, a blur of motion, but Sarah anticipated the move. She dodged sideways, heart roaring as she swung the plank in a desperate arc. It connected with Ethan's shoulder, a satisfying crack cutting through the intensity of the moment, but he barely faltered. The adrenaline high brought her an instant of hope, yet his expression turned from playful to furious in a heartbeat.

"You've made a mistake," he hissed, realizing he no longer held the upper hand.

Before she could react, he retaliated, lunging forward with surprising agility. She stumbled back, her feet catching on the uneven floorboards. In an instant, he was upon her, shoving her against the wall with a force that knocked the breath from her lungs. Pain radiated through her body, but she forced herself to focus, driving her knee up into his groin.

Ethan grunted, his hold on her momentarily loosening, just enough for her to break free. The hut felt smaller now, the walls closing in as they moved in and out of shadow, a perilous dance of predator and prey. She eyed a window, the faintest strands of silver moonlight spilling through, guiding her thoughts toward escape.

But this was no longer just about running. It was about survival and reclaiming her power. With renewed resolve, she turned to face him, anger sparking in her chest. "You think you're invincible because of your past," she shouted, her voice stronger now, echoing off the wooden walls. "But you don't own me. I will not be your victim."

Ethan's laughter echoed around her, unsettlingly calm. "You're amusing, Sarah. But this game is mine, and it's about to end." His eyes held a dark glimmer, and with a sudden shift, he lunged for her again.

She ducked instinctively, but he was faster than she anticipated. His hands grasped her arms, flipping her around, her forehead banging painfully against the wall. Stars burst in her vision, disorienting her, but the fight within her surged again.

She swung her elbow backward into his ribs, feeling the breath rush from him. He staggered back, momentarily stunned, and she seized her chance. With a roar of determination, she charged at him, her makeshift weapon swinging. The wooden plank caught him across the jaw, sending him crashing into the far wall, where he landed in a pile of old hay that sent particles of dust into the air.

She was bewildered by her own strength, but no time could be wasted. Heart hammering, she sprinted toward the door, but he was quicker, rising with an ominous anger.

"You can't escape your fate, Sarah!" he bellowed, as he lunged once more.

This time, she dodged, twisting away and tackling him to the floor just inside the door. They wrestled, bodies colliding, filled with desperation and raw instinct. Sarah was fueled by every moment he had stolen from her, every time she had cowered and fled. With each push and shove, she steadfastly refused to give in, becoming a whirlwind of defiance.

"Why did you do it?" Sarah screamed, pinning his wrists against the ground. "Why did you think you could take everything away from me?"

His breath was ragged, spewing a mixture of snorts and laughter. "Because… I can. Because I have the power."

The twisted logic they exchanged across the room, the painful rhythm of their struggle—it all finally unspooled her memories and thoughts like spiraling smoke. In that moment, something shifted deep within her.

"You think you know power? You don't know what it means to have it!" Her unwavering gaze locked onto his, a flicker of fire igniting within her. "I'm taking my life back, Ethan. This is where I reclaim my strength.

"With renewed vigor, she pushed harder, wrestling his hands away from her. She could feel the ropes of fear unraveling, the dawning understanding that she was no longer a victim but an empowered survivor. In one swift movement, she brought the edge of her plank down against his forearm, the satisfying crunch echoing loudly in the void surrounding them.

Ethan howled in pain, releasing her with a look of restrained fury. He scrambled to his feet, confusion clouding his eyes for a moment. But it quickly shattered as the true fury inside him erupted. "You'll regret this!" He advanced towards her, rage igniting every step he took.

No longer willing to cower, Sarah sidestepped, managing to sidle past him. She knew the hut's layout and was determined. She needed a plan. The old wooden hut, once a sanctuary, looked like a cage now, the memories of her terror weaving shadows around her.

"You won't get away," Ethan spat, the venom in his voice slicing through the air.

In a split second decision, Sarah dashed towards a large chest near the back of the room, desperately searching for anything she could use. She flung the lid open, revealing a collection of rusted tools, old nails, and dangerous-looking shards. Not entirely what she was hoping for, but something could work.

Ethan was hot on her heels, moving with the type of aggression that turned her blood cold. As he lunged again, she grabbed a jagged shard of metal, positioning it between her fingers like a dagger. It felt dangerous and powerful—just the way she needed to feel.

"You're a cornered animal now," she hissed, steadying her breath even as her heart thundered in her ears. "And I'm no longer afraid."

Their duel continued, a grim display of survival instincts colliding against sadistic pleasure. He swung first, a meaty fist aimed toward her head. She ducked just in time, feeling the whoosh of air as his fist narrowly missed her. With a primal scream, she retaliated, thrusting the shard toward his ankle.

Ethan yelped as it tore into his skin, a splash of crimson blossoming where he had once held dominion. She saw in that instant the manifestation of her fears turning into anger, a transformation rooted deeply in her struggle for survival.

He stumbled, glaring at her with a mixture of pain and fury, yet even now, she recognized a seed of fear lurking behind that madness. She pressed the advantage, chasing him into the murky edges of the hut, pushing him toward the door.

"You wanted me scared?" she shouted, her voice reverberating through the night air. "You're the one who should be afraid now!"

Ethan's laughter—a manic, desperate sound—only fueled her resolve. "You don't understand, Sarah. It's not fear that will save you. It's death. You're too weak to win this fight."

But she was stronger than she had been, fortified by the memories of who she was fighting for. In that moment, she realized her fear didn't matter. "No. You're wrong. I'm not afraid of you."

This fierce declaration transformed the atmosphere, charging it anew with urgency. Sarah backed him toward the doorframe, feeling the survival instincts kick in. She could not let him out; she needed to end it here.

Ethan lunged again, his animalistic growl echoing in the small space. But this time, she met him head-on, her resolve pushing back against the brute force he embodied. She used her body weight to knock him off balance, forcing him backward into the wall, hearing the thud of impact.

The world around her faded into the background, remnants of fear slipping away, forging her newfound strength into a fierce determination. She followed through, the shard plunging perilously close to his throat, drawing a line between submission and defiance.

"Admit it!" She pressed, her voice low but firm. "You were wrong to think I would ever be your puppet."

The fire in Ethan's eyes flickered between anger and disbelief. The realization of defiance washed over his features, and for the first time, he felt the weight of his own vulnerability.

"You think you've won?" he spat, the calm turning once more to rage. "This isn't over! You'll never be free of me!"

But with a fierce determination, she turned the shard slightly, applying pressure until he groaned in pain—not just physical, but emotional and primal, the sound reverberating through the cabin like a chilling echo.

"This ends now, Ethan," she declared, pushing back against her own fear. The conclusion to this confrontation was neatly written beneath the tension in the air, each moment pregnant with a sense of finality. "You will never hurt me—or anyone else—again."

And she meant it.

As she pushed the shard against him, ready to follow through, adrenaline mingled with fear. For just a heartbeat, she hesitated, a flash of dread overwhelming her thoughts. But as she stared down into Ethan's furious eyes—fear and rage mixed into a furious tapestry of emotions—the decision solidified.

With a swift, decisive action, she let the rage flow through her.

The clang of metal against wooden framework echoed as he fell back from her, the plank broken over her shoulder, a clear representation of her reclaiming strength in light of his violence. She stepped back as Ethan stumbled, gasping and wide-eyed, the dark intent flickering out of his eyes with each passing moment.

"You—I'll… you haven't seen the last of me," he choked, rage mixing with a hint of fear, reality dawning on him.

"No. I won't let you take that power from me again."

As he lay against the wall, defeated and desperate, Sarah finally understood the depths of her own determination. She would not be defined by fear any longer; she was alive, stronger than ever before.

And as the confrontation reached its harrowing conclusion, she felt the fierce heat of the struggle settle, knowing that even if he escaped, this night had changed her irrevocably. She could face the darkness, fighting back against the shadows, and emerge victorious against the hunter.

The schisms of doubt and fear that once corroded her spirit were dismantled. She had found her strength—the spark of resilience that had dimmed but never extinguished. Dust danced in the moonlight filtering through the windows as she withdrew from the scene, determination ignited in her heart.

In that small metaphorical promise lay the real victory: the courage to survive.

The Choice

The air crackled with tension, each breath Sarah took feeling heavier than the last. Inside the small, dimly lit hut, shadows danced eerily along the wooden walls, morphing into ghosts of doubt and dread. She clutched a makeshift weapon tightly in her trembling hands—a jagged piece of wood she'd fashioned in a desperate bid for defense. Outside, the chilling cries of jackals reverberated through the dark woods, but it wasn't their haunting howls that frightened her the most; it was Ethan's looming presence that sent waves of terror coursing through her veins.

A few moments earlier, she'd heard the unmistakable sound of footsteps approach her hiding place, slow and deliberate, echoing through her chest like a drum. Her mind raced, memories of the crime she witnessed flooding back. The violence, the blood, and the cold gaze of the man who had taken a life right before her eyes. And now, that very man was closing in on her, intent on ensuring she would never speak of what she had seen.

The weapon felt heavy, a burden as much as it was a tool for her potential salvation. She could hear him, catching a glimpse of his figure through a crack in the wooden walls. He was methodical, his focus locked onto the entrance as though he could sense her presence, as though he relished the thrill of the hunt. Each second that ticked by was a battle with her own thoughts. She thought of survival, she thought of justice, and most importantly, she thought of the cost of each.

Sarah had played the victim for too long. She was tired of feeling powerless, of being a pawn in a game where the odds were stacked against her. Survival instinct surged within her, urging her to fight back—to be proactive rather than reactive. But what would that mean? Would picking up the jagged wood and swinging it against Ethan make her a person filled with strength or just another killer? The morality of her choices twisted in her mind, a never-ending loop of justification spiraling out of control.

With every gut-wrenching moment, implications of her survival whirled around in her mind. She had seen what he was capable of; she'd felt the weight of another's life slip away in those brief, haunting flashes. In an ironic twist of fate, the crux of her situation was a reflection of those very choices that dictated life and death. She could protect herself, but in the act of doing so, what would she forfeit? Would she become the monster she so desperately sought to eliminate? What impressions would she leave if she struck back?

The weight of morality pressed down on her, suffocating in its intensity. Her thoughts flickered back to her life before this chaos—her routine, her aspirations, and the dreams that now felt like distant memories. She had been a woman with hopes, friendships, and an entire existence that had been stripped away from her in a heartbeat. Can someone who has witnessed such cruelty resist the temptation to let it collide with their soul? And if they do, what kind of life awaits them on the other side?

Ethan's silhouette loomed larger as he edged closer. Her heart raced, matching the tempo of her thoughts. She clenched her fists around the wood, its sharp edges digging into her palms, a reminder of the choice she had to make. She could defend herself against him, claim her right to survival. But in doing so, would she abandon the fragments of humanity that still resided within her? Would she consider her own life more significant than the lives he had taken?

Tears welled in her eyes, not from fear alone, but from the anguish of this moral quagmire. Each passing moment stretched into eternity, and the cacophony outside morphed into a haunting soundtrack of despair. The jackals' cries grew closer, a wild reminder of the savagery lurking in the world, echoing the turmoil in her heart.

The door creaked as Ethan finally pushed it open, the darkness swallowing her whole. His eyes gleamed with a predatory glint, and for the first time, a flicker of doubt crossed his face. Sarah could feel the primal instinct roaring within her now. She had officially entered the realm of fight or flight, but the choice was complicated; she was not simply running from a man but from everything she believed about herself.

"Did you think you could hide from me?" he hissed, his voice cutting through the heavy silence. Each syllable dripped with malice, and just like that, he cemented himself as the adversary she would have to face—not just for her life but for her very soul.

"Yes," she replied, her voice trembling but defiant. "I did! I thought I could escape your grip on my life. But now, I see it's not about hiding! It's about standing up for what is right."

The tension in the room shifted. Ethan's expression morphed, a mix of irritation and amusement. "You think you have a choice now? You think you matter? You're just another statistic, nothing more."

Fury ignited within her, fueling her conviction. "I refuse to be a statistic, Ethan. I am more than your next victim. I'll fight."

His laughter sent shivers down her spine, mocking her fragile strength. "Fight? What do you think you can do with that piece of wood? You think savagery will save you? You're too weak—a naive little girl pretending to be a warrior."

"Maybe you're right." A chill coursed through her as she spoke the words, feeling the reflection of truth settle deep within. "Maybe in a raw, primal sense, I am weak. But I know one thing—I will not become a monster like you."

The moment crystallized between them, time suspended in anticipation of what lay ahead. Sarah could feel the tides of fate swaying back and forth, and her heart echoed the pounding of the impending confrontation. She wouldn't let him strip her of everything she had spent years building—her dignity, her morals, and the belief that humanity could prevail.

With shaking hands, she steadied her grip on the jagged wood, breathing deeply to quell the storm inside. Was she ready to commit to whatever came next, to embrace the tempest of violence that would ensue? The thought of what stirring the shadows with violence could mean filled her with dread—but there was truly no other way. She didn't want to kill, yet it was as if the choice had been thrust upon her by circumstance.

Ethan stepped forward, and Sarah surged with resolve. She raised the wood defensively, her eyes locking onto his with newfound strength. "You might have taken lives, Ethan, but you will not take mine."

In that moment, the universe aligned, and the choice was no longer just about survival; it was her stand against darkness. She would become a beacon of hope in a world filled with fear. As she felt the warmth of adrenaline coursing through her veins, she couldn't shake the awareness of the life-changing choice she'd made in that instant—a choice where the echoes of her actions would linger long after this confrontation ended.

And then it happened. The burst of movement as Ethan lunged became a blur, a cacophony of chaos erupting in their confined space. The weight of her choice crashed down on her in waves, ignited by the primal instinct for survival

Sarah countered his advance with a fierce swing of the wooden weapon, fueled by desperation and the urgency of needing to claim her power. The jagged edge met resistance—a jarring collision that sent shockwaves through her arms—but she didn't flinch. Instead, she pressed forward, tapping into that core of non-negotiable strength that spoke of her resolve to survive.

In the ensuing struggle, panic surged alongside clarity—a mental fog lifted as adrenaline surged through her. She maneuvered with newfound agility, ducking and weaving, every action laced with purpose as she fought to uphold the breath of life against cruelty's grip.

Their fight danced around the room like a macabre tango—with each struggle, she was reminded of her choice to stand and defend herself, abandoning fear and denial in favor of a fierce tenacity.

But the deeper truth of her battle emerged amidst the thrall of chaos. This was never just a fight for her life; it was a fight for her values, her purpose, and everything she might become if she made it through. Each breath was tethered to the legacy of her actions. The ramifications of her choices didn't just belong to this moment; they would ripple throughout a life she longed to reclaim.

Ethan's strength was formidable, intimidating even. But with each move, each deflection, she could sense the tide shifting. She could feel him doubting, hesitating, the very core of his essence rattled by her refusal to capitulate. Chaos gave way to clarity, and the undeniable weight of her humanity emerged as the most potent weapon she wielded that night.

"Not today," she spat through gritted teeth, adrenaline bubbling through her veins as their duel reached a fever pitch. "You will not win."

Then, as the last vestiges of doubt coiled within her mind, she seized the moment. The jagged wood found its mark, a thrust that connected and forced Ethan back. In that instant, a realization washed over her—a visceral understanding of what it meant to truly fight back, not just in body but in spirit.

Yet as the struggle intensified and they battled for dominance, she faced another choice. A dilemma laced with profound implications once more pressed upon her conscience. She could secure her victory through violence, but in doing so, would she relinquish the last fragments of her humanity? Would she become just another savage in a world riddled with darkness?

"No!" she screamed, the word a visceral plea to herself and perhaps the universe. A fiery resolve washed over her. There would be a path forward that could preserve her humanity even amidst chaos.

The jagged weapon dropped from her grasp as she locked eyes with Ethan, her stare unwavering. "I may have to fight you, but I will not lose who I am in the process. I will find a way to end this without becoming you."

There was a moment of stillness, suspended in tension. She could see the confusion etched across his features, the flicker of uncertainty beneath the mask of cruelty. The very bedrock of their confrontation had transformed, and with it, her choice crystallized into something far more potent than mere survival—the choice to rise above the cycle of violence and reclaim her narrative.

But the moment was fleeting. With a swift move, Ethan lunged again, and instinct kicked in as Sarah reacted. She dodged, pivoting on her feet, reclaiming the momentum and wrestling control. This time, it felt different—her heart surged not with ferocity but with purpose.

With a calculated move, she disarmed him—a surge of strength carried her into a newfound clarity. Each breath resonated with the heartbeat of her convictions. While she could choose to strike out in vengeance, she would not enact the same monster that loomed before her.

Instead, she maneuvered to his side, gripping his wrist, forcing him back. Her voice broke through the chaos, steady and commanding. "This ends now, Ethan. You do not own my life; you do not dictate my fate. Not anymore!"

The resolve in her voice solidified as the weight of her choice echoed around them. She had not just fought for survival; she had battled for her essence, her humanity, and the very core of what it meant to rise above one's circumstances.

The tension broke, and with it, mutual understanding sizzled in the air—the fight was far from over, but she had emerged from the rubble of chaos fortified by the conviction that she could be more than a mere survivor. She could become a force for justice, for healing, and for hope amidst darkness.

As they locked eyes, the understanding that bound them transcended the violence of the night. She would carry the legacy of her struggle, stepping into the light that beckoned beyond the horizon, committed to reclaiming her truth.

In that final moment, definition crystallized—she had faced the choice between becoming a monster or retaining her humanity, and she emerged victorious, a testament to resilience amidst chaos. The struggles she faced mere precipitations of the journey that lay ahead, but now, she faced the battles forged anew, the future reclaiming its shape, aligning with the pulsating rhythm of her beating heart.

The world outside still awaited—filled with the cries of jackals lingering in the dark—but above all, it was now filled with a promise: of survival, hope, and the unyielding quest for truth. And no matter where the path led, she had made her choice.

Aftermath of the Battle

The moon hung low in the sky, casting an ethereal glow over the landscape as the first light of dawn began to push away the darkness. Sarah sat on a worn wooden chair in the small, dimly lit cabin that had sheltered her during the night of terror. The air was thick with a mix of adrenaline and fatigue, her heart still racing from the confrontation that had transpired only hours before. Every sound felt amplified in the silence; the creaking of the cabin walls seemed like a reminder of her vulnerability, the gentle rustle of leaves outside pressing upon her consciousness the fragility of her newfound freedom.

She wrapped her arms around herself, a futile attempt to soothe the growing storm of emotions within. The battle was over, and yet, it felt like she was still fighting—fighting against the memories that gripped her mind like a vice. The visceral images of Ethan, the desperate struggle for survival, and the feral nature of her fight flooded her thoughts, drowning out any remnants of peace. Her skin prickled at the memory of his cold, calculating gaze, and she flinched at the echo of his voice. In those harrowing moments, she had battled for her life, but the victory felt hollow now, tainted by the emotional debris left in the wake of violence.

The door creaked open, and Jenna stepped inside, her presence a welcome intrusion into Sarah's spiraling thoughts. She had seen the aftermath of that final confrontation, and there was an unspoken bond between them—one forged in shared trauma. Jenna's eyes scanned Sarah's face, searching for signs of the woman who had faced a monster and come out alive.

"Sarah," Jenna began softly, stepping closer. "You okay?"

"Yeah," she responded, though she didn't believe it. Her voice was hoarse, cracking under the weight of its own falsehood. "I think so."

Jenna's expression shifted as she studied Sarah closely. "You don't have to pretend with me. It's okay to not be okay right now."

A bitter laugh escaped Sarah's lips, surprising her. The statement held a truth she was still grappling with. "It feels like I should be celebrating, you know? Like I should be relieved. I survived." The words hung heavily in the air between them, each syllable a testament to what she had endured and yet, they were soaked in a melancholy that she couldn't shake.

"You are a survivor," Jenna said firmly, taking a seat beside her. "But that doesn't erase what happened. You're allowed to feel everything that you're feeling right now."

Sarah blinked back tears that threatened to spill over. "It's just... I didn't want it to end that way. I didn't want to have to fight. I thought I could somehow escape this. But Jillian, the officer... she didn't even believe me at first." The memory of the police station's sterile walls, the officer's skeptical gaze, and the realization that her life hinged on the words she spoke flooded her mind with fresh anguish.

Jenna reached out, placing a comforting hand on Sarah's knee. "You did what you had to do. This isn't your fault. Ethan made his choices. You were his target, and you fought back."

"But it's more than that," Sarah countered, a tremor in her voice. "I had to become someone else to survive. I lost part of myself in that fight. The woman who was just trying to exist in her small-town life is gone."

A heavy silence enveloped them, filled only by the faint chirps of morning birds and occasional rustles from outside. Jenna's grip tightened on Sarah's knee, grounding her. "You didn't lose yourself; you rediscovered what it means to fight for your life. That's something beautiful, too. You found strength."

"Strength," Sarah echoed, eyes drifting to the small window, where the light poured in, illuminating the dust particles dancing lazily in the air. That strength felt foreign, almost unrecognizable. She had fought not just against Ethan, but against the biases of a society that often dismissed the voices of women. The fear that had clung to her was now replaced with a new, heavier weight—the burden of knowing the darkness that existed beneath the surface of her community. The fear she faced was eclipsed by knowledge, and knowledge was a perilous gift.

"What's next for you?" Jenna asked gently, prompting Sarah to reflect on her future. "Have you thought about it? Where will you go from here?"

"It's hard to think about anything beyond... beyond this moment," Sarah admitted. The weight of her experiences loomed like a shadow, distorting her perception of what lay ahead. "I thought I could just walk away and forget, but now I know that's not possible. I have to confront what happened."

Jenna nodded in understanding. "And you're not alone. We'll figure this out together, one step at a time."

Outside, a rustling noise caught Sarah's attention, and her heart raced again. It was a reminder that the world she inhabited had changed. The tranquility of the early morning felt deceptive, masking the dangers that still lurked in the woods surrounding them. She had fought for her survival, yet the aftermath felt almost surreal. Could the images in her mind fade away or were they engraved within her forever, a constant reminder of her brush with death?

As if sensing her turmoil, Jenna pressed on, bringing Sarah's attention back to the conversation. "This isn't just about survival, though; it's about thriving again. Whatever that looks like for you."

"What if I can't?" Sarah whispered, the question draping itself over them, heavy with vulnerability. "What if I'm forever haunted by this? It's like I'm braced for the next blow. How can I move forward if I keep looking over my shoulder?"

The silence stretched between them yet again, as Jenna searched for the right words. "You take it one day at a time. You let yourself feel what you have to feel, and you don't rush through it. And you lean on your support system. I swear I'll be here every step of the way."

"I don't want to be a burden," Sarah confessed, guilt clawing at her insides like a feral beast desperate to escape. "Everyone's gone through something... Ethan hurt so many people. I can't just—make it all about me."

Jenna shook her head vehemently. "That's the thing, Sarah! It's not selfish to seek help; it's brave. You have a right to your pain just as much as everyone else who has endured this. You're not just some victim who has to tough it out—you're a person whose story matters. You survive first, and then we tackle the rest together."

Though Sarah felt a glimmer of hope flicker within her, it was accompanied by the relentless echo of Ethan's voice, slick and oily. *You think you can survive? You can't escape me.* She pushed the thought aside, willing herself to focus on the present, on Jenna sitting beside her.

"Okay," Sarah finally said, forcing herself to sound confident despite the uncertainty gnawing at her. "What do we do? How do I get past this?"

"We'll start with small things," Jenna suggested. "You could talk to someone professionally about everything you've experienced. I know a counselor who specializes in trauma—I can help set up a meeting. It could be a safe space for you to process your feelings, whatever they may be."

Sarah bit her lip thoughtfully, apprehension curling in her stomach. "And what if they can't help me? What if I tell them everything and they just look at me like I'm crazy?"

"Then we find another counselor. And another, if it comes to that," Jenna replied earnestly. "But you have to try, Sarah. You deserve to heal."

In the back of Sarah's mind, the question loomed—what if she couldn't heal? What if this was a wound that would never close, a scar that would mark her forever? Yet, seeing the fierce determination in Jenna's eyes sparked a flicker of something—a willingness to fight for herself, to reclaim the agency that had been stripped away from her.

"I'll think about it," Sarah said at last, half-fearful of those words. "But I think I need to confront my fears first, get a grip on this anger... and sadness... all of it."

Jenna offered a soft smile. "That's totally valid. Maybe we can even go for a walk. Not far, just around this area. Getting fresh air might help clear your mind."

"Will it really help?" Sarah asked, feeling skeptical.

"You won't know until you try," Jenna replied, her tone upbeat, optimism clinging to the words.

As they stepped outside, the warmth of the sun embraced Sarah, a stark contrast to the ice that had gripped her heart for so long. The woods surrounding the cabin felt nearly alive with morning sounds—the chirping of birds, the rustle of branches swaying, and the distant sound of water trickling. Each breath Sarah took filled her with a hesitating sense of possibility.

"I don't think I'll ever forget," she finally said as they walked further along the path, the ground feeling solid beneath her feet. "But maybe it doesn't have to haunt me."

"It won't." Jenna glanced sideways, determination radiating from every angle. "It will become part of your story. Just remember, after winter comes spring. Healing takes time, but you have a community that wants to support you."

The pair continued down the narrow path, Sarah allowing herself to lean on Jenna's presence. Natural light danced between the leaves, as she took a deep breath, exhaling slowly as she surrendered the grip of fear, at least for the moment.

"Can we talk about Ethan?" she asked suddenly, the name a bitter reminder of what she had faced, yet also a necessary conversation that hung in the air between them.

Jenna hesitated, then nodded. Of course. What do you want to say?"

"I want to understand him," Sarah replied, her brows furrowing as she sought clarity. "Not why he did it, but how someone could become that twisted. It's hard to reconcile the person I was with… the person I am now."

Jenna nodded thoughtfully. "That's okay. It's natural to seek understanding, even if it's painful. You're processing a lot right now."

A series of echoes rang in Sarah's mind—the look in Ethan's eyes, the manic glee when he thought he was in control. "It's just… I didn't see the signs. How could I have not known what he was capable of? Was I so naive?"

"No," Jenna replied firmly, stopping for a moment to meet Sarah's gaze. "You're not to blame. You were living your life. If he was able to hide his darkness, that's on him, not you. It's easy to let that guilt consume you, but don't. You've faced enough already."

Tears began to well in Sarah's eyes as she absorbed her friend's words. The guilt, the shame; they had burrowed themselves deep, exploiting the cracks of her mind. "I don't want to feel like this anymore," she whispered, her voice trembling.

"Then you take it one step at a time. It's okay to be angry—angry with him, with the world, and even with yourself. But you also need to give yourself compassion, Sarah. Remember you're a survivor. You broke the cycle."

As they resumed their walk, the sun began to rise above the horizon, bathing the forest in a surreal golden light. Sarah felt as if she were emerging from the shadows of her own mind, stepping into a world not entirely whole but one where hope flickered in the distance. She had survived. Though the scars would remain, they would also bear testament to her strength, a part of her story rather than its ending.

She glanced at Jenna, gratitude swelling within her. "Thank you for being here."

"I'll always be here," Jenna replied, a warm smile breaking across her face. "No matter what. And I mean that."

With fresh resolve washing over her like a spring thaw, Sarah knew that her journey had only just begun. Each step was a testament to her resilience, to the fight she had refused to abandon. With Jenna by her side, the burden felt lighter—perhaps not gone, but manageable.

And perhaps, someday, she would find a way to speak her truth and reclaim the narrative she had lost to fear. For now, she allowed herself the grace to heal, taking one step forward into the light.

AFTERMATH

Repercussions

The weeks following the confrontation felt like a quiet, unsettling dream for Sarah, where reality had stretched thin and every moment was punctuated by the jarring echoes of her bravest fight. The process of returning to her daily life seemed like an insurmountable challenge, with shadows of doubt clutching tightly to her heart. It was as if she was tiptoeing through a minefield, unsure of which thought or memory might detonate her fragile state of being.

At first, she tried to maintain as much of her normal routine as possible—working at the café, meeting with Jenna, and spending time with her family. The quaintness of the café infused her with moments of calm, or so it seemed. The aroma of freshly brewed coffee and the cheerful jingling of bells above the entrance lent a temporary sense of normalcy. But the laughter that filled the air was often muffled by an all-consuming silence that echoed within her mind. Familiar faces first brought comfort, but soon transformed into haunting reminders of how much had changed. She would often catch herself staring blankly at the customers, their conversations fading into a blur as her mind drifted into darker places.

One late afternoon, Jenna joined her for a coffee break, her vibrant personality serving as a bright contrast to Sarah's somber mood. Jenna animatedly recounted her recent adventures, her expressive hands painting vivid pictures in the air. Yet, as Sarah listened, she felt disconnected, a spectator rather than a participant in the life she once cherished.

"Sarah, you've been so quiet lately," Jenna said, her voice laced with concern. "You're not yourself. Talk to me."

"I don't know how to explain it," Sarah replied, her eyes glued to the patterned tiles beneath their table. "It's like… everything is different now. I can't shake the feeling that something's wrong."

Jenna reached across the table, her fingers gently squeezing Sarah's hand. "You survived something unimaginable. It's okay not to be okay right now. Healing takes time. Just remember, you're not alone."

Sarah blinked back tears as she took a breath. "Every time I close my eyes, I see him. I see that night replaying over and over. I can almost feel his grip on me again."

As the words left her lips, the dam broke. Jenna listened, her expression turning solemn. The realization that the traumatic experience was not just a fleeting shadow but a steadfast companion in Sarah's mind swirled heavily in the air between them.

"What you experienced was trauma, Sarah. It's normal to feel this way," Jenna reassured her. "Have you thought about therapy? It might help you process everything."

"Therapy?" The word felt foreign yet oddly familiar. "I just… I don't know. I don't want to relive it. I don't want to keep talking about it."

"But maybe that's exactly what you need. Talking about it doesn't mean you'll stay stuck there forever. It can be a step towards reclaiming your life."

After some silence, Sarah nodded reluctantly. "I'll think about it."

As Jenna chatted about inconsequential things, Sarah's thoughts wandered. The prospect of therapy felt like facing a powerful wave—inviting but terrifying. Would it help her piece together the shattered parts of herself, or would it drag her under even deeper?

In the days that followed, Sarah took tentative steps, searching for ways to navigate the aftermath. The pull of her old life was strong, but each shallow breath served as a reminder of the battle she wasn't sure she would ever truly win.

One evening, alone in her apartment, Sarah attempted to occupy her mind with a book she had put aside long ago. She had always loved the escape that reading offered, but the words now read like a foreign language—distant, devoid of meaning. She closed the book and leaned against the wall, allowing tears to slip down her cheeks. Every corner of the room felt charged with memories. The laughter with her friends, the warmth of the sunlight that streamed through the window, even the silence, which once felt comforting, now felt stifling.

It was during one of her solitary sessions when she decided to flick on the television. A crime show highlighted cases similar to hers, punctuating her already fragile emotional state. The reenactment of a woman's struggle against a faceless attacker stirred something primal within her. She felt anger rise, blending with her sorrow; the injustices of the world became too much to bear. Rage morphed into determination, and she picked up her phone and made the call Jenna suggested.

The therapist's voice was soothing, calm. "It's perfectly understandable to feel overwhelmed. You're not alone in this. Let's take it one step at a time."

Their sessions began as tentative explorations of her feelings. Each week, she peeled back layers of grief, fear, and anger—each a necessary part of her healing. The first few were excruciating, every word forcing her to confront the reality she had wanted to evade. Yet the therapist's patience, combined with gentle prodding, provided a safe outlet for her pain.

In one session, she said, "It's as if I'm viewing the world through a broken lens. I see everyone else moving on while I feel stuck. I should be grateful that I survived, but instead, all I feel is anger."

"That's okay," her therapist reminded her. "Anger is a valid feeling, especially after what you've endured. It's important to accept all your emotions as part of the healing process."

As these sessions continued, Sarah's feelings of isolation slowly began to dissipate. Jenna's unwavering support was integral. They ventured into the world together, even if just for small outings—a walk by the river, a café visit, or simply a quiet movie night.

In moments of vulnerability, Sarah would express doubts about her relationships. "What if they can't handle me like this? What if every little thing reminds them of what happened to me? Am I a burden to them?"

Jenna would roundly shake her head, her gaze steady. "You're not a burden, Sarah. You're human. You're allowed to lean on the people who care about you. That's what friends are for."

Gradually, it became clear that the shadows of her past were not meant to be banished, but acknowledged and integrated. While the scars would remain, she began to realize that she had the power to shape her new narrative.

One late afternoon, they found themselves in a small park, the amicable wind carrying the scent of blooming flowers. Sarah inhaled deeply, channeling the cool breeze that contrasted starkly with the warmth of the sun. She felt a flicker of resolve emanating from within her—an almost ironic sense of clarity among the chaos.

"Jenna, I've been thinking a lot about what happened, and about everything we've talked about," she said, turning to her friend. "I want to do something meaningful. Not just for myself, but for others who've been through what I have." Jenna's eyes brightened with encouragement. "What do you have in mind?"

"I don't know exactly, but I want to raise awareness. I want to be part of something that helps those who are affected by violence, by trauma. To show them they're not alone. That there's hope."

Jenna nodded in understanding as a smile flickered across her face. "I think that's a beautiful idea. You could start small—join a group, volunteer. There are organizations that focus on trauma support."

With conversation flowing, Sarah quickly became excited about the potential of engaging with others. It felt as though their shared dialogue had lit a spark within her; it now anchored her sense of agency. Perhaps she could find strength not just in her own journey but assist others as well.

As the weeks wore on, this determination became a staple of their routines. Sarah spent afternoons researching organizations while sharing her experiences on online forums, allowing her voice to ring out, even from behind a keyboard. Jenna, ever her cheerleader, suggested crafting a blog to share her journey, which Sarah found herself gradually embracing.

Yet alongside this newfound ambition, the echoes of past trauma lingered, still sending tremors of anxiety through her. She was often reminded just how fragile her emotional state could be, how quickly events could trigger memories of that night.

During those moments, Jenna stood by her, reminding her to take deep breaths, to embrace the present. "Recognize when you're feeling overwhelmed. Acknowledge it, but don't let it control you," she would counsel.

One fateful evening, at the community center where Sarah had volunteered to speak about her experience, she stood behind a podium, her heart pounding with apprehension. Her knees shook slightly, but her voice, when it came, was steady as she shared her story with a gathering of supportive individuals.

"I'm here to tell you that you can take back your power," she said to the audience, the words spilling out of her like a dam bursting. "You can choose to fight against the shadows of your past and emerge stronger."

It was a terrifying yet liberating experience. As she spoke, she noticed others nodding in empathy, compassion lighting their eyes. For the first time in a long while, she felt a surge—a connection to each of them born out of shared understanding and resilience.

That night, as she sat curled up in her bed, the warm glow of her bedside lamp casting light against the walls, a thought crossed her mind. Yes, she had survived. But her survival had transformed from mere existence into meaningful action. She was infusing her experience with purpose.

In the days that followed, Sarah dedicated herself to creating a blog, pouring her heart into posts that detailed accounts of her journey—each piece a small step toward reclaiming her narrative. She wrote about fear, healing, and the importance of community support, infusing her reflections with honesty while casting light on the darker shades of her experience.

And as Sarah engaged with her readers, the responses poured in— stories of shared struggles, glimmers of hope, and messages of gratitude flooded her inbox. For every story told, it felt as though she were building a bridge over a chasm she once thought insurmountable. As she read through their responses, tears of both sadness and joy flushed her cheeks.

In one particular message, a woman named Eliza wrote, "Your words made me realize that I'm not alone. Thank you for giving me hope when I felt so hopeless."

In those moments, the profound weight of her experience felt lighter. She began to see her trauma not solely as a burden but as a source of strength, a foundation to advocate for those whose voices had been muted by fear and silence.

However, the journey was not without its challenges. Late at night, the haunting memories of Ethan would creep back in, whispering reminders of the fragility of her newfound peace. It was during those sleepless hours that she learned to navigate her fear. Instead of drowning in it, she acknowledged its presence; she took ownership of it. In doing so, she could let it exist without allowing it to control her.

With each passing month, the emotional toll began to shift. The nightmare of the past remained, but it was matched by a growing sense of empowerment—and compassion for herself. She found solace in nature, took long walks, and engaged in mindfulness that allowed her to ground herself in the moment. All the while, Jenna remained her unwavering companion through the highs and lows, offering a steady hand and an open ear.

As summer transitioned into autumn, Sarah made another remarkable breakthrough in her healing journey. During one reflective evening, while watching the golden leaves drift from their branches, she realized that her life, like the trees shedding their leaves, held the promise of new beginnings. Shadows of her past no longer suffocated her; rather, they enriched her understanding of herself.

The leaves fell away, paving the path for the new growth that would emerge in its place. That metaphor blossomed within her chest, allowing hope to flourish, unfurling like petals in the sun.

One cool afternoon, deep in thought, Sarah found the courage to sit down once again and pen a letter—one to herself. The letter spoke of her journey, her fears, her strengths, and most importantly, her resilience. She detailed her future aspirations, the importance of reclaiming her narratives, and the determination to continue advocating for change.

As she sealed the letter, her heart felt full—not with burdens, but with promises. Promises to herself and to the community she committed herself to serve. With it, a renewed determination to stand against violence, an affirmation of truth in all its forms.

In the months that followed, Sarah reached out to local advocacy groups, eager to explore collaborative projects intended to support victims and spread awareness. The feeling of purpose coalesced, transforming her grief into action, solidifying her intention to become a beacon for others navigating dark waters.

But that night, as she lay in bed, a sudden anxiety washed over her. An unsettling shudder rippled through her, and she found herself anxious about the future. What if she faltered? What if all her progress crumbled under the weight of another panic? Behind her eyelids, visions of shadows danced, taunting her.

In that moment of vulnerability, she took Jenna's advice to heart. Instead of succumbing, she drew strength from her journey thus far. "I am not defined by what happened to me," she whispered to herself, "but by how I choose to rise."

As she breathed deeply, it hit her with profound clarity: the weight of her past may never fully dissipate. The shadows might linger like the crisp chill of autumn air, but they would not dictate her future. Sarah was learning to be gentle with herself, to give credence to the scars she bore while embracing the vibrant new chapters waiting to unfold.

And so, as twilight cast a tender glow beyond her window, illuminating the path ahead, she closed her eyes for a well-deserved rest. They were whispers of the past, but her future remained firmly in her hands—a canvas waiting patiently to be painted anew.

The Investigation Continues

Michael sat in his cluttered office, the dim light flickering overhead as he stared at the case files spread out before him. Evidence photos of Sarah's grim final moments mingled with notes scrawled in his own hurried handwriting and the fragmented reports from previous investigations. He leaned back in his chair, running a hand through his hair, the weight of the case heavy on his shoulders. The echoes of Sarah's story haunted him, a constant reminder of the darkness lurking in their town, and he was determined to bring justice to her memory.

Just days ago, the community had been shaken by reports of Sarah's tragic fate. While the official narrative suggested a girl lost to the jaws of the night, Michael couldn't shake the feeling that something was terribly amiss. He had seen far too many cases brushed aside in a system that favored silence over truth, and the lingering unanswered questions surrounding Sarah's death felt like a wound that refused to heal. His gut told him that the police's conclusion—that she had been killed by the very man she witnessed committing a crime—wasn't enough. There had to be more, and he was determined to find it.

The small-town dynamics complicated matters. The townsfolk were skeptical about outsiders, and as an investigator from the city, Michael was often regarded with thinly veiled disdain. Nevertheless, he was resolute. His motivation partially stemmed from personal loss; he had seen too many families suffer the consequences of violence without any answers. He would not allow another case to slip into obscurity. He owed it to Sarah, to her memory, and to the other victims whose voices were silenced by fear.

Michael reached for the first file on the pile—witness statements from locals who had seen Sarah the night she went missing. The reports were jumbled and vague, some offering scant details while others claimed to have heard screams in the night. He scrolled through each account, intrigued by the inconsistencies. "Why would witnesses differ so widely?" he pondered, tapping his pen against his desk. The details seemed scattered like breadcrumbs—a trail he was determined to follow.

With a resolve to speak directly to those who had witnessed Sarah's final moments, he grabbed his jacket and headed out. The chill of the autumn air immediately enveloped him as he stepped outside, the sun barely battling its way past the gray clouds. He felt the town's weight pressing down, heavy with unspoken fear and trepidation, but he pressed on.

The first stop was the local coffee shop, a gathering place for the community that often buzzed with gossip and chatter. Michael pushed through the door, the bell above jingling softly. The smell of freshly brewed coffee and baked goods filled the air, but the conversations abruptly hushed as he entered. He scanned the room and spotted a woman sitting alone in a corner, her eyes darting nervously to the door as if fearing unwanted attention.

"Excuse me, ma'am," he called gently as he approached her table. "Are you Rachel? I'd like to ask you a few questions about Sarah."

The woman nodded, her face pale and drawn. "Sure, I heard about what happened." She fidgeted, biting her lip, as he took a seat across from her.

"Can you tell me what you saw that night?" he prompted, trying to adopt a tone that might ease her fear.

"I saw her walking home… I swear, she looked like she was being followed," Rachel whispered, glancing around to ensure no one else was listening. "I… I thought it was just my imagination."

Michael leaned forward, encouraged. "But you're sure? Could you describe the person you thought was following her?"

Rachel's gaze dropped. "I couldn't see much. Just a shadow... and then... I heard the shouting. It was so loud, but then it stopped, and I thought maybe I should call someone, but..." Her voice trailed off, and her expression hardened with regret. "I didn't."

Michael felt a stab of frustration contrasting with empathy. "You're not alone in that. Many others felt the same—afraid to get involved. But if you saw anything, it's crucial. Every detail matters."

Rachel's eyes filled with tears, and he could see the harsh grip of guilt tightening around her heart. "I wish I had called. I thought... I thought it was just a fight or something. But that girl didn't deserve that. She was so nice."

Nodding, Michael sensed the raw emotion in her voice. "Did you see anyone else around? Anyone who might have been with her or the man who was following her?"

"I... I think I saw someone else around the alley. An older man. He didn't seem right. Just lurking in the shadows, watching."

Michael's heart raced. "Did you get a good look at him? Did he say anything?"

"No! Not really. I didn't want to look. I was terrified." She wrapped her arms around herself, shivering slightly.

"Thank you, Rachel. You've done the right thing by sharing this," he said warmly, determined to reassure her. "I might need to come back with some sketches, see if you can identify him or anything else. Would that be okay?"

She nodded, visibly relieved, and he left her to collect her thoughts while he moved on to his next interview.

Michael spent the following hours interviewing others—friends of Sarah, residents from the neighborhood, local bar patrons. Each encounter deepened his understanding of Sarah's life and the chilling implications surrounding her tragic demise. He unraveled a patchwork of relationships and networks that underscored the challenges he faced: perhaps knowing things, but still not knowing enough.

Returning to the office in the late evening, Michael sifted through the notes he'd taken, piecing together a mental map of the investigation. He barely noticed the light fading, lost in thought over the web of connections he was attempting to piece together. But then, the damning thought surfaced again—Ethan. The man who had killed her, or so the narrative went. Who was he, really? What motivated someone to commit such horrendous acts?

He gathered the gathered files on Ethan, pouring over any evidence he could find, determined to connect the dots. What had spurred him on to violence? How did a person come to stand on the precipice of such an abyss? Michael knew he had to dig deeper.

Internet searches revealed scattered information about Ethan—a troubled young man, a few run-ins with the law, some dubious associations. Michael could already see the outlines of a troubled past stretching out behind him—a boy whose childhood had been marked with neglect and perhaps violence. The road to his behavior seemed laden with the scars of a derelict upbringing. Michael was struck by how systemic failure often created a cycle of violence, feeding into the very tragedies that he was grappling with.

His determination to pursue justice for Sarah fueled him as he ventured out once more, this time seeking out the people in Ethan's life. The descent into Ethan's world felt grim, but it was necessary. He started with the edges—the friends, the acquaintances, the people who would tell him what they knew, even if it was only a fraction of the truth.

As he made his way to a run-down part of town, the atmosphere changed. The skirmishes with truth seemed more pronounced here. Sam, the first individual he found, was a former high school classmate of Ethan's, who now found himself trapped in a cycle of substance abuse. He was slumped against the wall of a dimly lit alley, rifling through a paper bag.

"Hey!" Michael called out, recognizing the hushed urgency around the matter. "I just want to talk for a moment."

Sam looked up, his sunken cheeks betraying a weariness that echoed the inability of people like him to escape their circumstances. "What's this about, man?

I ain't got time for cops." "I'm not with the police," Michael emphasized. "I'm just trying to understand the situation surrounding Sarah's death. I need to know what you can tell me about Ethan."

Sam shifted, sparks of recognition flickering in his eyes. "That dude's bad news. You have no idea. I mean, I heard about what happened, and I get it. Ain't surprised. He always had a temper."

"What do you know?" Michael pressed.

"Eh, just that he snapped, you know? He always had it in him. Something dark. But…he's a friend of mine, man."

"Were you close? Did you ever see this coming?" Michael countered, injecting urgency into his questioning.

"We hung out from time to time. I figured, like most people, that he just had it rough. But I didn't think he'd go that far. You know how the streets teach you to keep your mouth shut? Just keep your head down? That's what I did," Sam muttered, frustration seeping into his words.

"You knew about the anger? Did he talk about it?"

"Never said much, but it was there—always bubbling. There were times when I caught him with his fists balled tight. Like a bomb waiting to go off."

"Did he know Sarah?" Michael's heart raced at the prospect of drawing connections.

"Not that I know of," Sam replied distantly. "But he'd drink enough for a spin-off of a horror movie, you know? Got close to some wild people out there."

Michael sensed potential connections—the shadows of Ethan's life revealed a deeper darkness, perhaps fueled by resentment or abandonment. In his pursuit for truth, he felt conviction swelling; it wasn't just about Sarah, but about defying the shadows that plagued so many.

As he walked away from Sam, he felt the weight of unresolved questions pressing against him. Who would speak the truth? Who would risk their safety to speak for Sarah? He considered his next steps—reaching out to those who could reveal more, sifting through Ethan's remaining connections, feeling the urgency of time tick against him.

Days turned into weeks as he devoted himself to unraveling Ethan's existence. He interviewed former friends, learning of Ethan's pitiful attempts to fit into places he never belonged. He plunged deeper into the murky waters of drug circles, where loose lips occasionally offered grainy details regarding his violent outbursts. Michael understood that for every sound piece of information, he wasn't just battling Ethan; he was battling the pervasive silence that surrounded violence.

Every interaction, every witness he approached tore the mask off the events leading to Sarah's death, tightening the net of culpability around Ethan's looming figure. But even as the pieces fell into alignment, uncertainty still clouded the atmosphere. Just when Michael thought he was grasping the truth, another layer of complexity emerged. He found connections between Ethan and disturbing acquaintances, leading him down familiar streets that wove back through the community, all the while reminding him of the power of silence.

His tenacity earned him the ire of some, raising eyebrows among local factions wary of the 'outsider' unearthing their dark corners. The tension escalated as he received subtle threats, warnings veiled as whispers through hallways and restaurants. But he was undeterred; he knew real change required an unwavering pursuit of truth.

Finally, just as the chill of winter began to breathe new life into the dark months, Michael had a breakthrough. A new witness emerged—Ethan's former neighbor, an elderly woman who had observed suspicious behavior late at night. Her revelations, tied with descriptions from others, painted a more vivid picture of Ethan's erratic behavior leading up to Sarah's encounter.

"Sometimes, I would see him with others—strange people, the kind you want to avoid," she recounted, her hands trembling slightly. "They started to come around more, lingering, causing trouble."

"What kind of trouble?" Michael urged.

"The kind that didn't feel right," she wrung her hands. "Fights. Arguments. I thought they were just kids, you know? Stupid stuff. But then they'd go quiet, and it felt like danger was lurking."

Bile rose in Michael's throat as a knot of realization began to form. "Did you ever hear any names thrown around?"

"Just whispers. But… I heard someone mention Sarah once. I think I overheard a conversation through the wall," she admitted, her voice barely above a whisper. "It worried me, like they were targeting her."

"Targeting?" he echoed, the fear settling in his chest.

"Maybe. I couldn't make out the details, but there was talk of needing to silence someone… something about not letting her speak."

When he left her home, the weight of Sarah's loss clung to him, suffocating in its intensity. These revelations suggested a grimmer possibility: Ethan was not simply a lone wolf; he had companions in this gruesome game of violence. Were there others who lurked within the shadows? How far did this go?

Each encounter heightened the tension surrounding the investigation; he felt the web closing in as he pushed forward. The final pieces would soon fall into place, but he knew there was always the chance of failure. Days became consumed with uncovering secrets buried beneath lies, fueled by his desperation to honor Sarah's memory and give voice to the silent screams that had gone unheard.

In the final week before the conclusion of his investigation, Michael gathered all his notes, connecting each strand of information—a fleeting encounter, a word overheard, a twist of fate that had led him to this moment. He was exhausted but driven; with each revelation, he grew ever closer to the truth.

As the sun set on yet another relentless day, Michael resolved to confront the questions swirling within himself—the price of justice, the toll it takes, and the culpability of a system that often turns blind eyes. Raw emotion surged as resolve coalesced. The truth needed to be revealed, and he would see this through to the end.

Ethan awaited the unveiling of the truth; the darkness that resided within him was not going to stay buried much longer. As Michael prepared for the next steps, he knew the road ahead would be perilous—full of twists and unexpected turns, where shadows lurked and silent battles raged to bring forth the light that sought to uncover what had once been hidden. It was a fight for Sarah, for those lost in the shadows, and for justice yet to be served.

And as night began to fall, he found strength in the conviction that his pursuit, no matter how harrowing, was worth every perilous step. Michael steeled himself for the confrontation ahead, knowing that in a world steeped in silence, the truth would always seek a way to rise. 153 The jackals

A New Beginning

Sarah stood at the edge of the park, the light of the morning sun filtering through the branches of ancient oaks, casting dappled shadows on the ground. It was a new day, a fresh start, and for the first time in months, she allowed herself to feel the warmth on her skin. She took a deep breath, inhaling the crisp autumn air, rich with the scent of fallen leaves and blooming flowers. This was her sanctuary—her space to reclaim the life that had almost been taken from her.

As she strolled along the familiar path, Sarah noticed the small changes that had transformed the vibrant landscape of the park. There were children playing on the swings, their laughter ringing in the air, and the aroma of cinnamon and pastries wafting from the nearby café. Each sound was a reminder of normalcy and life moving forward, a soothing balm to her still-frayed nerves.

Since her harrowing experience with Ethan, Sarah had been on a journey—a path toward healing that she had not anticipated. The weeks following the confrontation were a blur of police interviews, therapy sessions, and sleepless nights filled with haunting memories. Yet, slowly, through the unwavering support of those around her, she began to piece her life back together.

Jenna had been her lifeline. The moment Sarah had stepped into the sunlight after her ordeal, Jenna had been there, hugging her tightly, promising to never let go. Their friendship had deepened, fortified by heartache and shared vulnerabilities. Jenna had become not only a confidante but also an advocate, encouraging Sarah to confront the trauma head-on rather than let it fester in the shadows.

"Let's start small," Jenna had said during one of their countless coffee meetups, her eyes filled with determination. "Why don't we take a walk in the park together? It's a safe place. Just you and me."

That simple suggestion had turned into a routine that anchored Sarah in reality. Their walks became sacred rituals—opportunities for laughter, tears, and the sharing of dreams once shelved in the depths of fear. Sarah found herself speaking openly about her experiences, expressing feelings she had struggled to articulate. Each conversation acted as a release valve, a way to diffuse the intensity of her emotions and ease the weight she carried.

As they walked today, Sarah turned to Jenna, who was animatedly discussing the upcoming community fundraiser. "I really think we should volunteer together. It's a way to meet new people and give back. Plus, it'll help you take your mind off ... well, everything," she said, hesitating momentarily before continuing.

Sarah smiled, appreciating Jenna's thoughtful approach. "I'd love that. What kind of events are they planning?"

Jenna's eyes sparkled with enthusiasm. "There's a bake sale, a charity run, and even a silent auction! We could bake some cookies together. You know how much I love your chocolate chip recipe."

The mere mention of her baking brought warmth to Sarah's heart. She hadn't made cookies in a long time; the act of creation, of infusing pleasure into something tangible, felt foreign yet inviting. "That sounds perfect, Jenna. Let's do it!"

The weeks that followed were peppered with activities that seemed mundane to others but felt monumental to Sarah. She began volunteering at the community center, rediscovering her love for art as she helped with children's craft sessions. The tactile experience of working with paint and clay acted as a therapeutic outlet, allowing her to channel her feelings into something beautiful.

Sarah also joined a support group for trauma survivors. The group, consisting of men and women from different walks of life, created a safe haven where vulnerability was met with understanding. Each shared story resonated with her; the narratives echoed her own fears and struggles. Here, Sarah started to realize that she was not alone. With each meeting, she felt the shackles of shame loosening, replaced by a network of shared strength.

During one session, the group facilitator encouraged them to create vision boards—collages that illustrated their dreams and aspirations. Sarah hesitated at first, unsure of what lay ahead. However, she was struck by an overwhelming longing for joy, growth, and adventures that transcended the confines of her past.

That night, armed with magazines and scissors, Sarah sat at her kitchen table, scissors in hand. With every cut and paste, she envisioned her future. Pictures of vibrant landscapes, tranquil beaches, and laughter filled her board. She included snippets of quotes urging resilience—wildflowers growing through cracks and artists painting bright murals on drab walls. This exercise reignited a flicker of hope inside her.

With each passing day, Sarah noticed her confidence slowly returning. She found herself laughing more spontaneously, crying less frequently, and dreaming bigger. Days that initially felt heavy now held the promise of possibility. She discovered a newfound 156 The jackals appreciation for the little things—a cup of coffee in the mornings, a cozy sweater that hugged her just right, and the vibrant colors of the sunset painting the horizon.

One afternoon, as Sarah stood in line to grab her regular coffee, she spotted a flyer pinned to the community board: "Local Arts Festival—Open Call for Artists!" Her heart raced as she read the details. The festival aimed to highlight local talent and inspire creativity in the community. It would take place in a month, and she could submit her artwork for display. Something deep within her stirred, a sense of excitement pushing through the remnants of self-doubt.

"Hey, do you want to get involved?" Jenna's voice broke through her reverie, and Sarah turned to find her friend holding a stack of flyers with her eyes gleaming with excitement.

Sarah took one of the flyers, her fingers trembling slightly. "I want to, but I haven't displayed my work since... since everything happened. What if no one likes it?"

Jenna's expression softened, and she grabbed Sarah's shoulders gently. "You cannot let fear dictate your life anymore. You've been through so much; don't let it stop your creativity. This is about sharing your story, your perspective, and your healing."

Sarah's pulse quickened. Despite her apprehension, she felt a flicker of courage igniting inside her. "You're right. I won't let my past define my future. I want to do this."

In the weeks that followed, Sarah immersed herself in her art, pouring her emotions onto canvas. Colors flowed like blood from a wound previously hidden. As she created, she confronted her inner turmoil—the chaotic swirls represented her struggle, while moments of clarity blossomed into vibrant landscapes filled with hope and serenity. With every stroke of her brush, she painted a narrative of survival, resilience, and rebirth.

The day of the festival arrived, and despite her nerves, Sarah set up her work alongside other talented local artists. The festival buzzed with energy; laughter mingled with the scents of food stalls and the sounds of live music. As she stood by her artwork, she watched attentively as people walked by.

Occasionally, someone paused to catch sight of a particularly striking piece. Their appreciative nods and smiles filled her with warmth and pride.

One elderly woman approached Sarah with tears in her eyes. "This piece speaks to me," she murmured, pointing to a vibrant canvas depicting a field of wildflowers under a bright, expansive sky. "It reminds me of hope after loss. Thank you for sharing this."

The sentiment hit Sarah deeply. The woman's words validated everything she had poured into her art—the emotion, the healing, and the longing for joy beyond darkness. They were all interconnected. In that moment, Sarah felt a connection to something larger than herself, the profound reminder that her journey was not only her own but woven into the fabric of shared human experiences.

The festival was a turning point for Sarah. The conversations she had, the stories she shared, and the encouragement she received from the community ignited a fire within her heart. She began to see herself not just as a survivor but as a storyteller with a voice that mattered.

In the weeks that followed, the momentum of her transformation gained speed. Sarah found herself pursuing other creative outlets— writing poetry, learning guitar, and even contemplating a blog to share her journey and inspire others. She wanted to connect with individuals who might be facing their own battles, showing them that there is light at the end of the tunnel.

With each step she took, Sarah felt the shadows of her past beginning to fade. Although the scars remained, they were no longer chains that bound her but rather badges of honor—marks that told a story of a woman who had faced the abyss and emerged stronger.

Support from Jenna and the community only fueled her desire to help others. Together, they organized workshops at the community center, bringing together survivors to explore art as a healing tool. It was rewarding to watch participants open up, sharing their struggles while creating, knowing they were no longer alone.

One evening, as Sarah packed her materials after a successful workshop, she felt an overwhelming sense of gratitude wash over her. The journey had not been easy, but it had led her to profound realizations about herself and the world around her. She was becoming the person she had longed to be—a woman of strength, compassion, and purpose.

As they sat outside the center under the twinkling stars, Sarah and Jenna often reflected on the incredible progress Sarah had made. "Do you remember when you thought you'd never feel happy again?" Jenna asked with a smile, nudging her arm.

"I do," Sarah replied, her voice soft but resolute. "But now I know happiness is within reach, even in the face of darkness. It's not a destination, but a journey—a choice I make every day."

Days turned into weeks, and Sarah continued to forge ahead, balancing her art, community involvement, and self-discovery. She often visited the park, her sanctuary, to soak in the beauty around her. She could breathe easier there, reveling in the serenity that once felt inaccessible.

It became a place of reflection, where she set intentions and gazed toward the horizon, envisioning a life filled with possibility. One evening, standing in the park, staring at the sunset painting the sky in hues of pink and orange, Sarah closed her eyes and took a deep breath.

As she opened them, she smiled at the beauty surrounding her. Life held promise, and she was ready for it. Each joyful moment pushed the fear further into the past, lessening its grip on her spirit.

With every brushstroke, every shared story, and every breathed-in whisper of hope, Sarah knew she was reclaiming her life. She was ready to embrace the future fully—ready to live, create, and love again.

The shadows would always exist in her mind, reminders of what she had faced. But they no longer defined who she was. Instead, she had emerged from the darkness, a woman transformed, driven by purpose, and armed with resilience.

Longing for adventure, Sarah allowed her excitement for the unknown to flourish. There was much more to explore, far beyond what she had once known. She could create her narrative, filling it with vibrancy, joy, and the promise of new beginnings.

And so, with an open heart and renewed spirit, Sarah stepped into her future, ready to shine bright against the backdrop of life.

THE UNBELIEVER

The Doubt

Michael sat at his cluttered desk, the faint light of his desk lamp casting long shadows across a stack of case files. The room was filled with the monotonous hum of a nearby heater, a sound that often drowned out the chaos swirling in his mind. He had dedicated years of his life to law enforcement, veterans' cases, and even domestic disputes, but nothing had prepared him for the darkness that seeped into his thoughts since Sarah's disappearance.

For many in his department, the narrative was clear: Sarah Evans was dead, her body hidden among the shadows of the crime-ridden landscape of their small town. A witness to violence, a victim of the chaos that often lurked just beneath the surface of their seemingly idyllic lives. But Michael could not surrender to that narrative. Something about it felt wrong, an uneasy weight that pressed down on his chest, squeezing his heart with each beat. The absence of concrete evidence haunted him, gnawing at his conscience.

He stared at the case file spread open before him, a different kind of chaos alive in the photographs and reports. The smiling face of Sarah in one photo danced before him, her bright eyes reflecting a warmth that seemed to belong to a world far removed from the jagged edges of the reality he was grappling with. Her laughter echoed faintly in his ears, and for a moment, he could almost see her walking through the precinct, determination in her stride, oblivious to the tragedy that awaited her.

A few weeks ago, the community had mourned her presumed fate. It was simple for them to accept the loss, to wrap their grief in the neat package of closure that came with believing she was gone. But Michael was not so easily satisfied. The more he dug into the details, the more he found inconsistencies that didn't fit the narrative—a narrative spun from fear and speculation rather than facts.

In the beginning, the case had seemed straightforward. Witnesses had reported seeing a commotion in a nearby alley, and those who had crossed paths with Ethan, the man suspected of committing the crime, were quick to label him a monster. Yet, as Michael pored over witness statements and cross-examined rumors, he found that no one had actually seen Ethan commit the act. There was an absence of evidence that gnawed at him.

What had happened in that alley? Why had Sarah chosen to walk that way? His thoughts spiraled, intertwining with memories that felt too personal. Michael had his own ghosts—lost loved ones that whispered in the silence of the night. But what drove him now was not only the specter of memory, but the fierce desire to give Sarah a voice, the chance to reclaim her story from those who had reduced her to a mere statistic.

He rose from his desk, pacing the small space in an effort to clear the fog clouding his thoughts. The walls seemed to close in on him, memories of failed cases creeping like shadows in his peripheral vision. He unclipped the badge from his belt, rolling it between his fingers, contemplating the purpose it once held for him. Justice. That had been his call, his reason for waking each day. But now, he felt the weight of his badge like an anchor, dragging him down into despair.

"Hey, Detective." The sound of his colleague, Officer Lin, broke him from his reverie. She leaned against the doorframe, arms crossed, her expression wary. "You still looking into Sarah Evans's case?"

"Yeah. Why?" He closed the case file and turned to face her, masking the tumult of emotions storming within.

"You know how it is. People move on. We put out the word she's gone, and most are willing to leave it at that," she replied, her voice laced with a mix of sympathy and exhaustion. "You're a good cop, Michael, but sometimes you have to let go."

"Let go?" The words left his mouth with a bite that surprised even him. "Letting go isn't an option, not when we don't have answers. Not when her family deserves to know what happened."

Officer Lin sighed, pushing herself off the door. "I get it. But this isn't just about the case anymore. You're losing yourself in this. You've been working late, pulling double shifts, skipping meals. It's not worth it, Michael. Not when there are other cases that need our attention."

He opened his mouth to argue, but the conviction in her eyes stopped him. Deep down, he knew she was right—he had been ignoring his own needs, slipping further down a path that led only to darkness. But he couldn't shake the feeling that Sarah deserved better than what the world was willing to offer her—a silence that threatened to swallow her entire existence.

"Let me show you something," he finally said, gesturing for her to follow him. They made their way to the evidence room, a dimly lit space stacked with boxes and unmarked files. A faint musty scent lingered in the air, like the weight of forgotten stories begging to be retold.

Michael led Lin to a table cluttered with evidence bags and photographs related to Sarah's case. "Look at these," he urged, pulling out a series of witness statements, the ink slightly smudged from hasty notes. "Every single witness saw something different. One person thinks they saw her arguing with someone. Another insists she was alone. How do we reconcile that?"

Lin leaned closer, scanning the pages. "People see what they want to see, Michael. Emotions cloud judgment. Maybe they don't want to admit that it could have been worse."

"But that's exactly it! No one has given Sarah the benefit of the doubt. It's as if we've written her off without taking the time to understand what happened." He felt the fire of his passion light beneath him, an ember growing stronger with each assertion.

"Okay, okay. I get it," Lin said, raising her hands in a surrendering gesture. "But you can't battle the world alone. You need to get the department on your side, not take them on as enemies."

Michael released a bitter laugh, the sound echoing off the cold walls. "You think anyone here would care if I pushed harder? After all, I'm just a cop with a passion for a woman who is presumed dead. I'm one of them—just as easily dismissed."

In that moment, Michael recognized the truth behind Officer Lin's words. It was not only Sarah's story that needed to be uncovered, but his own burden as well. He had buried his past, always focusing on others' pain rather than dealing with his demons. The loss of his sister in a hit-and-run accident had turned him into a willing martyr, pouring himself into a hollow existence of vigilante justice.

As he took a deep breath, his resolve crystallized. "I won't stop," he finally declared. "I owe Sarah that much. I owe it to myself."

Lin nodded, a flicker of understanding passing between them. "Then let's figure this out together. But please, allow others in. Don't shoulder this alone. It's going to take a whole lot more than just you to find the truth."

"Thanks, Lin," he said, genuine appreciation filling his words. "I know it sounds crazy—obsessive even—but…" He trailed off, unsure how to articulate the depth of his feelings.

"Yeah?"

"But I can't shake the nagging feeling that something bigger is at play here. Sarah's case—Ethan's actions—there's a connection we need to unveil," he finished, determined.

"Alright. Let's get back to work," she said.

As they walked back to the precinct, a sense of camaraderie bloomed between them. Michael was still haunted, but with Lin by his side, the darkness began to lift just a little.

Days turned into weeks as Michael threw himself into the case, poring over archives and records, interviewing anyone who even remotely crossed paths with Sarah. He noticed patterns forming, and with each conversation, the doubts of his peers echoed louder—filling spaces with questions rather than answers.

"Detective, I heard you've been talking to the barista from that café Sarah frequented," said Officer Finley, a curt man with little faith in the power of discussion. "Don't waste your time. She'd probably forgotten what she had for breakfast, let alone the mundane details surrounding Sarah."

"Then we need to jog her memory," Michael retorted, his frustration rising. "Maybe her memory can unlock new leads. Just because you deem something irrelevant doesn't mean we should dismiss it."

"Go ahead and break a sweat then," Finley muttered as he retreated to the breakroom, leaving Michael brooding. With each passing day, he could feel the weight of doubt settling onto his shoulders. It nearly immobilized him—like a thousand tiny stones slowly piling up, threatening to crush his resolve.

After one particularly grueling day, Michael returned to his apartment, exhaustion wrapping around him like a heavy blanket. He poured himself a whiskey, needing something to numb his mind. But instead of drifting into oblivion, his thoughts circled back to Sarah.

What would she think if she knew he was fighting for her? Would she appreciate his determination or see it as futile? More than anything, he longed for a glimpse of her spirit, the fierceness behind her laughter. The fire in her eyes that commanded respect and authority. The courage to stand up against adversity. He craved justice—not just for her memory but also as fuel for his own healing.

That night, he lay on the couch, the whiskey bottle empty by his side, and tried to sleep. But echoes of the case flooded his mind, seeping into every crevice of his subconscious. Instead of dreams welcoming him with ease, night terrors invaded, clawing at any sense of comfort. He couldn't escape the visions: Sarah's face twisted in fear; Ethan lurking from the alley; closures denied in muffled whispers.

A bright sliver of light broke through the haze the next morning. Upon returning to the precinct, Michael discovered something new—an anonymous tip had surfaced. The words were vague, a cryptic promise of "knowing what happened" if he was willing to continue the search. More than a beacon of hope, it ignited a fire in his gut, reminding him that quitting was not an option.

He wasted no time—gathering his notes, shaking off the remnants of doubt. An unyielding determination pushed him forward as he worked tirelessly to track down the source of the tip. Every moment counted now; Sarah deserved that from him.

As the sun dipped below the skyline, painting the precinct with hues of orange and purple, Michael honed in on the lead. It led him to a rundown diner at the edges of town, one he hadn't visited often—the kind of place where secrets were shared under the cover of greasy plates and low voices.

Pushing through the door, he was greeted by the familiar smells of fried dough and coffee. A young waitress caught his eye, and he made his way to the booth where she was hunched over, scribbling notes. She looked up, surprise flickering across her face.

"Detective," she began, glancing around as if concerned someone might overhear, "I heard what you're looking for."

Michael felt a surge of adrenaline. "You know something about Sarah? Anything at all?"

She hesitated, gaunt eyes searching for confirmation that he would keep her secrets. "I don't want to get involved, but… I saw a guy. He wasn't a regular but came in a few days before… everything happened. He was watching her."

A thread of excitement weaved through his veins, but he knew better than to jump to conclusions. "Do you know who he was?"

"No. I can't remember names. But I can remember faces, and he'd been hanging around a lot that week."

A wave of frustration threatened to surface, but he squeezed it down. "Do you remember anything specific about how he looked?"

She thought for a moment, biting her lip, before offering. "He had this ugly scar right over his eyebrow. It made him look… dangerous. Like he was always ready for something to go wrong." She winced at her own words, as if they summoned the threat itself.

Michael scribbled notes, heart racing. "Do you have any idea why he was watching her?"

"I… I think he was waiting for someone. Maybe something was going down."

The pieces were coming together, sealing the cracks of uncertainty that had opened since Sarah vanished. "Thank you," he said, sincerity coloring his words. "This could really help."

As he walked out of the diner, deeper shadows clung to him, but now they felt different—more tangible, more ailing. A glimpse of hope peeked through the cracks, bolstering his resolve. He now had a thread to pull, a piece that might unlock a darker truth than he had anticipated.

Each step he took back to his car fueled ambition, the passion igniting inside him. Sarah would not remain a lost fragment of their community, bereft of memory. He owed her the truth, and as Michael flipped through his notebook, he felt something shift within him. A flicker of recognition: the elusive truth was waiting for him to uncover it, and he would not back down.

In the days that followed, Michael threw himself into the investigation, piecing together testimonies that hinted at the enigmatic scarred man. The tip he received wouldn't be the end of the search; it was merely the beginning of something much larger. It reignited a flame within him, a thirst for resolution that felt long overdue.

With each late night in the precinct, with every sentence he typed in his ever-growing report, Michael drew closer to the truth—one that would unravel webs of deceit and challenge the foundations of what many had long accepted. With renewed vigor, he embraced the responsibility weighing upon him, determined that Sarah Evans's voice would be heard, even if he had to raise it for her.

The journey wouldn't be easy, but he wouldn't stop until he finally unveiled the answers hiding in the dark.

At last, doubt began to melt away, replaced by a relentless pursuit toward justice. And as the shadows nestled deeper into the world around him, Michael steadied himself for the fight ahead, unwavering.

Connecting the Dots

The sun hung low in the sky, casting long shadows across the street as Michael parked his car outside the local diner. The place was a staple in the community, a hub where townsfolk shared gossip over coffee and pie. He had spent years coming here, forging relationships with the community, the kind that made people talk—even if it was slowly at first. Today, however, he felt a weight pressing down, a mix of urgency and dread that had driven him back to the scene of the crime.

As he stepped inside, the bell above the door jingled, announcing his arrival. The familiar scent of bacon and fresh coffee enveloped him, a stark contrast to the grim atmosphere that had settled over the town since Sarah's disappearance. The diner was quieter than usual, a handful of regulars seated in booths, eyes shifting cautiously at the sight of him. He felt their stares, the whispers pooling into murmurs that filled the air.

"Coffee, Michael?" Doris, the waitress, asked, her voice laced with that warmth he had always appreciated. But today, he hesitated, knowing that the comfort of caffeine wouldn't ease the burdens weighing on his conscience.

"Not right now, Doris. I'm looking for some people who might have seen something. I could use some leads," he replied, scanning the room for familiar faces. He spotted Marv, a grizzled old man who always seemed to be at the diner, nursing a cup of coffee and his stories.

"Mind if I join you, Marv?" Michael asked, sliding into the booth across from him.

"Sure thing, detective," Marv replied, rubbing his chin thoughtfully. "You look like you've got something heavy on your mind."

"I do," Michael admitted. "I need your help. I'm trying to get some information on Ethan Hayes. Anything you've heard, even if it seems small."

Marv leaned back, folding his arms as he considered the request. "Ethan, huh? That boy's trouble. We all knew it, even before what happened to that poor girl."

"Why's that?" The more Michael spoke to the community, the clearer it became that Ethan wasn't just a simple bad apple; he represented something darker.

"Oh, come on," Marv scoffed. "His family, for starters. They were always on the outskirts. Nobody wanted to associate with them. You know the type, always stirring the pot, always finding excuses for bad behavior. His old man was a piece of work."

Michael nodded, his pen poised over his notepad. "What do you mean by that?"

"Abusive. Everyone knew it. Kept a tight rein on Ethan. He was a good kid once, but after his mother left, things changed. I remember hearing him scream sometimes. It wasn't just the boy; it was the whole family. They rarely came into town unless they had to. For a long time, they were ghosts."

"Figures," Michael said quietly, scribbling down the details. He had already gathered pieces from various witnesses, but this contextual lens was crucial. "Were there any incidents? Anything that stands out?"

Marv rifled through his memory, brow furrowing in concentration. "The usual stuff for kids, I suppose. Fights. A few petty thefts. But you know how these things work. The law's always harder on the kids from the wrong side of the tracks. Ethan was one of those. Once you're marked, it's hard to shake."

Michael felt a knot in his stomach twist tighter. "Do you think anybody actually cared? Did anyone ever step in to help?"

"I don't know, Detective," Marv said, his voice lowering. "You'd have to ask someone who was around more. Folks like to turn a blind eye. When you've been around as long as I have, you learn that most people only really care about their own problems."

Michael sighed, sensing the pattern emerging. A broken system; broken families. It was a cycle that bred despair and violence. "Any other information about his associates? Friends?"

Marv paused, eyeing the coffee pot on the table as though it held all the answers. "There was a boy, Tyler. Always ran with Ethan. Trouble followed them like a shadow."

"Tyler?" Michael wrote the name down, the ink dark against the white page. "Where can I find him?"

"Probably still at the park, if he hasn't skipped town. Those boys are always hanging around the old playground, reminiscing about the trouble they used to get into. But be careful—Ethan's got some loyal followers, and they don't take kindly to outsiders."

Michael nodded, a sense of urgency igniting once more. He handed Marv a couple of bills for the coffee he hadn't ordered, signaling that the conversation was over for now.

"Thanks, Marv," he said, rising from the booth. "Keep your ear to the ground."

As he left the diner, a feeling of unease settled over him like fog, obscuring his thoughts. The broken fragments of Ethan's life felt painfully clearer now, and as Michael drove to the park, he prepared himself for more unsettling truths. The landscape changed as he moved through the town, the familiar buildings now stripped of their comfort. Each corner echoed the stories of those forced to live in shadows.

When he arrived, the park was all too quiet. The sun was fading, casting long, eerie shadows in the playground. Michael stepped out of his car, scanning the area for signs of life. He spotted a group of boys huddled near the swings, their laughter a stark contrast to the grim tone of the town.

He approached cautiously, letting their carefree chatter draw him just close enough. "Hey, fellas!" he called with feigned lightheartedness, forcing a smile. The boys turned, eyes widening before they straightened up.

A taller one, with messy hair and an oversized hoodie, stepped forward. "You a cop, mister?" his voice tinged with suspicion.

"I am, and I'm looking for information about Ethan Hayes." He watched as their expressions shifted, recognition dawning like a slow sunrise.

"Why do you wanna know about him?" The taller boy's voice lowered defensively, an instinctive barrier of loyalty rising.

"I just want to know how he's been. What he's been up to." Michael kept his tone neutral, carefully gauging their reactions.

"Why are you asking that?" a younger boy piped up, shifting nervously. He could feel the unease ripple through them, an invisible tether linking their apprehensions.

"Because he's important to me. I heard he might be in trouble, and I want to help him," Michael replied, hoping to soften their defenses.

"Help him? He's a loser. Always getting into stupid shit," the tall boy scoffed, crossing his arms again.

"Maybe. But that doesn't mean he deserves what's happening now. Look, any help you can give me is important."

The boys exchanged glances, uncertainty hovering in the air like heavy storm clouds. Michael could see the flickers of their memories dancing behind their guarded eyes. With gentleness, he pressed on. "What kind of trouble has he been in? What do you know about his home life?"

Silence fell as they hesitated, the younger boy shifting uncomfortably. "It's not our business," he finally mumbled.

"But it is, if you're his friend. Friends look out for each other," Michael said, his voice gentle yet firm.

"His dad's a drunk," the tall boy muttered under his breath, breaking the silence. "Yelling, hitting, all that stuff. Ethan didn't have it easy."

"What about his mom? Where's she?" Michael pressed, encouraging him to continue.

"Just left one day. Packed up and went. No one knows where."

Pain struck Michael like a bolt of lightning. Another thread tying Ethan to a life of neglect and abandonment. "What about you? Did you ever talk to him about it?"

The boy shrugged, looking away. "What good would it do? He just kept getting worse. Acting out, missing school... He became the kid no one wanted to play with."

Michael felt a surge of anger and sadness. This wasn't just about Ethan anymore; it was about a systemic failure that left children stranded in a cycle of despair. "Thanks for telling me. If you ever think of anything else, I need to know, okay? It could help him."

As he turned to leave, Michael caught a fleeting glimpse of the pain in their eyes, laden with regret and fear. It was a reflection of a deeper issue—the struggle of the forgotten youth in a broken system that often turned away from the dark corners of their lives.

Stepping back into his car, Michael glanced at the diner across the street. Familiar faces blended into the background, the weight of their stories pressing down on him as he prepared to head to the next lead: Tyler.

The drive seemed fleeting, each road a reminder of the obstacles laid before him. He parked outside an old rundown house, the paint peeling, the lawn unkempt. The memories of children playing once littered that space, but now, it felt haunted by ghosts of lost opportunities.

Knocking on the door, he felt the pulse of uncertainty in his chest. After a moment, it swung open, revealing a disheveled woman in her forties, her features hard and tired.

"Who are you?" she asked sharply, narrowing her eyes at him.

"Detective Michael. I'm looking for Tyler," he said, offering a brief nod of acknowledgment. "I need to talk to him about Ethan Hayes."

"Tyler!" she hollered over her shoulder, a sharp command echoing into the house. Michael heard shuffling in the distance, a small voice mumbling complaints as it drew closer.

In moments, a lanky teen appeared, his hair tousled, his clothing rumpled. "What do you want?" he asked, his defensiveness palpable.

Noting the anguish in his eyes, Michael softened his approach. "I just want to talk, Tyler. I'm trying to understand what's been going on with Ethan. Can you help me?"

"Why should I?" Tyler shot back, crossing his arms defiantly.

"Because people's lives are at stake. I need to know if he's okay. All I'm asking for is to hear your side of things." Tyler hesitated, glancing at his mother. The decision hung in the air like a pendulum, swinging between distrust and the instinct to finally speak up. "Fine," he muttered, stepping outside and closing the door behind him. "What do you wanna know?"

"Just tell me what happened. Why did he start turning to violence?"

Tyler scowled. "He just couldn't take it anymore. His dad—he's a piece of crap. Can't keep a job, barely takes care of him. Drinks all the time. You know how that is, right?"

"I know it can be tough," Michael replied, careful to keep his tone gentle and understanding.

"We did a lot of stupid stuff together. At first, it was just messing around, like breaking stuff or sneaking out late. But after a while, it got worse. He didn't know how to stop."

Michael jotted down notes, steering the conversation. "Did Ethan ever talk about his mom?"

"Just that she left. Said she didn't want him anymore. I think that messed him up. Made him angry. Like he wasn't worth anything."

The weight of Tyler's words pressed down on Michael. The cycle of neglect, rage, and violence poured from their recounts, the shadows growing longer. "Tyler, did you ever think about helping him?"

"Help him? We were kids, man! I had enough of my own problems. Besides, no one cared about the trouble he got into until it was too late.

Everybody just looked the other way." His voice broke, the bitterness surfacing.

Michael remained silent, his heart aching for them all, but he knew that he had to keep pressing forward. "Tell me more about the last time you saw him."

Tyler's expression darkened. "A couple of months ago. He was acting different... more angry. Said some weird stuff about how he'd show everyone he wasn't just some loser."

"Show them how?"

"Thought he could do something crazy. He was talking about taking it to the next level like he wanted to prove something to everyone. It scared me, you know? I didn't see him again after that."

"Scared you how?" Michael probed, heart racing as he sensed a breakthrough.

"Just...he was off, like he was losing it. I thought he was gonna do something stupid. But I was tired of being the guy who saved everyone else. I didn't wanna get dragged down too."

The young man's admission hung in the air, the recognition of a broken system settling heavily in both their hearts.

"Tyler, thank you. If you think of anything else—anything at all—you can reach me. I just want to help."

Tyler nodded warily as they exchanged goodbyes, sadness etched deeply into their expressions as he returned to his broken home, silhouetted against the backdrop of despair and filth.

As Michael drove back to his office, the air felt thick with truth—utterly exhausting, yet invigorating. He began to connect the dots, weaving a web of Ethan's life that painted a tragic picture. Each fragment of a story revealed patterns, threads tied together by pain, neglect, and systemic failures.

He arrived at his dreary office building, parked, and made his way up the stairs. It had been hours since his inquiries began, but it felt like the revelations were only just beginning to surface.

In the solitude of his office, he spread the notes before him, each word a bead in a necklace of long-spun pain. Names began to float across his mind as he mentally slipped through each thread he'd captured—Sarah, Ethan, Tyler—and he knew it was essential to go deeper. The investigation had to reach beyond mere surface details.

He picked up the phone, dialing the local child protection services. Navigating the bureaucracy was daunting, but for Neil's sake, he pressed on. If Ethan was a product of his environment, then there might be records; there had to be something.

"Hi, this is Detective Michael," he said, excitement threading through him despite the weariness. "I need to inquire about a boy named Ethan Hayes. Could you help me?"

"Ethan Hayes?" The woman's voice on the other end was cautious. "We have had some involvement with his case in the past."

Michael's heart surged at the confirmation. "Can you tell me what kind of involvement?"

She hesitated. "There were reports of neglect. Behavioral issues, aggression. The office investigated a few times, but without a willing participant, it's hard to act on what we find."

"Did he receive any help?"

"Only briefly. The family wasn't responsive or cooperative. When the mother left, it really didn't help matters. Ethan became a ward of the state for a short period, but he was returned to their care. It's a sensitive issue—the family has rights, even if they're not the best guardians."

"Are there any records of complaints or visits made?" He could feel the pieces finally coming together, weaving a narrative of neglect, some deeply-rooted issue that demanded action.

"I can't share specific details, but I can tell you that the community often looks away. We have to follow legal procedures to act."

The sentiment echoed loudly in Michael's mind—community indifference year after year producing children like Ethan, left to the wolves. "Thank you. Please let me know if anything else comes in."

As the call ended, Michael leaned back in his chair, contemplating the weight of responsibility pressing on him. It was vital to continue uncovering truths; Ethan's story couldn't end as one more statistic in a broken system.

He felt energized to take the next steps. Those next steps would lead him down a corridor of hidden horrors. But sometimes, to see the light, you needed to delve into darkness. And Michael felt more determined than ever to connect each fragment and reveal the truth.

With renewed purpose, he reached for his notepad once again, preparing to draft a plan for the next stage of his investigation. The broken system was daunting, but knowing he wasn't alone made fighting back worthwhile. Finding justice for Sarah would be the catalyst for change in Ethan's life, one way or another. And Michael was determined not to let either of their stories be buried in the shadows any longer.

The Breakthrough

Michael sat at his cluttered desk, papers strewn about, the remnants of countless leads and interviews forming a chaotic tapestry of Sarah's case. Coffee stains marked the edges of some pages, a testament to countless sleepless nights spent unearthing truths that eluded him. The dim light of the desk lamp flickered above him, casting shadows that danced on the walls, mirroring the turmoil brewing within his mind. He took a deep breath, pushing his fatigue aside as he sifted through the evidence again. He couldn't shake the feeling that he was on the precipice of something monumental.

It was quiet in the precinct; most of his colleagues had gone home, leaving only the distant sounds of muffled voices and the occasional clatter of office furniture. The solitude felt suffocating at times, but it also provided a space for clarity. He needed to focus, to connect the dots that had been laying scattered in front of him.

As he rifled through the documents, something caught his eye—a small detail that had gone unnoticed in his previous assessments. It was a list of names from the local bar where Ethan had been known to frequent, a list compiled from witness reports that indicated he was often seen in the company of a questionable crowd. Michael leaned closer, scanning the names again, and then it clicked. One name stood out—a former associate of Ethan's who had served time for assault. He had heard bits and pieces about this man, but nothing concrete enough to connect the dots in his mind.

With renewed energy, he grabbed his phone and began to search for recent information related to the man. It didn't take long before he found a lead—an arrest a few weeks prior linked to a series of violent incidents escalating in the area. Each detail he uncovered felt like a piece of a sinister puzzle slowly coming into view.

Michael's heart raced as he recalled the interactions he had with Sarah's friends. They had mentioned a group of people who often loitered around the bar, a group that seemed to have a connection to Ethan, but no one had identified any potential threats. Now, it was beginning to make sense. Ethan didn't act alone; he had a network that supported his twisted ambitions.

He quickly dialed Jenna's number, knowing she would still be in the area, diligently supporting Sarah through the aftermath of the ordeal. While his personal life had taken a backseat to this investigation, Jenna had essentially become a lifeline for Sarah—and Michael couldn't shake the feeling that they needed to converge their efforts.

"Michael? Is everything okay?" Jenna's voice came through, laced with concern.

He could hear the weariness in her tone. "Jenna, I think I've made a breakthrough. I need you to meet me at the station as soon as you can."

"On my way."

With the call ended, he took a moment to mentally prepare, running through the implications of what he had just discovered. It wasn't just enough to identify threats; he needed actionable intelligence. The connection to this man could provide insight into Ethan's methods and encourage further investigation into the bar scene, which seemed to harbor a dangerous undercurrent.

As he waited for Jenna, he considered the implications. What if Ethan's vendetta against Sarah had deeper roots in that world, linked to obsessions or rivalries that Michael had yet to uncover? The thought gnawed at his mind and kindled a sense of urgency that went beyond procedural investigation—this was about justice for Sarah and every woman who had suffered in silence.

The moment Jenna arrived, she was a whirlwind of energy, rushing into the precinct with eyes wide with anticipation. "What did you find?"

"I think I've discovered someone connected to Ethan," he replied, guiding her into his cramped office. "A man named Derek Weston. He's got a violent history and was recently arrested for a string of assaults in the same neighborhood where Sarah saw the murder take place."

Jenna leaned against the desk, absorbing each word. "So, you think he's somehow linked to Ethan? Like a partner in crime?"

"Exactly. If we can find Derek and connect him to Ethan, we might be able to expose this entire operation before more innocent lives are harmed. It could also give further credibility to Sarah's statements."

"But how do we find him?" Jenna asked, her brows furrowed. "He's probably laying low after his recent arrest."

Michael leaned back, contemplating the next steps. "I have to go back to the bar where Ethan and Derek frequented. There must be someone there who knows something, something I missed. We need to put pressure on the right people."

Jenna nodded, her determination matching his. "I'll come with you. If they see a familiar face, it might help break the ice."

"Let's go then." The two of them left the precinct, their minds racing in unison like a finely tuned engine.

As they drove to the bar, Michael's mind was flooded with a collage of thoughts and emotions—the fear for Sarah's safety, the urgency of the investigation, and an ever-increasing sense of dread about what their pursuit might uncover. What if Derek really was an integral part of a more extensive, darker underbelly that connected back to Ethan?

The bar was located on a dimly lit street, partially obscured by overhanging trees and a haze of humidity that hung in the air. Michael parked the car, and they stepped out into the lingering twilight. The sounds of laughter, music, and the clinking of glasses filtered through the air, contrasting sharply with the tension building inside him.

As they entered the bar, the atmosphere shifted—a mix of euphoria and danger. Michael's eyes scanned the room, trying to identify anyone that might offer leads. He spotted a familiar face—a bartender he had briefly spoken to during his last visit.

"Stay close," he whispered to Jenna, making their way to the bar counter.

"Hey, Tom," Michael greeted the bartender, who looked as disinterested as usual. "Do you have a minute?"

"Sure, what's up?" Tom replied, wiping down the counter.

"We're investigating the recent incidents around here, and I need to know if you've seen Derek Weston lately. He's a dangerous guy, and we believe he may be connected to other serious crimes."

Tom's demeanor shifted slightly, a flicker of recognition in his eyes. "Derek? Yeah, I've seen him. He was here about a week ago, causing trouble."

"Trouble how?" Jenna chimed in, eager for more information.

"He was with a couple of other guys—real sketchy types. They were loud, making threats to some people in a corner," Tom said, glancing around nervously as if checking for lurking ears. "But you didn't hear that from me."

Michael leaned forward, tapping the counter lightly, urgency punctuating his voice. "Where did he go? Do you know if he's been back since?"

"After that night, a few guys I know who run in those circles said he was heading out of town to lay low for a bit. You know how it is—when the heat's on, you gotta get out. But that wasn't long ago, so he could still be around."

"Who are his associates?" Jenna probed, her voice steady but insistent.

Tom hesitated, eyeing the door as though afraid of being caught in their conversation. "The guys he rolls with are real pieces of work. I don't want any trouble, alright? But there's a guy named Vinny, runs with him. You might want to check him out."

Michael felt a surge of adrenaline at the mention of another name. "Where can we find Vinny?"

"Last I heard, he was hanging out at a place on Old Mill Road. That's all I know. Just… watch yourself, alright?"

"Thanks, Tom. We appreciate it," Michael said, exchanging a knowing glance with Jenna as they stepped away from the bar counter.

Once outside, they both exhaled deeply, a rush of accomplishment mixed with concern.

"He's still out there," Michael said, voice taut with urgency. "Derek is likely hiding out—and he knows Ethan. If we can find Vinny, we might discover more about the connection they all have."

Jenna nodded. "I'll follow your lead, but be careful. This could get dangerous."

Michael quickly made their way back to the car, adrenaline coursing through him. The truth felt closer than it had ever been, but he couldn't shake the feeling that every new lead brought with it danger—danger that could threaten Sarah's safety.

Driving towards Old Mill Road, each red light felt as if it was tautening the moment—the uncertain wait adding to the suspense.

"This is the place," Michael said, pulling into a dimly lit parking lot, scanning their surroundings carefully. The building was worn down, graffiti marking the entrance where loitering individuals eyed them with curiosity.

"Let's stick together," he urged Jenna as they stepped out of the car.

As they walked toward the entrance, Michael's heart raced, fueled by hope and fear of what they might find. He stepped inside the bar, noticing the smell of stale beer mingling with the lingering scent of smoke. The place was filled with an eclectic crowd, laughter bouncing off the walls, but the sense of danger hung thick in the air.

They moved toward the bar, and Michael immediately recognized the bartender, who bore a striking resemblance to Tom, though he did not harbor the same familiarity.

"What can I get for you?" the bartender asked, eyes darting between them as if questioning their presence.

Michael leaned on the bar, confidence masking his nerves. "We're looking for someone—Vinny. You know him?"

The bartender's eyes narrowed slightly, sizing them up. "Aren't many people asking for him these days. What do you want with Vinny?"

"Someone's in danger, and we think he can help. We need to talk to him." Something flashed in the bartender's eyes—was it fear? Michael couldn't tell.

"Vinny doesn't just talk to anyone," the bartender replied, lowering his voice. "You'll need to earn that privilege."

"Tell him we're here about Derek Weston," Jenna added softly, her voice steady with authority.

The bartender hesitated before leaning back, glancing toward the far corner of the bar where a group of men were seated. Michael followed his gaze, his stomach tightening at the sight of a rough-looking character that appeared to be the focal point of the group.

The bartender finally sighed, "I'll see what I can do, but keep your heads low. Vinny isn't one to be trifled with."

They waited, tension pooling in the air like a coiled spring. Soon after, the bartender returned, gesturing for them to follow him. Heart pounding, Michael exchanged a glance with Jenna before moving toward the back of the bar, following the trail toward a dimly lit lounge area.

As they approached, he could see Vinny—a burly man with tattoos covering both arms and a glare that could freeze fire. He sat with several other low-lifes, laughter peppering their conversation, but he fell silent upon noticing the approaching figures.

"Vinny," the bartender announced, his authority fading in the wake of apprehension. "These two want to talk."

Vinny leaned back, assessing Michael and Jenna with narrowed eyes. "You looking for trouble, or what?"

"Just some answers," Michael replied, straightening his posture and trying to remain calm. Jenna stood beside him, stealing occasional glances at the surrounding characters watching intently.

"And why would I give you answers?" Vinny shot back, a smirk playing at the edges of his lips.

Michael took a breath, choosing his words carefully. "We think Derek Weston's connected to a murder—and we know you know him. The lives of innocent people depend on this."

Vinny's expression shifted slightly, interest piqued, but distrust lingered in his eyes. "And what's in it for me? You think I'm going to risk my neck for some stranger?"

Michael leaned forward, using his best persuasive tone. "There's something bigger at play here. If Derek is involved, you might be in danger too. We can help protect you—but we need to know everything you know."

Another glance exchanged between Jenna and Michael. The weight of their truth hung in the air, and the moment stretched as Vinny considered.

Finally, he chuckled darkly, leaning forward. "Fine. I'll tell you what I know about Derek. But if you waste my time, you'll wish you hadn't shown your faces here."

Michael nodded, feeling the weight of this moment. They were getting closer; he could feel it. Behind the bravado of the dangerous men around them laid a visceral fear that Michael knew he could exploit—fear for their own safety, the same fear Michael felt for Sarah's well-being.

"Derek's been dealing with some bad people lately," Vinny continued, his voice lowering. "He's involved in something shady, and it goes deeper than any of this petty gang nonsense. There are whispers of other unsolved cases—cases like Sarah's."

The blood ran cold in Michael's veins. "What do you mean?"

"Let's just say that getting too close to Derek involves ties to others, more influential people than he can handle. If you're looking to take him down, you better be ready for what comes next."

"Where is he now?" Michael pressed, urgency spilling over as he recognized the delicate urgency of the situation.

Vinny leaned back, crossing his arms, an inscrutable expression on his face. "I can't say for sure. He's probably keeping it quiet for now with the heat around him. But I'd steer clear from asking too many questions if I were you. You might end up on someone's radar."

Just as Michael was considering how to dig deeper, the air shifted. A low murmur of tension stirred among the group near them, and a man with a menacing presence slid closer. He whispered something to Vinny, who nodded slowly, his gaze darting to Michael and Jenna.

"Looks like our time's up," Vinny remarked, his expression turning serious. "You need to go before the situation escalates. Just… be careful, alright?"

Michael felt the pressure mount as they stepped back from the table, regret spilling into his mindset as they retreated. They couldn't afford to push it now, but this lead had changed the entire game.

Exiting the bar, adrenaline coursed through his veins. They had discovered a connection, but it fell into the realm of danger that loomed over them like a storm cloud. They raced to the car, the weight of uncertainty accompanying them as they sped off into the night.

"Do you think we can get to Derek before he disappears?" Jenna asked, her voice steady but laced with concern.

"We have to try," Michael replied, heart hammering. "We need to find a way to connect the pieces, but we have to tread carefully. There are more players in this game than we realized, and it's escalating."

As they hurtled down the dark road, the stakes felt higher than ever. They were close, so close to the truth—and yet, it seemed to glimmer just out of reach, like a light flickering amidst the shadows.

He felt the weight of responsibility bearing down on him; this was about more than just finding a murderer. This was about Sarah and ensuring that her story was heard, her truth revealed. As they headed toward whatever awaited them, Michael could only hope they wouldn't be too late.

With each turn, the thrill and danger intertwined, leaving them teetering on the precipice of discovery, ready to uncover the dark underbelly that connected them all. The sense of urgency surged within him, driving Michael onward—into the darkness, searching for the light of justice that remained just beyond the horizon.

CHASING SHADOWS

The Pursuit of Truth

The rain drummed against the windshield of Michael's car as he navigated the gloomy streets of the small town. Each raindrop felt like a reminder of the weight of the investigation pressing down on him. The echoing silence that filled the car was unsettling. He could not shake the feeling that he was constantly being watched. He had awakened those shadows, and now they stirred uneasily in response.

After weeks of following leads and piecing together the fragmented evidence surrounding Sarah's disappearance, Michael found himself staring at the same wall of silence that he had encountered time and time again. The tight-knit community held secrets that didn't want to see the light of day. It was frustrating—no, infuriating. He had made a promise to Sarah's family that he would get to the bottom of this. Yet with every door that closed in his face, the pang of doubt crept closer.

His first stop today was Jill's Diner, a local hub where gossip flowed as freely as the coffee. Michael pushed open the door, and the bell jangled above him. The familiar scent of greasy breakfasts and sweet pastries enveloped him like an embrace, but it was a reminder that he was there on business, not pleasure. He took a seat at the counter, nodding to Jill, the owner, who was busy flipping pancakes on the grill.

"Hey, Michael! The usual?" she called out.

"Yeah, please," he replied, his mind racing through the potential conversations ahead. He needed information, but getting it would take more than just his badge and charm.

As Jill poured him a cup, he scanned the diner. A table of locals whispered and glanced his way, their laughter fading into suspicious murmurs. He took a sip of his coffee, trying to mask his frustration.

"Any news on that missing girl?" A man's voice broke into his thoughts. It belonged to an older gentleman, creased and worn like the vinyl stool he sat on.

"Still working on it," Michael said, trying to keep his tone casual. "Do you know anything about Sarah? Or maybe how she was connected to Ethan?"

The man's eyes widened slightly, but he glanced around the room, lowering his voice. "I wouldn't want to get mixed up in this, son. You know how folks around here are."

Michael felt the familiar weight of the community's unease. "I get that. But keeping quiet won't help her family. They deserve answers."

Jill placed a plate of eggs and bacon in front of him, cutting off any chance of further conversation. Michael's hopes for a breakthrough extinguished as he took a bite. Every mouthful became a reminder of how little progress he had made.

After finishing his meal and tossing a few bills on the counter, he stood to leave. "Thanks, Jill," he said, glancing back at the table of locals. They were whispering again. Their faces were shrouded in a layer of apprehension.

He stepped outside, letting the chill of the rain hit him. A comforting embrace amidst the uncertainty. He had a few more people to talk to, and every moment wasted pushed him further from the truth. He drove to the local community center, a place he had previously visited for various town meetings. This time, he was in search of a woman named Marissa – someone who had seen or heard something the night Sarah had gone missing.

The community center bustled with activity. A group of children painted murals on a large canvas, their laughter painting the air vibrant with energy. It struck him hard—life moving forward while Sarah's case lingered unresolved. He found Marissa at a table, circulating information for an upcoming town hall meeting. She looked up, her face warming with recognition. "Michael, right?"

"Yeah. Do you have a moment?" he asked, trying to remain professional despite the urgency burning in his gut.

"Sure, what's up?"

They found a quieter corner of the room. "I'm following up on Sarah's case, and I got the sense you may know something," he prompted.

Marissa shifted uncomfortably. "I saw the news report, but I don't really interact with that crowd. You know how it is. People like Ethan keep to themselves."

"Have you spoken to anyone who may have? Someone who might have seen something?" He leaned in closer, his voice low.

She looked around before continuing. "People are scared, Michael. Some saw what happened, but they held back. No one wants the trouble that comes with it." 195 The jackals

"Trouble?"

"There's talk—unsavory types involved. Drug dealing, gang activity. You know how it goes in small towns. You don't want to rock the boat. It's easier to look the other way."

Michael's heart raced. This was the lead he was looking for, yet frustration knotted in his stomach. "So you're saying people know, but they're afraid to speak up?"

"Exactly," she sighed. "I wish I could help more. But if I hear anything, I'll let you know."

As he turned to leave, Michael felt a flicker of hope. Maybe if he learned more about this network, he could unravel the threads tying Sarah's case to something larger. He knew he had to dig deeper, but he couldn't do it alone.

Meeting with his partner, Detective Harris, was next on his agenda. They sat at a small diner across town filled with deputies and officers. Michael glanced around, feeling as if everyone's eyes were on him, scrutinizing him for pursuing the truth.

"What's going on with the case?" Harris asked, leaning back in his chair. "I heard you visited Jill's."

Michael nodded. "Same old story. Nobody wants to talk about Ethan, and they're too scared to bring him up."

"That's part of the problem. This small-town culture protects its own, even when it comes to wrongdoers," Harris said, frustration thick in his voice. "If there's something bigger happening here, we need to discover it before it's too late."

"I think there's more to it. Marissa mentioned some sort of drug network or gang ties—something that could involve more than one crime," Michael shared.

"And you think that connects to Sarah's case?"

"Could be. If I can find someone willing to talk, we can start unraveling this."

Harris leaned forward, his interest piqued. "Let's look into it. I'll pull some background on Ethan and see if he has any known associates."

Just as Michael opened his mouth to respond, a wave of familiarity crashed over him—his phone buzzed in his pocket. He fished it out, glancing at the screen.

"Hello?"

The voice on the other end was a whisper, strained and frantic. "Michael, it's Jenna. You need to come quickly."

"Where are you?" Michael's pulse quickened.

"I'm at Sarah's old apartment. Someone's been here. I can feel it…"

Before Jenna could finish, the line went dead. Panic fluttered in his chest. He quickly looked at Harris. "I need to go. Something isn't right."

He raced back to his car, adrenaline surging through him as he drove to the apartment complex. Heart pounding, he jumped out and burst through the front door.

The hallways were eerily quiet, the air thick with tension. Michael charged up the stairs, calling out, "Jenna!"

He reached the door to Sarah's apartment, noticing it was ajar. With a push, he entered. The place was dim, the only light coming from the afternoon sun poking through the curtains. His eyes swept the room, searching for any signs of Jenna.

And then he saw it—a piece of fabric caught on the corner of the couch, the color matching the sweater he'd seen Jenna wear earlier.

"Jenna?" he called again, fear creeping in.

Just then, a noise came from the back room—a scuffling sound. Michael rushed toward it, his heart racing. The door creaked as he pushed it open, revealing a dimly lit bedroom.

There she was, crouched in a corner, her face pale. "Michael!" she gasped, relief flooding her voice.

"Thank God you're okay. What's going on?" He hurried to her side, scanning the room carefully for any threats.

"I was checking the place for clues when I noticed something strange—footprints near the back window."

His blood ran cold, realizing the implications. "Did you see anyone?"

"No but—" She swallowed deeply, visibly shaken. "I heard voices outside just moments before you got here. They were talking about Sarah... about making sure no one ever found her."

His mind raced. "We need to call for backup."

As she grabbed her phone, Michael stepped back to listen, straining to hear any signs of intruders. He felt that familiar sense of urgency driving him forward. Sarah's case was not just another job—it was turning into a full-blown conspiracy, a race against people who would go to any lengths to protect their secrets.

But just as quickly as the urgency swelled, it was punctured by an uneasy silence. Footsteps approached from outside—a low murmur, barely audible but vibrant with threat.

"Hide!" he hissed, pushing Jenna further back into the shadows of the closet.

Michael's pulse thundered in his ears as he quietly moved toward the door. Slowly, he unsheathed his weapon, holding it tightly as he prepared for whatever was coming.

The door swung open, and two figures stepped inside. They were men of average build, dressed casually but carrying an unsettling air of menace. Michael could see their faces etched with determination.

"Where is she?" one of them asked, scanning the room.

Michael's throat tightened. "This was not how it was supposed to go."

In that moment, the tension crackled like electricity, and Michael's mind clicked into action.

The stakes had just risen dramatically. He was standing in a room with two dangerous individuals, with Jenna's life at risk and the truth more elusive than ever. The pursuit of truth was turning deadly, and he had to keep them talking, keep them occupied.

"Looking for someone?" he said, stepping into the room with a false sense of bravado, even as his heart raced.

The men turned, surprise flickering across their faces, quickly replaced by irritation. "Who the hell are you?" one of them sneered.

"I'm the guy standing between you and your target," he shot back, keeping his stance steady, ready for anything.

"Better step aside, officer. We got some unfinished business here."

One of the men moved toward him, but Michael couldn't let them advance. "If you're looking for Sarah, you're chasing down the wrong lead. She's already dead," he bluffed, hoping to draw them in, hoping to stall for time.

The words had barely escaped his lips when a resounding crash echoed outside, followed by yelling. The pounding of boots surged into the building, and the men exchanged glances, their expressions shifting from irritation to alarm.

"We need to go," one of them hissed.

They turned to stumble out, but Michael seized the moment and lunged forward, grappling with one of the men to push him back against the wall.

Everything erupted into chaos. Jenna screamed as the second man whipped around, his fist connecting with Michael's jaw. The world buckled as pain seared through him, but he pushed through, ducking low to tackle the man who had just hit him.

A flurry of blows exchanged between them, fueled by adrenaline. The fight carried them crashing deeper into the room, throwing items carelessly around as they struggled for dominance.

Somewhere outside, Michael heard shouting—backup was coming.

In one swift motion, he shoved his opponent back, sending him crashing into the nightstand. The man fell with a groan, momentarily stunned, and Michael quickly repositioned himself to focus on the second attacker.

But before he could act, the door burst open again, and a squad of officers stormed in, weapons drawn.

Michael seized the moment. "Get them!" he shouted as the remaining thug scrambled toward the window in a last-ditch effort to escape.

The officers acted without hesitation, apprehending both men quickly and efficiently.

"Are you alright?" one of the officers asked, concern flooding their tone.

"I'm fine, but we need to keep these guys contained. They're connected to everything—the drugs, Sarah's case," Michael urged, letting his breath settle. "We have to find out what they know."

As they cuffed the men and led them out, Michael turned to Jenna, who was visibly shaken. "You okay?"

"I think so," she replied, taking a shaky breath. "What just happened?"

"You just helped uncover something bigger than we thought," he said, feeling a mix of adrenaline and anxiety.

Yet, as relief washed over him, Michael couldn't shake the lingering fear that a web of organized crime was intertwining with Sarah's fate. The truth was lurking in the shadows, but it was becoming clear that the deeper he dug, the more perilous the path would be.

With newfound urgency igniting within him, he left the apartment, stepping back into the rain-soaked world outside. The chase for truth was far from over; it had just intensified, leading him into a tangled web of deception and danger. And he was determined to uncover every last clue. The pursuit of truth would be relentless, and Michael was ready.

Danger Lurking

Michael adjusted his tie as he stepped out of the police station, the sun dipping low in the sky, casting long shadows on the pavement. He couldn't shake the feeling that someone was watching him. The hum of the busy street felt more like a buzz of danger than the comforting noise of a community at peace. He had 202 The jackals spent the day piecing together the fragments of Sarah's life—reviewing her statements, examining the crime scenes, and now he was poised to dive deeper into the darkness that surrounded Ethan's actions. Words like "witness" and "perpetrator" echoed in his mind, but they were just the surface of a convoluted reality he was determined to unravel.

Michael's heart raced as he moved toward his car parked along the gutter, a nondescript sedan that had seen better days. The faint sound of laughter from a nearby park felt like a cruel reminder of the normalcy that had been shattered by violence. Sarah's face lingered in his memory—a blend of fear and resilience that stirred something within him. He had an obligation not only to her but to the very fabric of their community to ensure it was safe again.

He slid into the driver's seat and started the engine, its growl punctuating the silence of his thoughts. Tonight, he would follow up on a lead—the name of a man who had crossed paths with Ethan before. He was a source known for mingling on the fringes of the law, a place where truths often lay buried under layers of deceit. Michael had no idea what he was walking into, but he felt the weight of urgency pressing down on him, an invisible hand urging him forward.

The drive through the quiet streets of their small town felt surreal, as if he were in an alternate dimension where darkness lay over every neighborhood like a shroud. Michael's mind raced with constant reminders of the stakes involved, but even more pressing were the questions that pounded in his head. Who was Ethan, really? What twisted realities had shaped him into the monster he was? Each question was a thread, leading him deeper into the heart of a mystery intertwined with pain.

As he approached a dilapidated bar on the outskirts of town, the atmosphere thickened with menace. The sign swung lazily in the wind, its paint peeling in large, rusty letters that spelled "The Vortex." He parked a distance away, wary of drawing attention. The dim light spilling from the windows painted silhouettes of patrons engaged in hushed conversations—a breeding ground for secrets.

Michael stepped out, his senses heightened; every sound and shadow felt amplified. He moved carefully toward the entrance, scanning the surroundings for anything out of the ordinary. The smell of stale beer mingled with the scent of despair as he pushed through the dusty door, chilled by the contrast to the warm air outside.

Inside, the low hum of conversations mixed with the clinking of glasses, creating a haze of casual disinterest. His eyes quickly adjusted to the dimly lit room, its corners obscured by shadows. A couple of men at the bar turned their heads, sizing him up with wary eyes. Michael's intuition screamed that he didn't belong here, but the truth he sought was buried somewhere within these walls.

He moved toward the bar, taking a seat at an unlit corner. The bartender, a bulky man with a scruffy beard and tattoos snaking up his arms, approached. "What'll it be?" he asked, his voice indifferent but his demeanor definitely cautious.

"Just water, thanks," Michael replied, scanning the room for any sign of the person he was supposed to meet—Tommy, a rumored informant who had dealings with Ethan. It felt as if time stretched, lulling him into a false sense of security, but he remained vigilant. Tommy was a name whispered in the shadows, the kind of person who blended into the darkness and returned with secrets that could prove deadly.

Minutes dragged on, and just as Michael considered leaving, a lanky figure slipped through the door. Tommy. He moved with a nervous energy, eyes darting around as if expecting to be followed. Michael cocked his head, intrigued by the aura of anxiety surrounding him. Taking a deep breath, he raised a hand to catch Tommy's attention. Their eyes locked, and Tommy hesitated—an instant of recognition and fear passed over him before he trudged towards Michael.

"Are you sure this is a good idea?" Tommy mumbled as he slid into the seat beside Michael. His voice was almost lost in the ambient noise of the bar.

"Just talk to me," Michael urged, leaning forward. "I need to know what you know about Ethan."

Tommy shifted nervously, glancing around as if checking for invisible threats. "Ethan's bad news, man. He's not the kind of guy you want to cross. I've seen what he can do to people he thinks might snitch."

Michael's heart raced at Tommy's warning. "I know he's dangerous. But I need to uncover the truth about what happened to Sarah. She's alive, and I believe she can still come forward with her story."

"Alive?" Tommy echoed, his brow furrowing. "That's a bold claim. People don't just disappear without a trace. If he's behind it, he's likely dealt with her."

The anxiety in Tommy's voice was palpable. Michael caught the bartender's eye, a silent request for that water. When it arrived, the bottle seemed heavy with implications: this could be their last conversation.

"Tell me everything," Michael insisted, "every detail, no matter how small."

Tommy's eyes darted again. He lowered his voice. "I saw him the night of the incident. He was acting strangely, all jittery, like he was waiting for something. Or someone. After it happened, he hit the back roads. But the thing is, he didn't just disappear—he was back again a few nights later, same old Ethan."

Michael leaned in closer. "What about his connections? Does he run with a crew? Anyone you think could help or hinder my investigation?"

"Ethan's got ties to some pretty serious players," Tommy replied, his voice trembling. "You muck around in this, and you pull in those bigger fish. You could end up not just putting yourself—" he gulped, "but Sarah in danger. You can't go asking questions without a plan."

"What do you mean?" Michael pressed further, feelings of impatience bubbling beneath the surface. "People like him don't scare easily, you know? The kind of people you need to talk to are dangerous. They might know where she is, but they won't give up that information freely. Or they could just decide to silence you—forever."

Realizing the stakes were even higher than he'd imagined. Michael took a moment, fear mingling with resolve. "I have to do this. I can't let fear dictate my actions."

Michael sensed Tommy gathering courage. "If you want to get the truth, you'll need protection. There's a lot of eyes watching and ears listening. It's safer for you to stick to the shadows, especially this close in."

As they continued to exchange whispered revelations about Ethan's possible whereabouts and connections, Michael caught sight of movement from the corner of his eye. A trio of burly guys entered the bar, their body language shouting intimidation. They moved with a predatory air that sent a shudder through him.

"Remember what I said about staying out of sight?" Tommy hissed, his eyes wide with panic. "We need to bail. Now!"

Michael felt the urgency of Tommy's warning, but he was rooted to the spot, a sense of foreboding rising as he saw the men head toward them. The trio was scanning the room, and it was all but certain they were looking for someone. His gut roared with alarm, urging him to move. He grabbed the edge of the bar to steady himself and signaled to Tommy, who was already shifting uncomfortably in his chair.

"Let's go out the back," Michael suggested, urging Tommy to follow as they stood. The closer they got to the exit, the more it felt like shadows closed in around them.

Just as they reached the back door, one of the men called out, "Hey! You! Tommy!"

Instinct kicked in; they needed to run, but not without a plan. Michael bolted through the door, pulling Tommy alongside him. The alley was dark and narrow, littered with garbage and the residual smell of despair. They maneuvered through the maze of backdoors and fences, the echoes of the men's laughter behind them a chilling reminder of the danger they faced.

"Where now?" Tommy gasped, breathless and panicked.

"Just keep moving. We need to get to my car." Michael put on a burst of speed, forcing Tommy to keep pace. Together they weaved through the darkness, heading toward the parking lot that felt agonizingly far away.

Suddenly, Michael heard a crash reverberate through the alley—a swift movement behind them. The hairs on the back of his neck prickled as adrenaline surged. "We're being followed!" he shouted.

Heart pounding, they rounded a corner, and Michael spotted his car just ahead. He sprinted toward it, fumbling for his keys as they approached. "Get in!" he ordered, his voice a mixture of urgency and fear.

Tommy dove into the passenger seat as Michael slid behind the wheel. Just as he turned the key, he caught a glimpse of movement from the alley. The three men emerged, their expressions twisted with malice. Michael's breathing quickened—he had no intention of letting them close in. He hit the gas, the engine roaring as they tore out of the parking lot.

The car swerved onto the main road, and Michael risked a glance at Tommy, whose face was pale with terror. "You okay?" he asked, anxiety creeping into his tone.

"Yeah… just please don't stop. I don't want to go back to that place." Tommy's words emphasized the fear coursing through him.

Michael's hands gripped the steering wheel tightly as they sped away, heart racing in time with the engine's growl. He felt the weight of the truth still looming ahead—the dangers still lurking. But there was no going back now; their lives were intertwined with the shadows, and he was committed to bringing them into the light.

"Once we're clear, we need to find somewhere safe to discuss our next steps," Michael urged as they turned onto an empty road lined with trees.

"Right." Tommy nodded, but Michael could tell his mind was racing with questions. "How do you plan to get any answers? The guys back there… they won't let this go easily."

"I'll find a way," Michael vowed, though deep down he wrestled with doubt. The deeper they dug, the more danger they faced. He needed to keep pushing for answers, not only for Sarah's sake but for his own.

As they wound through the darkening woods, it was hard to shake the feeling of eyes watching them from the shadows. The whisper of the branches in the wind felt like a warning, and every little sound turned sinister in the depths of the night.

Michael knew he was now caught in a game that could end in violence or worse. But if there was a flicker of hope left for Sarah, he had to keep moving, keep searching. And he would do so, no matter the cost.

Tonight, he was more than just a badge; he was Sarah's last hope, and despite the dangers looming large, he had no intention of letting the truth remain buried.

The Final Clue

As Michael pushed through the heavy door of the small, cluttered precinct, an unfamiliar sense of resolve washed over him. The weight of the case had been pressing down on him for weeks, and he knew that every moment he wasted could mean the difference between catching Ethan or losing him in the shadows forever. He had felt the pulse of urgency quicken in his veins, driving him forward as he rifled through papers suppressing the gnawing anxiety that threatened to overwhelm him.

Ethan's name was only cemented further in the folds of every report scattered on the desk before him, his face a ghostly shadow appearing in the margins of notes taken in haste. Michael didn't know exactly why, but he felt an unsettling connection forming between Sarah, Ethan, and a series of other unsolved crimes in the area. The thought kept him awake at night, gnawing at him like a persistently unanswered question. What if those women—those innocent souls who had been so cruelly snatched from their lives—were somehow intertwined with Sarah's story? What if there was a pattern he was missing?

With determination, Michael began taking notes. At first, he was simply tracking the timeline of Sarah's case—the day she witnessed the murder, the date she reported it, and then the moments leading up to her disappearance. He noted the details of the case: an unsolved homicide from years prior, a woman seen stumbling out of the same alley where Sarah had first encountered Ethan. He didn't believe in coincidences; too many strange events seemed to accumulate, coalescing into something that felt like a map, promising clarity.

Each detail had begun to form a web in his mind, stretches of string arching from one case to another like a carefully orchestrated crime board neglected in an old detective's office. He went through the piles of case files one by one, tracing the connections with focused intensity, his pen scratching fervently across his notepad as he mentally pieced together a narrative that had eluded him for weeks.

Halfway through the files of the unsolved cases, something striking caught his eye—a name, an address, a connection. He blinked hard, steadying himself against the edge of the desk as realization flickered like a faulty lightbulb in his mind. The street where Sarah first encountered Ethan in that alley. The same street had ties to other cases—cases that had gone cold. He felt a surge of excitement coupled with dread. There had to be something there, a clue he'd overlooked, a latent thread waiting to be tugged.

Breathless, Michael raised a finger to tap the computer keyboard, pulling up old police reports, photographs of the crime scenes—see if she matched, he told himself. If he could connect Sarah to the previous victims, he might understand the extent of Ethan's depravity. It wasn't just about solving one case anymore; it was about piecing together a tragic tapestry of lost lives.

Scrolling through file after file, he began to see the threads weaving intricately together. The victims' reports began to list similar circumstances: late-night sightings, brief interactions with a man whose description was becoming achingly familiar. Most notably, they each lived within a close radius of where Sarah had been that night. In his mind, he began to map their journeys, drawing invisible lines that connected their fates. The adrenaline rushed through his veins, pushing him forward.

Then he stumbled across a photo—one he had dismissed earlier, overshadowed by the weight of Sarah's case. It was grainy and out of focus, taken from a distance, but Michael could make out enough details. Framed against the black night, a figure loomed just a few meters away from the last victim's home. The posture, the stance. It was unmistakable. He grabbed the file that was open beside him, opened it wide, and created a stack, aligning various dates, reviewing the angles of the reports as if trying to telegraph the meaning embedded within.

"I can't believe I missed this," he murmured, mostly to himself. But he couldn't be distracted by the past. Squinting at the monitor, he tried to hone in further. The last sighting of Sarah echoed in his mind—the struggle, the chaos. Ethan was still at large, and he could feel the heat growing under the collar of his shirt. The deeper Michael delved into the records, the more prevalent the chilling notion became, the connection between Sarah and these victims was gnawing at his gut, itching for affirmation.

With each connection illuminated, the urgency of time swelled around him like a tightening noose. He glanced toward the clock on the wall—it was ticking away relentlessly, reminding him that Ethan was still out there, lurking, possibly aware of the eyes that sought him. He jumped from the chair, paced the small confines of the room, glancing out of the window at the fading daylight. He needed to act, and now.

His heart raced as he considered the implications of the evidence he had just cobbled together. The thought hung heavy in the air—if he was right, if these women were victims of the same predator, Sarah's disappearance was just one piece of a larger, more sinister puzzle. Justice hung in the balance between Sarah's fate and the lives of the others who had suffered. Michael knew what he had to do next: he needed to track down Ethan's last known whereabouts and see if there was any indication of a pattern leading him back to the missing piece of this convoluted investigation.

Clutching the little evidence he had acquired, Michael rushed to his car, barely acknowledging the officers that greeted him. His mind was preoccupied, calculating the significance of the threads he had uncovered. They wrapped around his thoughts, squeezing tighter, pushing him toward the unparalleled urgency of his mission: justice for Sarah and the other women that had fallen victim in Ethan's shadow.

As he navigated through the town, he replayed the details over and over in his head, pulling facts apart like a puzzle. He headed towards the last known street corner—the same one where Sarah had reported her sighting, in the depths of darkness where he believed Ethan lingered. He parked the car in the shadows, sweat beading on his brow with both excitement and fear.

Gathering what little resolve he had, Michael stepped into the night, determination charging his steps. He surveyed the cold, blue-lit streets, remembering what Sarah had described and envisioning the path she took. Adrenaline surged through him as he recalled how the raging ambience of violence had thrummed in her voice.

But he wasn't merely motivated by justice; there was an emotional rage brewing beneath the surface, a protective instinct towards the victims of this hunted beast. Each error, every overlooked detail, could not be allowed to repeat.

With every step down the familiar road, the hairs on the back of his neck prickled. An uncanny chill slithered through the night, as if the darkness itself were listening. He clenched a fist, feeling the magnitude of his mission wrap around him, a dark embrace that drove him forward.

Suddenly, he noticed something lodged in the cracked pavement just ahead of him. As he approached, his heart began thumping wildly once again. There, half-buried amid debris, was a twisted piece of metal. Michael dropped to his knees, brushing aside the dirt. It was a keychain, one bearing the logo of a gym Sarah was known to frequent.

Michael felt a rush of triumph, an electrifying jolt that surged through him. This keychain—had it belonged to Sarah? Had it fallen from her bag during her encounter with Ethan? Just as the idea took root, he spotted a small piece of fabric threaded through the metal ring. A memory flickered—he recalled seeing a similar fabric in the police photographs from the crime scenes involving the other victims.

The minutiae of this single piece began to unravel exponentially in Michael's mind. With a racing heart, he stood, pocketing the keychain carefully. The fabric was his link, a crucial piece that could tie Sarah's case to a multitude of other unsolved crimes involving the women who had also suffered at Ethan's hands.

Realizing the significance, he felt the thrill of discovery pumping through him. This was no longer just about tracking down Ethan; this was about undertaking a hunt for the truth to illuminate everything that had been obscured. He needed to connect with other victims' families and gather their stories to understand the full spectrum of Ethan's terror.

The reality of what he uncovered weighed heavily; he realized that lives depended on the truths he might unearth, and that realization propelled him. He hurried towards his car, thoughts racing and the chill of desperation renewed in the air. As he turned the key in the ignition, his heart thudded against his ribcage, but he forced himself to breathe, to center. He needed clarity in this storm of urgency.

And yet as the headlights pierced the opalescent night, a figure passed through the shadows ahead, flickering as if a mirage. Michael pressed the pedal harder, instinctively seeking to close the distance, racing toward the truth.

The figure paused just on the edge, silhouetted against the blinding lights. Michael's heart pounded as he felt the tipping scale of fate precariously balanced. He could potentially have a lead, a confrontation with who knew what. The tension hung thick in the air, as every instinct in him screamed to prepare.

He strained his eyes, searching the night for clues—the way they moved, the cadence of their breathing, a slight flash of white that could signify a jacket or a balled fist ready to strike. All at once, uncertainty weighed heavy, but the newfound evidence began to tease the shadows into fullness.

Ethan could be anyone, lurking in the flares of light or hidden in darkness, but he had clues now—real clues that would point him in the right direction, back to the killer in this twisted game of cat and mouse.

As Michael prepared to leap from the car to confront whoever stood there at the edge of the road, he heard a whispered name swept away by the warm wind.

"Sarah."

The name coalesced into urgency driving him forward. He had to uncover the truth behind every lost soul, behind every thread that Ethan had sewed into the fabric of their shared horror. The fabric of lives bound too tightly together, their stories intertwined.

Michael's adrenaline surged once more as reality began to take shape, the truth illuminating the path ahead. In the thrill of possibility and dread for what lay beyond, he braced himself to finally confront the shadows that had haunted not only Sarah but the entire community torn apart by violence.

Before he could step out and catch the dark figure, a roar echoed from deep within the wooded shadows nearby. They were not alone, and the time for reality to vindicate itself had arrived. What now lay ahead was not just another false lead but a confrontation with the truth that had been waiting in the wings, ready to unveil itself in a rush of dark inevitability.

Michael fought the instinct to retreat. He was so close—too close to let go now. With a prayer whispered under his breath, awareness heightened, he dashed from the car, propelled by the desperate need to unearth the mysteries hidden in the night. The truth was near—he could feel it in his bones, connectitude alive in the silence. Tonight, the weight of revelations would shift, and whatever was lurking just a breath away would either emerge into the open or disappear forever under cover of darkness, clear into the hinterland of the unresolved.

The chase was on once again.

THE TRUTH REVEALED

Unmasking the Killer

The dawn broke reverently, casting fragile shafts of light through the window of the small office where Michael hunched over a dense stack of files. The remnants of yesterday's rain clung to the glass, but the haze above the town was slowly dissolving, revealing the potential for a new day. But for Michael, this day held a weight heavier than any storm. He could feel it in the pit of his stomach as he flipped through clippings and notes, his finger trailing across a photograph of Ethan's face.

The image was grainy, taken from a security camera in a place Sarah had visited—a gas station, he recalled. A banal backdrop, yet now it resonated with the significance of the truth it cloaked. Michael's phone buzzed aggressively, tearing his thoughts from the mess on the desk to the screen that lit up. A new lead.

He jumped, heart racing, and snatched the phone, scanning the message. Another witness had come forward, a passerby, someone who had seen something crucial. Michael's pulse quickened. He scribbled down the address and barely took a breath before he was out the door.

As he navigated the damp streets, the weight of Sarah's ordeal loomed in his mind, a relentless haunt. Each step reminded him of the lives intertwined by horrific chance, at the center of which stood Ethan—a killer, a haunted ghost of the past. Michael couldn't escape the nagging thought that Ethan's life story intertwined with Sarah's—not just in crime, but perhaps in more personal ways.

Arriving at a modest coffee shop where the witness was waiting, Michael took a moment to compose himself. He inhaled deeply, letting the aroma of sweat-slicked palms mix with the rich scent of brewing coffee. The bell above the door jingled softly as he entered, scanning the room until his eyes landed on a young man in a baseball cap hunched over a coffee cup, visibly shaking.

"You're Michael, right?" the man asked, his voice a hesitant whisper.

"Yeah. You're Chris?"

"Yeah." Chris glanced around nervously, as though fear itself might walk through the door. "I don't want anyone to hear."

Michael nodded, motioning for Chris to follow him to a secluded corner. As they slid into a booth, Michael leaned forward, his eyes locking on Chris. "What did you see?"

The young man shifted uncomfortably, his eyes darting to the door. "I wasn't supposed to be out that late," he confessed. "But I saw something… something that's been haunting me."

"Take your time," Michael urged gently.

"I was walking home—cutting through the alley behind the diner when I heard shouting. At first, I thought it was just two guys messing around. But then…" Chris swallowed hard. "Then I saw him. The guy in the hoodie. He was… he was hurting her."

Michael's stomach twisted into knots. "Were you able to see her? Was it Sarah?"

"I don't know," Chris admitted, shaking his head. "I couldn't see her face. Just the struggle. The guy was tall, and the way he moved… it was like he was trained. Cold, you know? I thought I should call the cops, but then I saw the knife."

Michael's heart raced. "Did you get a good look at him? Anything you remember about his face, scars, tattoos?"

Chris hesitated, rubbing his hands together. "I don't remember much, but… I think I saw something written on his arm. It was… like a symbol or something. I wish I could remember more."

"Did you tell the police?" Michael pressed.

Chris flinched, his eyes darting to the side. "I… I didn't think they'd believe me. I mean, I'm just a nobody. I thought maybe it was better to keep quiet. But then I heard about what happened to Sarah, and I started to feel guilty."

Michael felt a surge of anger. "You have to speak up! This could help us—help her!"

Chris looked lost, a boy caught in a storm. "I'm scared. What if he finds out? What if he comes after me?"

"We'll protect you," Michael assured him. "You aren't alone."

As Michael exchanged numbers with Chris, he leaned back, reflecting on the urgency of it all. The pieces of the puzzle were coming together, but they were laced with dread. A killer was still out there, and Sarah—the heart and soul of this nightmare—was nestled in that web of uncertainty. He needed to make connections, not just superficially, but the kind that revealed truths buried deep.

Driving back to the office, a shadow crawled over the horizon. Michael's mind spun. Images danced before him—Ethan's face, Chris's trembling voice, Sarah's desperate eyes pleading for help. Everything collided within him, a storm brewing physically and emotionally.

Once inside, Michael dove back into the files. Flipping through various reports, he sought connections—anything to link Ethan not just to Sarah, but to Chris as well. And then he caught a glimpse of something familiar. The tattoo. He fished out a photo of Ethan from previous investigations and scrutinized it—there it was, a faint impression of a symbol spiraled on Ethan's wrist.

Adrenaline surged through him. He was onto something. He rifled through the papers, connecting dots until a clearer picture emerged. All these years, Ethan had danced on the edge of darkness, and now his web of intrigue ensnared Sarah.

Meanwhile, Sarah slid down into a familiar memory, darkness creeping in on the edges. She was sitting on her bed in her home, staring at old photo albums, laying bare times of joy mingled with the ignorance of who would emerge from the shadows later. She had seemed so... naive.

Flipping through the pages, she came across a photo of a summer day, laughter making the air light—her friends gathered, flavors of ice cream thick on their tongues, their futures waiting to unfold like the petals of a blooming flower. Everything enveloped in sunlight. But then her eye caught a figure in the background, cementing another memory inconspicuously woven into her happiness—a young Ethan, smiling shyly as he hovered near.

Connection after connection veiled in the past, only for her to be pushed into the ugly clutches of violence. She fought against the pervading dread, knowing now that the stories we tell through fleeting glimpses might spiral into something darker, something devastating.

The echoes stirred within her half-formed thoughts, leading her back—revisiting the empyrean day at the diner, the noise and the laughter that fled listless second after second. Ethan's arrival at her periphery of memory illuminated everything. She shifted uneasily in her sleep, the weight of those memories crashing in waves, but beneath it all was a resolute strength; she wouldn't be just a victim; she would fight back.

Michael's phone rang, jostling him from the mire of his notes. It was Detective Walsh. "Michael," she called, the urgency in her voice slicing through the haze. "We may have found a connection between the killer and Sarah. I need you at the precinct now."

The words spiraled into action, and he was out the door before she even finished speaking. The precinct was bustling with officers. Tension crackled in the air as he pushed through to find Walsh, whose brow was furrowed with a sense of impending gravity.

"Did you get Chris to talk?" she asked, urgency threading through her words.

"Yeah, he's on board," Michael replied, trying to gauge her expression. "He mentioned a symbol on Ethan's arm, and I witnessed something similar."

Walsh's eyes widened. "Recently, we recovered a notebook from one of Ethan's known associates. Inside, diagrams and sketches that represent things important to him. Symbols, affiliations… it looks all too connected to what Chris described."

Panic surged within him. "We have to confront him."

"We will. But first…" She paused, taking a breath, steadying herself. "We need Sarah's input. She must know."

Michael felt an ache growing larger in his chest. "But she's vulnerable. We're risking her safety."

"She deserves to know the truth," Walsh replied firmly.

They moved toward Sarah's recovery center, a place that had become synonymous with both respite and trauma. As they approached, Michael's heart raced, a complex blend of fear and determination. Would she want to confront her past head-on?

The door creaked open to reveal Sarah, sitting at a small table, the morning sun pouring in around her. She looked fragile yet fierce, the scars of her experiences reflected in the depths of her eyes, determined not to fade into a past lived at the mercy of another.

"Michael," she greeted softly, a wary smile tugging at her lips. "What brings you here?"

Michael exchanged a glance with Walsh. "We need to talk about Ethan. There are connections."

Sarah's expression tightened, walls rising while vulnerability flickered behind her eyes. "I don't know if I can face this."

"We think you need to see the evidence—the links that connect you both," Walsh spoke gently, her voice a mix of empathy and resolve.

Sarah blinked, the weight of the world languishing on her shoulders. "I need to know, don't I?"

Every heartbeat coursed through Michael's body, a fight or flight instinct, merging with the sense of dread tightening around them. "Yeah."

"Okay," she whispered. "Let's do this."

Michael led her into a private room where the boards filled with photographs, notes, and timelines formed a chaotic map of her life intersecting with Ethan's. He watched her eyes widen with disbelief as they settled on the grainy images of the man who had turned her life inside out. The tattoos revealed in the scrawled notes, the symbols, and echoes of childhood roared back, tightening the threads connecting them.

"It's him," she murmured, voice tremulous. "I trusted him… I've seen him before."

A silence enveloped them, heavy and still. "He's tangled in more than just the crime against you, Sarah," Walsh interjected softly. "We think he may have ties to a larger network."

Sarah turned to Michael, surfacing disbelief colored with fear. "He's dangerous. If he finds out…"

"We'll prevent it," Michael assured her, a fierce determination gripping him. "If we stay ahead of him."

Moments faded into eternity as vulnerability washed over them, a shared understanding forged in silent promise.

"Then we need to act," Sarah finally spoke, her voice steadying, a flicker of resilience igniting. "I won't let him own me anymore."

Michael nodded, forging a path forward. They needed to confront the past, to face Ethan head-on. Backing down was no longer an option.

As they prepared to take the fight to the killer, shadows loomed in the corners, unseen and threatening. The truth was emerging, each piece fitting like an imperfect jigsaw. Each connection pulling them closer to a moment of confrontation, a dark conclusion brewed in the callous wake of vengeance.

Despite the terror, the dread, the pulsating reality of horrendous truths clawing at them, Michael felt an undying surge within. They had this chance to shift the balance. With everything on the line, the stage was set for the showdowns that would draw out the masked killer lurking in the depths of darkness—both within the shadows they feared and in the haunted echoes of memories that intertwined their lives.

Michael took a deep breath, feeling the ground beneath him shift in anticipation as they prepared for what lay ahead—the unraveling of a killer. The final standoff between darkness and the pursuit of truth awaited them, and he was determined to unmask it.

The Showdown

The night pressed heavily as Michael crept through the dimly lit corridor of the abandoned warehouse. Shadows danced eerily against the concrete walls, twisting and contorting like the fears gnawing at the edges of his mind. The flickering light from a solitary bulb overhead created an atmosphere thick with suspense, punctuated by the echo of his footsteps against the hard floor. He had spent countless hours tracking Ethan, piecing together clues that had led him here, to the heart of danger.

Michael's mind raced. He was driven by the faces that haunted him—Sarah's wide, terrified eyes, the horror of that night when she had slipped through his fingers, and the chilling knowledge that her life had been played as a game of cat and mouse. It was a struggle that he could not ignore, a mission bordering on obsession. He had to put an end to Ethan's reign of terror, not only for Sarah but for every potential victim lurking in the shadows, too afraid to speak their truth.

The scent of rust and oil lingered in the air, mixing with the faint trace of decay, the remnants of the building's discarded past. Each inhale was a reminder of the stakes at play. He tightened his grip on the flashlight, its beam cutting through the darkness as he scanned the surroundings for any sign of his adversary. Ethan was clever, cunning, and a thrill-seeker who derived a perverse joy from the hunt. Michael had to remain one step ahead, or risk finding himself in the killer's crosshairs.

A soft creak echoed behind him, causing his heart to slam against his ribcage. Michael froze, straining his ears, muscles coiled like springs, ready to react at the first sign of danger. The warehouse was a maze of steel beams and crates, a perfect hunting ground for someone like Ethan. Every corner could hide a trap, every shadow a threat.

"Come out, Ethan," he called, trying to project confidence he didn't feel. "This game ends tonight."

Silence hung frozen in the air, but Michael could almost feel Ethan's presence lurking just out of sight. The mind game they played danced at the edges of his thoughts, escalating the tension. He recalled every detail from the investigation—the interviews with friends, the discovery of Ethan's previous crimes, the chilling drawings he uncovered—symbols of the very madness dwelling within this man. This wasn't just a confrontation; it was a battle against the scars of trauma Ethan had inflicted on countless lives.

"Does it feel good, Michael?" Ethan's voice echoed from somewhere in the darkness, taunting and smooth. It slithered through the air, chilling Michael to the bone. "Playing the hero when you're just a pawn in my chess game?"

Michael's breath hitched, anger surging beneath his skin. "This isn't a game. It's a chance to stop you once and for all."

The light flickered ominously, and then Ethan stepped into view, a shadow from the depths, his features obscured but his cold smile evident. It was a smile that disarmed and disoriented, the kind that made Michael's skin crawl. He felt his heart race not only from adrenaline but from the sheer weight of the moment.

"What do you think you can do, Michael?" Ethan stepped closer, his presence oppressive, a predator in his element. "You're still just a detective, arms full of investigation papers. You know nothing of the game I play—the control I wield over life and death. You can't stop the inevitable."

Michael's hands clenched into fists. "You think control is power? You've only created chaos." Rage bubbled beneath his cool demeanor, and his voice hardened. "You thrive on fear, but tonight, that fear is going to be your downfall."

The air crackled with tension as the two men circled one another, each attempting to predict the other's next move. Michael's thoughts raced—a plan formed, a mental map of the terrain and possibilities, but Ethan's unpredictable nature was a formidable obstacle.

"Variations of chaos," Ethan mused, a deranged gleam in his eye. "Isn't it beautiful? Every act of violence is a ballet, every scream a note in my symphony. You see… you don't understand my artistry."

"No, I don't," Michael countered, taking a step forward. "But I'm going to show you what true justice looks like."

Ethan laughed, a low, menacing sound that reverberated through the empty space, feeding Michael's anger. "Justice? This city chews people up and spits them out. You think a badge gives you power? You're just another soul in the crowd, trying to do what's right when the world has already failed."

With that, Ethan lunged, and the warehouse erupted into chaos. The two men collided, grappling for dominance as they spilled across the cold floor. Michael fought back, fueled by adrenaline and the weight of his convictions. He couldn't allow Ethan to escape again; the thought of Sarah haunted him as he pushed against the weight of his opponent. The physical struggle was accompanied by a flurry of words—shouted accusations and desperate pleas.

"Why do it, Ethan?" Michael gasped, forcing Ethan back. "You had a choice!"

Ethan's face twisted in delight as he countered, "Choices? I relish in making others suffer. You're all so predictable." He twisted free, sending Michael sprawling to the floor.

Pushing back onto his feet, Michael swung a fist, connecting squarely with Ethan's jaw—a satisfying moment as the killer staggered back. But Michael knew, from countless hours spent studying his adversary, that this was just one confrontation amidst a vast game of strategy. They both circled again, calculating, waiting for a moment of weakness.

"Tell me about Sarah," Michael growled, using the emotional weight of her name to distract Ethan. "Was she another trophy in your twisted collection?"

Ethan's eyes flashed with anger, and for a brief moment, there was a vulnerability that passed through his manic facade. "You think you can play the good guy? Didn't you let her down? You could have saved her."

What do you know?" Michael shot back, determination fueling his next move. "I'm the one here now, and I won't let you hurt anyone ever again."

With a roar, Ethan lunged again, and they clashed once more. It was a blur of fists and fury, each man intent on breaking the other. The fight escalated—a dance of survival fueled by vengeance and justice. Michael's instincts kicked in as he maneuvered, driving Ethan toward a stack of crates.

"Now you'll know what it feels like to be hunted," he growled, finally managing to knock Ethan off balance, crashing him against the crates.

But the moment of victory was short-lived. Ethan recovered quicker than expected, grabbing hold of a slim blade from his belt. Michael's heartbeat quickened as he saw the glint of metal beneath the fluorescent light. He barely dodged the first swipe, but silently cursed himself for allowing Ethan even an inch. The blade swung dangerously close as he evaded, adrenaline coursing through his veins.

"Do you see how easy it is?" Ethan taunted, dancing back. "You can play hero, but the truth is, there's always a monster lurking."

Enough!" Michael bellowed, his voice echoing, commanding and fierce. He pushed past the pain of exhaustion; he had come too far and lost too much to falter now. Michael lunged instead, aiming for a disarming blow.

The two men became a blur of motion—Ethan was fast and deadly, but Michael was relentless. They crashed against the crates yet again, and what had begun as a calculated battle devolved into a desperate struggle for dominance.

Then, in the midst of their fight, a sharp pain shot through Michael's side as Ethan's blade found its mark, slicing through fabric but, by some miracle, missing anything crucial. Gritting his teeth against the pain, Michael retaliated, landing a punishing blow to Ethan's midsection that forced the air from his lungs.

Both men staggered back, panting, sweat mingling with blood. Michael's gaze locked onto Ethan, fueling his resolve. He had to end this—not just for Sarah, but for every victim this monster had ever claimed.

"What are you afraid of, Michael?" Ethan sneered, wiping blood from his mouth. "The darkness? Or the light that guides the way? You're as lost as you think I am."

"I'm not afraid of you," Michael shouted defiantly, his breath coming in sharp gasps. "I'm afraid of what you represent—the violence, the chaos, the pain you inflict on innocent lives. That's what I'll fight against to the very end."

Their eyes locked, and in that moment, Michael knew the truth—Ethan was a manifestation of everything broken in the world, a danger that needed to be extinguished. He had to bring light back, even if that meant putting his own life on the line.

With renewed vigor, Michael lunged forward again, catching Ethan off-guard. The blade went wide as they struggled, and adrenaline surged through him, igniting a fire within. This was it—the defining moment.

In a whirlwind of movement, Michael managed to wrestle the knife from Ethan's grasp, the weapon clattering to the ground. The look of shock on Ethan's face ignited a fierce satisfaction within him as he pressed the advantage, pressing Ethan against the crates once more, his palms pinning the man down.

"This is your end, Ethan," he declared, the weight of his mission sinking in as he caught his breath, adrenaline fading and clarity rushing through him. "No more victims. No more pain."

Ethan struggled beneath him, fury twisting his features. "I'm not done yet!" he growled, twisting violently, but Michael was prepared. He tightened his grip, the strength of determination pushing him further, squeezing until the fight began to leave Ethan's body.

As Ethan's resistance waned, Michael's grip finally loosened enough for him to take a breath, but he wasn't prepared for what came next. In a final desperate act, Ethan barked a laugh, his eyes glinting with a manic hope. "You're just like me, Michael! You wear the badge, but there's darkness inside you—just waiting to come out!"

In that moment, Michael felt the weight of his own darkness threaten to rise, but he met it with resolve. No matter the struggles he faced within, he would never become the monster Ethan had chosen to be. He would remain a protector, a beacon of hope against the shadows.

"Maybe you're right," he admitted, fighting against the dull ache of exhaustion that threatened to pull him under. "But I choose not to let it control me. You, on the other hand, have made a hundred different choices, each one leading you down a darker path."

The truth resonated in the air like a gunshot, and Ethan's bravado faltered. An odd flicker of doubt crossed his face, a moment where the mask of the predator slipped for just a second.

Yet before Michael could capitalize on this, a sudden noise broke the moment—a scuffle of footsteps echoing from deeper within the warehouse. A team of officers, drawn by the chaos, rushed into the fray, their presence filling the space with renewed hope.

"Freeze!" They shouted, weapons drawn, a tide of authority flooding in to support him. It was exactly what Michael needed.

"Don't think this is over!" Ethan spat at Michael, anger glistening in his eyes as officers descended upon him. "You're just delaying the inevitable!"

As they restrained Ethan, Michael took a step back, the adrenaline draining from his body as the reality of the night set in. He felt battered and bruised, physically and emotionally, but there was a sense of relief that washed over him as the threat was finally contained.

"Take him away," Michael commanded, his voice steady despite the chaos of a thousand tumultuous emotions raging within him. He watched as they led Ethan out—the killer that had haunted both him and Sarah, now firmly in custody.

Breath slowing, Michael turned as the last remnants of the confrontation faded into the night. He knew that this was not merely a battle won; it was a turning point in a delicate dance with darkness that would reach beyond this moment.

Behind him, he felt the presence of his comrades, people who had rallied for their community. They offered supportive words and claps on the back, reassurances that whispered of new beginnings. Yet, he couldn't shake the weight of the conflict—the implications of his choices, the lives still at stake, and Sarah still haunting his thoughts.

"Sarah," he murmured, his heart heavy. He needed her to know that she was safe, that he would not let this fight go unanswered. She had fought long before him, and he had a duty to honor everything she had endured.

With determination ignited anew within him, Michael stepped forward into the light of dawn, the shadows receding behind him, grasping onto the hope that surged; the truth would be revealed, and justice, though sometimes delayed, would always find its way back into the light.

Resolution

In the quiet moments that followed the chaos, Sarah sat on the porch of her small house, the sun dipping below the horizon, casting long shadows across the yard. The stillness felt foreign, almost oppressive. She was alone with her thoughts, each one prickling her skin like static electricity, remnants of the adrenaline that had coursed through her veins just days before. She clutched a mug of tea, its warmth offering a comfort that belied the tempest inside her mind.

Michael, on the other hand, stood by the window in his office, staring out at the fading light of day. The investigation had closed, the killer brought to justice, but the weight of what he had witnessed clung to him like a heavy cloak. He had seen the darkness in humanity, the depths to which one could sink. He had witnessed Sarah's terror, her fight for survival, and the price she had paid to reclaim her life. Now, he was left with a mixture of relief and guilt, aware that closure could never truly erase the scars left behind.

Both Sarah and Michael had been irrevocably altered by their experiences. For Sarah, the battle for her life was not just a fight against Ethan but also a struggle against her own fears and insecurities. She had been thrust into a situation where she had to grapple with her own identity—the woman who was once invisible was now a survivor, marked by the shadows of her past. Each time she closed her eyes, she was confronted with memories that haunted her, fragments of the night that had changed everything. The screams, the adrenaline, the sense of powerlessness—it all felt insurmountable.

"It's just a nightmare," she whispered to herself, though the soothing cadence of her voice felt hollow. The reality was that the nightmares lingered long after the dawn broke, and the scars of her ordeal were etched deep within her psyche.

Meanwhile, Michael paced the room, recalling every detail of the events leading to the confrontation. He had stayed in the shadows, working tirelessly to protect Sarah, yet he felt a profound sense of failure. The darkness of the case weighed heavily on him—the victims, the tragic stories, and the indifference of a system that often left those in peril to fend for themselves. It made him question his role as an investigator, the very purpose of his work.

He found solace in the idea that justice had been served, but at what cost? Sarah had almost paid the ultimate price for her bravery. The realization made his chest tighten; he had known the risk, yet the fight and the chaos had pushed him forward with reckless abandon. The faces of the innocent lingered in his mind, and he was left wrestling with the notion of whether the darkness he had witnessed was a reflection of humanity or merely its shadow.

As the sun set on the horizon, Sarah found herself surrounded by her friends, a small gathering of warmth and laughter that acted as a balm for her frayed spirit. Jenna, ever observant, did her best to coax Sarah out of her shell, her infectious energy lighting up the room. They shared stories, memories of simpler times that brought laughter into the space, but occasionally Jenna's eyes would reflect concern, searching for the Sarah she knew before the incident.

"Are you okay?" Jenna asked, her tone soft, the laughter receding for a moment as she studied Sarah's face.

"I... I don't know," Sarah admitted, her voice barely above a whisper. "Some days, I feel fine, and others, it feels like I'm still in that moment, fighting for my life."

Understanding flickered in Jenna's gaze—a mix of empathy and sorrow. "It's okay to feel that way. You've been through so much."

The words hung in the air, laden with an emotional truth that resonated deeply within Sarah's heart. She wasn't just grappling with fear; she was reconciling her identity as a survivor and the emotions that came with it—pain, relief, guilt, anger. It was a tumultuous cocktail that left her reeling, but being surrounded by her friends reminded her that silence was no longer her refuge; she could lean on them to navigate these turbulent waters.

On the other side of town, Michael stepped away from the window, allowing the last rays of sunlight to spill into his office. His phone vibrated against the desk, snapping him back to reality, and he glanced at the screen—an update about a community meeting aimed at readdressing the issue of safety in their town. He remembered how the citizens had come together after the tragedy, sharing not just their fears but also their hopes for a future where something like this could never happen again.

He had made a promise to himself and to Sarah that he would work to ensure justice went beyond just the courtroom. It needed to transform into action—the kind that spared others from experiencing the darkness he and Sarah had faced. So, he resolved to attend the meeting, not just as an investigator but as a member of the community, ready to foster a more significant dialogue about violence and survival.

The following day, Sarah stood in front of a mirror, staring at the reflection that looked back at her. The woman who gazed back had changed; she wore the marks of her battle, both visible and invisible. The scars on her body had mostly healed, yet the emotional wounds seemed raw, tender, as if someone had struck them too soon.

Determined to reclaim some semblance of normalcy, she dressed for the day, selecting an outfit that felt like armor. Something comfortable yet feminine, something that reminded her she was still a woman with dreams, laughter, and the ability to thrive. She resolved to face the world outside, to meet those willing to support her journey toward healing.

Sarah walked to the local community center, where the meeting was being held, the crisp morning air invigorating her. As she entered the room, she felt the energy of the assembled community—a mix of concern, determination, and hope. She spotted Michael at the front, his presence steadying as he prepared to address the gathering. Their eyes met, and she felt an unspoken bond between them—two survivors navigating the aftermath of violence together.

The meeting began, with individuals sharing their stories, expressing their fears, and voicing a collective desire for change. Sarah listened intently as parents spoke about their children, young women shared their experiences of harassment, and community leaders discussed initiatives that could improve safety for everyone. The honesty in the room was palpable, filling in the hollow spaces that echoed with silence in her life since the crime.

In a moment of courage, she rose to speak, and for the first time since her ordeal, she felt empowered. Standing in front of her community, she poured out her heart, sharing her story not from the perspective of a victim but as a warrior—a survivor who refused to remain silent. "We can't let fear dictate our lives anymore. We must speak up, and we must come together," Sarah's voice rang with conviction.

The response was overwhelming. She felt the community rally behind her, and with each word she spoke, she could sense a collective shift—a recognition that true strength lies in solidarity. By sharing her truth, she was somehow paving the way for others to do the same, transforming her pain into a beacon of hope.

When the meeting concluded, Sarah felt a weight lift off her shoulders. She had taken a step in the right direction—one where she was not just a statistic but a voice of change. The community buzzed with conversation, a tapestry of shared experiences that bound them together. She caught Michael's eye once more, and he smiled, pride radiating from him in a way that made her heart swell.

"Hey," he said, approaching her after the meeting wrapped up. "That was incredible."

"Thanks," she replied, the warmth flooding through her. "I didn't know if I could say anything, but it just… flowed, you know?"

"I think that's how healing works," Michael responded softly. "You find your voice when you least expect it."

They stood together, encased in the warmth of others' conversations, soaking in the shared humanity surrounding them.

"Do you want to grab some coffee? There's a nice café on the corner," he suggested.

"Yeah, I'd like that," Sarah replied, her heart feeling lighter than it had in weeks. As they walked side by side, venturing toward the café, she felt the subtle shift within her—one toward healing, connection, and new beginnings.

As they settled into a cozy corner of the café, Sarah recounted the details of the meeting and her experiences. They laughed as they shared anecdotes, and the conversation flowed easily between them. For a moment, the weight of the world fell away, replaced by the warmth of human connection.

After several moments of shared laughter, Michael leaned back in his chair, assuming a more serious expression. "I'm really proud of you, Sarah. You took a huge step today. This is a start, not just for you, but for others who might feel the same way."

"Thank you," she said, her voice earnest. "But I couldn't have done it without you. You believed in me when I didn't believe in myself."

"I think we both helped each other through this," he replied, the sincerity in his gaze making Sarah's heart flutter. "You brought me back to why I chose this path—to fight for those who can't fight for themselves. Together, we'll keep pushing for change. You're part of this community now, and your voice matters."

Their shared journey, though fraught with adversity, had forged an unbreakable bond. As they finished their coffee, they made plans to collaborate on community outreach, pushing against the barriers that violence had erected in their lives. Together, they envisioned a safer world built around understanding, compassion, and proactive measures.

Days turned into weeks as they tirelessly worked to raise awareness and foster connections within the community. Their initiative gained momentum, garnering support from local businesses, schools, and residents eager to create a safer environment. They organized workshops, bringing in experts to discuss safety, mental health, and the importance of honest communication—tools that were essential in preventing violence and nurturing resilience.

Sarah found herself blossoming in her new role. She presented at schools, creating safe spaces for students to talk about their feelings, fears, and hopes. Each time she shared her story, she witnessed the transformative power of vulnerability. Young girls approached her, thanking her for giving them courage, often sharing their own stories of wanting to be heard.

Michael stood at her side, always a few steps behind, encouraging her, guiding her as they championed their cause. The sense of purpose they both felt imbued their lives with meaning. They were not simply haunted by the past—they were shaping a future filled with hope and solidarity.

The community meetings became regular events where people shared not only their fears but also their triumphs. They began creating a network of support that extended far beyond one-on-one interactions. Sarah's voice was among many, creating an anthem of unity that resonated deeply.

As each month passed, the emotional weight of the ordeal still lingered, but it was now woven into something greater—the beginning of healing, an understanding of the bond forged through shared trauma. They both took strides toward acceptance, learning that scars, while painful, are also reminders of survival, resilience, and, ultimately, strength.

One evening, as Sarah and Michael strolled along a quiet path in the park, she inhaled deeply, feeling the cool breeze tussle her hair. The sunset painted the sky in hues of orange and purple, and for the first time in a long while, she felt a sense of peace wash over her.

"Do you ever think back to that night?" she asked, her gaze fixed on the horizon.

"Sometimes," he admitted. "But I try not to let it consume me. It's part of the journey, but it doesn't define us."

She nodded, feeling a flicker of hope ignite within her. "If I didn't go through that, I don't think I would have found this—this purpose, this community. It's as if every painful moment led me here."

Michael stopped, turning to face her, their eyes locking in a moment that felt timeless. "And it led us here together, to help others in the same way. We turned into warriors for change."

"Warriors for change," she echoed, savoring the words as they fell from her lips. "I like that."

"Me too," he grinned.

As the night settled around them, Sarah took a deep breath, feeling an unshakable bond form between them. She knew their journey wasn't over; there would be challenges ahead, but at that moment, as the stars began to twinkle overhead, they found solace in their shared story—a testament that they could redefine their lives, forging a future molded by hope and strength.

Their laughter filled the air, intertwining with the sounds of the night—the chirp of crickets and the rustle of leaves. It was a symphony of resilience, a promise of new beginnings where scars transformed into symbols of survival.

As Sarah glanced at Michael, she marveled at how they had both emerged from the shadows into the light. They had not only sought justice but had become catalysts for change—reshaping their narrative, inviting others into the fold, and igniting a spark of hope that could illuminate even the darkest corners of their existence.

In the camaraderie of their shared struggles, Sarah understood that healing was neither linear nor easy, but it was profoundly possible. They found strength within themselves and each other—two warriors, stepping boldly into a future where their voices would carry the truth, pouring light into the shadows that had once threatened to consume them. Together, they were not just survivors; they were torchbearers of change, ready to illuminate the path ahead.

Justice Served

The Aftermath

In the weeks following the tumultuous events that forever changed her life, Sarah found herself slowly emerging from the shadows that had enveloped her. The memories of the confrontation with Ethan haunted her dreams, replaying in vivid detail—his menacing presence, the oppressive haze of fear, and the primal instinct to survive. Yet, as the days turned into weeks, she realized that the nightmares did not define her; they became a testament to her resilience.

The community had rallied around her in a way she had never imagined possible. They offered not only their support but their unwavering belief in her truth. In the aftermath of Ethan's apprehension, Sarah's story became a beacon for others who had suffered in silence. Local groups advocating for victims' rights organized meet-ups, marches, and awareness campaigns. They explored the narratives of those who had suffered violence, illuminating the often-hidden scars that many bore.

On a particularly rainy afternoon, Sarah attended a community gathering held in the town square. It had been organized to honor victims of violence, a poignant reminder of the battles fought in silence. As she stood among a crowd of familiar faces, she felt a swell of emotion rising in her chest. Each placard held a name—each name a story, a life lived, a battle fought. She could see the determination etched upon the faces of those around her, a unity forged through shared pain and strength.

Jenna, her steadfast friend, stood by her side, holding a sign that read "Justice for All." The energy of the crowd was palpable, an electric current of hope that reverberated through the air. As Sarah looked around, she noticed the faces of those who had once been strangers. They were now allies—people who understood her journey, who shared the same mission of transforming pain into purpose.

"Hey, are you okay?" Jenna asked, turning to Sarah, her brow furrowed with concern.

Sarah nodded, though her heart felt heavy. "It's just… I never realized how many stories there are. I feel like I'm just one of many now."

"That's exactly it," Jenna replied. "You've shown them they're not alone. You're a part of something bigger now—a movement for change."

The sound of applause broke Sarah from her thoughts as speakers began taking the mic. Local leaders, activists, and survivors shared their experiences, each story weaving a tapestry of resilience. Their words struck a chord deep within Sarah, igniting a fire she hadn't known existed. They each told their truth, their road to recovery and the impact of community support. As their voices rose, she could feel the weight of shame and fear begin to lift from her shoulders, replaced by a sense of belonging.

After the speeches concluded, the crowd gathered for a candlelight vigil. As Sarah lit her candle, she thought of those who had not survived their battles, the ones whose voices had been silenced forever. The flickering lights danced in the darkening sky, a constellation of hope against the backdrop of their shared struggle. She closed her eyes, allowing the warmth of the flame to settle over her, igniting a fierce determination within.

In the days that followed, Sarah engaged in therapy – a crucial step in her healing journey. She initially attended individual sessions, where she faced the fragmented memories of that fateful night. With the help of a compassionate therapist, she began to piece together the remnants of her trauma, transforming them into narratives of strength.

She also discovered group therapy, where she connected with other survivors in a safe space. Hearing their stories mirrored her own experience and allowed her to express the swirl of emotions that had once seemed insurmountable. Sarah shared her story of survival; the details poured out, unearthing the depth of her pain but also the strength it had inspired. Slowly, the shame she had felt transformed into a commitment to stand for those unable to speak.

As her healing deepened, she became involved with a local organization dedicated to victims' advocacy. Each week, she volunteered to help organize workshops aimed at educating the community about violence prevention and the importance of supportive resources. Helping others empowered her in a way she had never anticipated; this phase of her life was no longer just about survival but about advocacy.

One afternoon, as she prepared materials for a workshop, she received a heartwarming message from a woman named Lisa. Lisa had reached out to share how Sarah's story had inspired her to report her own experiences of abuse. "Your courage has given me the strength to speak up," Lisa wrote, "and I just wanted you to know that you're making a difference." Sarah smiled through her tears, realizing this was what she had hoped to achieve.

The culmination of these experiences led Sarah and Jenna to brainstorm an event that would provide a platform for survivors to share their stories publicly. They envisioned a community open mic night, showcasing the voices of those who had been silenced. It was an ambitious undertaking, but Sarah felt alive with purpose and enthusiasm. Together, they painted flyers announcing the event, plastering them around town, inviting anyone with a story to tell.

The day of the open mic night dawned, and Sarah felt a mix of emotions—excitement, trepidation, but mostly hope. The venue buzzed with energy as survivors and allies streamed in, filling the room with laughter and camaraderie. Sarah stood backstage, her heart racing as she watched the first speaker take the mic. The words flowed, each story adding to the atmosphere of solidarity that enveloped the room.

As Sarah's turn approached, she reflexively gripped the notes she had prepared. It was daunting to share her story again, but this time, she was not just a victim; she was a voice of hope for others. When she finally stood before the microphone, she could see familiar faces in the audience—friends, family, and even strangers who had traveled to hear her story. For a moment, she felt a swell of fear rise, but the warmth of their support steadied her.

She spoke about her journey, the darkness, and the light she had found in community and connection. "I learned that silence is a prison we build for ourselves," she said, her voice steady. "But with courage, we can break those chains and forge a life of freedom and healing."

As she finished, the crowd erupted into applause, and Sarah felt alive, enveloped in a wave of love and support. In that moment, she understood that she was not alone, nor had she ever been. The vast web of interconnected stories created a tapestry woven intricately with resilience, hope, and healing.

The weeks turned into months, and Sarah continued to find strength in her advocacy work, engaging with lawmakers to push for policy changes focused on victims' rights and protections. The community buzzed with discussions on consent and awareness, determined to eradicate the stigma surrounding trauma and to dismantle the systems that had so long silenced victims.

One sunny afternoon, Sarah received an invitation to speak at a local high school about her experience and the importance of recognizing and reporting violence. She felt honored and apprehensive as her heart raced once again at the thought of sharing her story with young people.

When she entered the auditorium, the room filled with curious faces, and her nerves began to dissipate. Yet another opportunity to shed light on a topic that needed discussion. Sarah spoke candidly—her voice echoed in the hearts of those listening. She knew that each story was powerful, and she felt a surge of determination to empower others to find their voice.

As spring turned into summer, Sarah's dedication to her cause made ripples throughout the community. She watched as more and more students began to attend workshops, engaging in conversations that had once been taboo. There was a new understanding blooming in the air, a shared responsibility among the community to stand together against violence.

In the twilight moments of summer, Sarah, Jenna, and their community organized an event to commemorate the first anniversary of Sarah's confrontation with Ethan—a Day of Hope. The ceremony would serve not just as a way to honor victims but to provide survivors a space to share their journeys toward healing.

The day arrived, and a sense of palpable anticipation filled the air. People gathered, lighting candles in remembrance of those who had suffered. Survivors took the stage to share their stories, showcasing the healing journeys that came through bravery and community support. When Sarah stepped up to pay tribute, her heart swelled with gratitude; she wanted everyone to know how far they had come collectively, how much brighter the light could be when they stood together.

As she closed her speech, Sarah looked out at the sea of faces, a mixture of solidarity and hope: "Today, we stand together—reminded that our strength lies not just in fighting our battles alone but in lifting each other up. Let us change the narrative. Let us speak for those who cannot. Together, we can create a world where every voice is heard, every life is valued, and every story is honored."

When the event concluded, the community gathered for a symbolic release of lanterns, each representing a wish, a hope, a healing journey. As Sarah watched the lanterns float into the dusky sky, illuminated in warm hues, she felt a lightness wash over her. It was as if her past was finally shifting—no longer a burden but a catalyst for change—a story retold with newfound power.

Back in her apartment that night, while looking at her reflection in the window, she saw not just a survivor but a fighter, a woman who had found her voice in her darkest hour. Through her journey, she had transformed her pain into purpose, igniting a passion for justice that resonated far beyond herself. The community she had cultivated was now a tapestry woven through shared stories, love, and resilience.

As she settled into bed, Sarah felt a deep sense of closure blanket her. The fear was still there, but it was different now—it was intertwined with hope and a newfound commitment to ensure that the truths heard today would echo into the tomorrows of countless others.

With every challenge she faced, she would remember that she was never alone; she had fostered a community that would rally together. The spirit of justice would forever dwell in her heart, pushing her to advocate for those without a voice, turning ripples of support into waves of change.

In the quiet of the night, Sarah closed her eyes, embracing the light emanating from her journey, grateful for the beauty that arose from chaos. The past had shaped her, but it no longer defined her. She was not just a survivor; she was a force for justice, committed to rewriting narratives and breathing hope into the world. 248 The jackals

A Future Reclaimed

As the sun began to rise, casting soft golden rays through the window of her small apartment, Sarah sat on the edge of her bed, staring at the reflection in the mirror. The bruises on her body had faded, remnants of an ordeal long thought to be behind her, yet the emotional scars still lingered, etched deeper than any visible mark. She gazed into her own eyes, searching for the woman she used to be before the chaos of the past few months swept her life into a downward spiral.

For too long, fear had dictated her existence. It had robbed her of joy, turned her days into a blur of anxiety, and transformed the vibrant woman she once was into a mere shadow of herself. But today was different. This morning, she felt a subtle shift within her—a spark of determination ignited by the trials she had endured. It was time to reclaim her life, to redefine her identity, and to embrace the future that lay ahead.

With a deep breath, she pulled herself to her feet. The sunlight poured into the room, illuminating the clutter that had gathered over the weeks. Books laid abandoned on the floor, their pages curled from neglect, while art supplies collected dust in a corner. Once, Sarah had been passionate about painting—expressing her emotions through color and form. Now, they felt like distant memories, forgotten in the wake of fear and uncertainty.

Taking a tentative step toward the easel, she felt a flutter of excitement mixed with trepidation. Could she really go back to painting? Could she unleash the creativity that had been stifled for so long? She brushed her fingers against the textured canvas, feeling the roughness beneath her touch—a reminder that art could be as beautiful as it was raw, just like her journey.

In that moment, Sarah understood that the act of creating was pivotal, not just for self-expression but for healing. She set to work, eager to feel the paint glide across the canvas. As her brush moved, strokes transforming into vibrant hues, she poured her heart onto the canvas, channeling her pain into something meaningful. Shadows morphed into light, chaos transformed into order, and amidst the uncertainty, she found clarity. Each stroke represented a piece of her—a celebration of resilience, a reclamation of her spirit.

Days turned into weeks, and each morning carried with it a newfound energy. Sarah dedicated herself to her craft, reconnecting with a passion once thought lost. Paintings began to accumulate, vibrant reminders of her journey—a testimony to what she had overcome. She no longer shied away from her experiences; instead, she embraced them, acknowledging that they shaped who she was now. The struggle had wielded a profound influence, imbuing her art with depth and authenticity that she had never explored before.

But her canvas wasn't just her art; it became a metaphor for her life. Each day was a new blank space, waiting for her to fill it with purpose and intention. Slowly, the small apartment transformed into a sanctuary, a reflection of the reclamation that took place within her. She painted walls with colors that made her heart sing—a warm terracotta, a serene azure, shades that symbolized hope and renewal.

While the physical changes in her environment lifted her spirits, the emotional transformation was even more significant. Each time she picked up a brush, she confronted her fears, allowing the colors to whirl around her doubts. Occasionally, memories would resurface—the dark shadows of that fateful night, Ethan's chilling visage striking fear deep within her soul. But instead of succumbing to the memories, she chose to weave them into her work, fostering a sense of empowerment in facing her past.

Sarah began to exhibit her artwork at local galleries, something she had always dreamed of but never had the courage to pursue. The first time she stood in a gallery filled with her paintings, a rush of exhilaration washed over her. The air was thick with the murmur of voices and the distinct features of admiration as visitors took in the depth of her work. Faces lit up with understanding—deep calls from her tumultuous journey reverberated in the hearts of those who observed.

"Your art is captivating," one woman remarked, her eyes glistening. "It tells a story that resonates."

The words struck a chord within Sarah, an affirmation of her strength, her survival, and her metamorphosis. Each piece was a chapter of her life, a testament to the battle she had fought and the beauty she couldn't have imagined emerging from the ashes.

But the path to healing wasn't linear. There were still moments when darkness threatened to engulf her. On sleepless nights, shadows morphed into haunting reminders of the past, and her heart would race, pounding against her chest like a wild beast. However, in those moments, Sarah learned the importance of grounding herself—she would hug her beloved paintings, finding comfort in the colors she had poured her soul into. Each color was a reminder of the joy she had captured, of the life she was reclaiming.

As the months went on, not only did Sarah's confidence strengthen, but so did the relationships around her. Jenna, her steadfast friend, played an integral role in this transformation. The ls bond they shared blossomed, woven tighter by their examinations of every dark corner and every triumph. Jenna's encouragement pushed Sarah toward new horizons—whether joining a local art collective or attending community events where healing conversations swirled in the air.

One autumn evening, after a day of painting, Sarah and Jenna found themselves sitting beneath a spreading oak in the park, the golden leaves swirling around them like a gentle rain of blessings.

"I can't believe how far you've come," Jenna marveled, her voice warm with admiration.

"I still can't believe it either," Sarah admitted, a smile tugging at her lips. "I had lost myself for so long, but I'm finally beginning to feel whole again."

"What's next for you?" Jenna asked, genuine curiosity emanating from her friend.

"I want to explore more," Sarah replied, her heart racing with a surge of excitement. "I've thought about using my art to support others—maybe workshop sessions for survivors of trauma. I want to help them heal through creativity, just as I have."

Jenna's eyes sparkled with pride. "That's incredible, Sarah. You have so much to offer the world."

For the first time in years, Sarah envisioned a life that extended beyond her fears. She would no longer be shackled by the threats of her past but would embrace a path of hope—bridging her journey with those who had walked similar roads. Her art would be the medium, a vessel through which she could inspire resilience, strength, and recovery.

As winter approached, Sarah organized her first workshop at the local community center, an idea born out of necessity and desire to give back.

She'd prepared a space that felt inviting, with candles flickering, soft music, and vibrant colors decorating the walls. The turnout exceeded her expectations—women and men who carried their own burdens entered the room, their expressions rife with uncertainty, yet tinged with a flicker of hope.

Through shared stories and creativity, they ventured into a realm of self-discovery. Sarah witnessed her small group transform—their hesitation melting away as they picked up brushes, poured their pain and experiences onto canvases. Emotions flowed like rivers, woven together by their shared camaraderie. Each moment became an affirmation of what they had survived.

"I never thought I would express myself like this," one participant exclaimed, her voice shaky but alive with newfound energy. "I feel free."

The echo of that phrase didn't just resonate within the walls of the community center; it reverberated within Sarah's heart. It was a moment of clarity—a realization that healing was not a solitary journey but a collective experience that forged unbreakable bonds.

As the sun dipped below the horizon, marking the end of their workshop, Sarah felt a wave of gratitude washing over her, a reminder of the strength she had discovered not just within herself, but alongside others. The darkness that once threatened to consume her life had evolved into a beacon of light—a path that led to purpose.

However, the most poignant revelation came when she confronted the ghosts of her past. One evening, while standing in front of a canvas that depicted her journey through darkness and into light, she experienced an epiphany. Rather than viewing Ethan as a figure of fear, she began to see him as a chapter of her life—a chapter that, while painful, had ignited a fire in her spirit that could never be extinguished.

She no longer sought to erase the past but to own it, to integrate it into her story. With each brushstroke, she converted anger into colors, pain into forms; she transformed negativity into a canvas of triumph. That night, she painted a large mural—a tribute to the journey of survival, a testament to her strength, and a call to others to embrace their paths.

The unveiling of the mural at the community center was attended by friends, family, and the individuals she had worked with. As her brush caressed the final strokes, the audience held its collective breath. In that moment of silence, Sarah understood that this was more than just a piece of art; it represented hope for those who had felt lost, a symbol that even in the depths of despair, there was a way out.

When she stepped back, the mural revealed a powerful message—one of healing and hope, a vivid landscape of color depicting a journey through darkness toward a horizon bursting with light. It was a reflection of Sarah—a survivor, an artist, a woman who had transformed her struggles into something beautiful, offering solace to others embracing their own battles.

As applause enveloped her, the warmth flooded her chest and tears streamed down her cheeks, not out of sorrow but gratitude. She had found her voice again. Sarah felt alive.

That evening, walking back home with Jenna by her side, Sarah marveled at the transformative power of sharing her truth. The future, once clouded by uncertainty, now glistened with possibility. Each day, she faced healing with open arms, embracing the beauty of the journey ahead.

"I can't believe how far we've come," Jenna said softly, her voice tinged with emotion.

"It's only the beginning," Sarah replied, a smile blooming on her face as she contemplated the endless possibilities awaiting her. "I can't wait to see where this leads."

The threads of her life now intertwined with purpose, passion, and connection—each one a testament to the resilience of the human spirit. As she gazed toward the setting sun, Sarah felt an unwavering certainty within her heart: the future was reclaimed; it was time to live boldly, unapologetically, and with every ounce of vibrancy she could muster.

Legacy of Truth

The sun began to dip below the horizon, casting a warm glow over the small town that had once been a backdrop to fear and turmoil but was now emerging renewed, glistening with the promise of change. The streets held whispers of resilience, of lives interwoven in tragedy yet bound together in healing. Michael stood on the edge of the park, watching children play on swings, their laughter pealing into the crisp evening air like a distant bell tolling a joyous note. This was a sight he had yearned for—normalcy, innocence restored after a year plagued by chaos.

His past months of investigation had led him to countless faces, each bearing their own shadows of sorrow and sadness—families disrupted, dreams shattered, lives lost under the veil of brutality. For every effort he had poured into uncovering the truth behind Sarah's life and the pain inflicted by Ethan, he now felt a weight lift, even if just slightly. The town had rallied together, and in that collective spirit was the seed of change.

The trial had ended with a verdict that echoed through the community: justice had been served. Ethan was sentenced to life in prison, and though the gavel had struck down with finality, Michael knew that the impact would resonate far beyond the courtroom. The dialogues it had sparked, the conversations about violence, protection, and the vital need for advocacy, would continue long after the echoes of the court room faded. As he reflected on all that had transpired, he found solace in the connections he had forged and the battles he had fought—not just for Sarah but for every other unheard voice silenced too soon.

He stepped into a local coffee shop, the scent of roasted beans wrapping around him. Gathering courage from this familiar environment, he made his way to a small table in the corner. A framed photograph adorned the table's wooden surface—a vibrant image capturing Sarah surrounded by friends, laughter lighting up her eyes. It had been taken at the charity event that celebrated her resilience, an event organized to honor the victims of violence and providing hope to survivors. Michael's heart swelled with pride as he thought of how far Sarah had come, how she had transformed her trauma into advocacy, becoming a beacon of strength in a once-dark landscape.

Conversations swirled around him, patrons sharing stories of bravery and survival. Yet, amidst the chatter, he could hear the gaping needs for change echoing from the community. How many families were still affected by violence? How many voices remained silenced? He couldn't help but feel that his work was far from over. Justice was not an endpoint but a continual quest, a journey demanding vigilance and commitment.

"Michael!" A familiar voice broke through his reverie. Jenna approached him, her face radiating warmth. "I haven't seen you in ages!" She slid into the seat opposite him, her eagerness pulling him from his thoughts.

"Been caught up in everything," he confessed, running a hand through his hair. "But I'm glad to see you."

After exchanging pleasantries, Jenna leaned forward, her expression growing serious. "Have you thought about what you'll do next? You know, with the foundation and everything Sarah started?"

His mind whirled, recalling the plans they had briefly discussed for a non-profit aimed at aiding victims of violent crime. "It's something I want to get off the ground," he admitted, "but it needs more than just desire. It requires community involvement, awareness, resources."

Jenna nodded. "It's crucial, Michael. People need to feel supported when they've faced something so horrific. Violence spreads, but awareness can stem the tide and soothe the wounds. Sarah's speeches at the events have helped mobilize people. I've seen donations come in, and the volunteer response is overwhelming."

He smiled, recalling the fire in Sarah's speech at the last gathering, how she had shared her journey, moving the audience from sorrow to solidarity. "Her tenacity has been inspiring," he remarked, pride warming his chest. "It shines a light on what healing truly looks like. Yet I can't shake off the feeling that we need to do more—to educate, to prevent, rather than just treat the symptoms."

They spoke late into the evening, designing plans that would transform advocacy from a dormant impulse to a living movement. Each idea felt like a thread weaving into a larger tapestry—a community awakening to the perils surrounding them, taking a stand against violence, advocating for educational programs, and encouraging people to voice their stories.

As their planning session drew to an end, Jenna leaned back, her excitement palpable. "With everything we've been through, this could lead to a legacy—a living testament to the truth. If we can help just one person," she gestured towards the bustling coffee shop, "to stop the cycle, then it's worth it."

Michael nodded thoughtfully, contemplating the gravity of her words. A legacy of truth—a strand threading through every life touched by violence, highlighting the importance of support for victims and the steadfast commitment of the community to ensure justice was not merely a word, but a way of life.

Days turned into weeks as he embraced the challenge ahead, his heart fueled not by the ghosts of the past but by the living realities of the present. The foundation was born from their shared dreams. They rallied compassion and courage, spawning initiatives that educated community members on the signs of domestic violence, offered counseling services, and fostered open dialogues where survivors could share their experiences.

Michael found himself swept back into the whirlwind of purpose, leading seminars where voices would break through the silence that so often engulfed victims. He saw the faces of people, once burdened by shame and fear, step forward to reclaim their narratives. Their stories, once shrouded in darkness, transformed into declarations of hope and revival, thrusting forward the urgent message that every life mattered— even in the face of unimaginable pain.

Through their collective efforts, the community transitioned from passive observers to proactive agents of change, cultivating an ethos of solidarity in the aftermath of chaos. Sarah frequently echoed the message of hope, instilling belief that vulnerability was not a weakness but an opportunity for connection and growth. Laughter broke through the shadows as people found solace among one another and began to rebuild their lives for a brighter tomorrow.

The media began to take notice, reporting not just on the foundation or Sarah's triumph but on a community rising against violence. Interviews showcased strength, resilience, and the importance of community action, echoing Michael's sentiments about the necessity for continual pursuit of justice. The narrative had shifted from one of tragedy to a reflective exploration of healing and hope, affirming the idea that violence does not have to be an accepted truth of society.

Months later, he found himself back at the park where it had all begun, back to where life once felt heavy with fear. A small event to raise awareness about advocacy and support was about to unfold, and people had gathered in droves. Banners were raised and children painted faces with smiles, laughter bubbling from the depths of happy hearts.

Stepping onto the small stage, Michael felt the pulse of the community surge around him. He took a deep breath, scanning the crowd filled with familiar faces—survivors, advocates, families, and friends—united by common goals and shared understanding.

"Today," he began, his voice steady, "is not just a celebration of what we have accomplished, but a reminder of what we can continue to do. Each one of us holds a power—the power to change the narrative, the power to give voice to the silence that surrounds violence. The legacy we build together speaks of hope, resilience, and unwavering truth."

He felt a swell within him, a rush of emotions as he looked out into the sea of faces—each one a testament to the collective journey they had undertaken against violence. "Let us advocate for those who cannot speak. Let us reflect the light of hope into every dark corner that exists. We can honor those we've lost by making our community a sanctuary—a place where love triumphs over fear."

As loud applause erupted, cheers mingled with the breeze, their combined energy weaving a tapestry of resilience and solidarity. Michael stepped down, filled with renewed purpose and gratitude for the shared journey. The efforts to foster change continued, reaching farther than he had ever imagined, instilling a sense of justice that would resonate through every layer of society.

In the days that followed, combined efforts bore fruit—educational programs were implemented in schools. Workshops blossomed in community centers, inviting discussions around understanding relationships built on respect rather than fear. Support groups grew, allowing individuals to gather, share, and heal together under the umbrella of collective strength.

Through all these moments, Michael felt the profound truth that justice is an ongoing endeavor—a legacy that evolves, nurtured by continual awareness, connection, and the courage to face uncomfortable truths. The work went beyond mere laws and verdicts; it birthed a movement. Michael saw the slow shift in culture, a society willing to confront its complexities rather than shy away from discomfort.

And as the seasons changed, so did Michael. He grew into the role of community leader, bridging gaps between law enforcement and advocates to promote understanding and healing. Discussions became more common, leading to a culture where people were encouraged to speak up rather than remain silent. His path crisscrossed with many others—each unique story adding a layer to the understanding of violence and its far-reaching impacts.

Yet tragedy remained present, lurking like shadows ready to pull at the frayed edges of momentum. There were still instances of violence, lives lost in silence, but the foundation had built a scaffolding strong enough to support countless voices intent on fostering change. Advocacy became a reflex, a mantra in the community aimed at shifting the paradigm.

Sarah, too, flourished in her renewed capacity—her voice sharpened like a blade as she navigated the nuances of story and truth, guiding others toward light. Together, they forged bonds that transcended individual scars, building a legacy threaded through various life experiences yet united by the same truth—they all sought justice, healing, and the reclamation of their voices.

The journey had not been free of struggle, but with each challenge, Michael gathered representatives from community fields—educators, healthcare professionals, law enforcement—to build resilience against violence. Their voices carried forth a mantra: there is strength in honesty, and truth must permeate through every layer of society—education, healthcare, justice—all intertwining to create a matrix of support for every individual.

Days turned into years, with Michael at the helm of transforming a once carved narrative of sorrow into one rich with resilience and understanding. His commitment stemmed not from the need for accolades but from the urgent call to ensure that every survivor found their voice amidst the cacophony of societal expectations.

As an evening fell softly around him once again, he felt a profound connection to this community he had come to know and cherish. They had risen from the ashes of a shared past into a future vibrant with possibilities, working tirelessly to keep the conversation alive. The events organized became lessons taught in schools, dialogues initiated among families.

And in those reflections, Michael found solace. The legacy they created shaped a society that embraced justice, one that underscored the essential truth: every voice matters, and advocacy keeps that voice alive. It was their mission to ensure that no life was left in shadows, no story ended unheard, and for every truth that surfaced, there would be another piece of light to illuminate the darkness.

As he ventured forward in this shared pursuit, he held onto the notions that time could heal, that communities could thrive through unity, and that together they could create a ripple effect of change, where truth echoed through every corner of society, challenging the darkness, and igniting hope for every heart that beat for justice.

****

Hey, Amazing Readers!

Wow, you made it to the end! First off, a massive shoutout and thank-you for sticking with me through this electrifying journey of survival, fear, and relentless pursuit. As the pages turned, I hope you felt the rush of adrenaline and the hair-raising chills that came with each cliffhanger. It's been nothing short of wild, and your company has made it even sweeter!

The truth revealed and justice served aren't just the conclusion of our story; they echo the real struggles we face in life. My hope is that through the highs and lows of this tale, you encountered a reflection of your resilience in the protagonist and maybe even glimpsed a slice of the shadows we all carry. Life imitates art, right? And in art, there's often a raw portrayal of survival; it's about persevering against the odds, fighting through terror, and ultimately grasping for that sliver of hope.

As you close the book, take a moment to ponder the characters that danced in your mind and left their impressions. Trust me, their stories won't evaporate quickly. Need I remind you of the thrill, the intensity, and maybe even the moral dilemmas we tackled? This book doesn't just end; it opens the door to discussions about justice, truth, and the unyielding spirit we all possess.

And if you felt even a tingle of excitement while flipping through these pages, let that be your fuel! Because, remember, the fight for truth and justice doesn't just end when the last word is read. It continues in our everyday lives, and if this story inspired a glimmer of courage or a nudge to question things, then I've achieved my goal.

So go ahead, keep chasing those shadows, seek the truth, and never forget to trust your instincts. Thank you for embarking on this thrilling ride with me, sharing in the heart-stopping moments, and delving deep into the narratives that remind us of what it means to be truly alive. I'm beyond grateful for your time, enthusiasm, and adventurous spirit throughout this journey! Remember, this isn't just my story; it's ours now!

Let's keep our conversation alive even after the last page has turned. Your thoughts, feedback, and interpretations mean the world to me and can fuel more stories down the line. Until next time, keep those lights on and your hearts open to adventure!

With wild excitement

Alice D.